FEVER

BOOKS BY MICHELE SLUNG

Fever: Sensual Stories by Women Writers
Murder for Halloween (co-editor)
Hear! Here! Sounds Around the World
Shudder Again: 22 Tales of Sex and Horror
Slow Hand: Women Writing Erotica
I Shudder at Your Touch: 22 Tales of Sex and Horror
The Only Child Book
More Momilies®
The Absent-Minded Professor's Memory Book
Momilies®: As My Mother Used to Say®
Women's Wiles: An Anthology of Mystery Stories by the
Mystery Writers of America
Crime on Her Mind: Fifteen Stories of Female Sleuths from
the Victorian Era to the Forties

FEVER

Sensual Stories by Women Writers

Edited by

MICHELE SLUNG

HarperCollins*Publishers*

Designed by Alma Hochhauser Orenstein

Library of Congress Cataloging-in-Publication Data

Fever : sensual stories by women writers / edited by Michele Slung.
  p. cm.
  ISBN 0-06-017038-7
  1. Erotic stories, English—Women authors. 2. Erotic stories, Canadian—Women authors. 3. Women—Sexual behavior—Fiction.
  I. Slung, Michele B., 1947– .
PS648.E7F48 1994
813'.01083538'082—dc20   94-9367

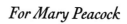

For Mary Peacock

CONTENTS

Preface   xi

THE BREAK   1
Toby Vallance

MARIAN'S EARS   17
Susan St. Aubin

QUEER   31
Elizabeth Clarke

WEDDING NIGHT   45
Francesca Ross

AN HONEST TRANSACTION   57
Marion Callen

LILITH   65
Francine Falk

SHOES   77
Lawanda Powell

A SLOW FREIGHT   81
Phaedra Greenwood

THE NIGHT MARE   91
Susan Dooley

G.T.T. (GONE TO TEXAS)   103
L. M. Lippman

CLIMACTERIC   117
I. Buguise

WHERE THE CYPRESS PAINTS THE SKY   125
Laurel Gross

LOVE IN THE WAX MUSEUM   141
Nancy Holder

YARN   153
Jenny Diski

A DISH FOR THE GODS   169
Kay Kemp

LAST TANGO IN GENEVA   175
Jacqueline Ariail

POLISHING MY SKIN   189
Nazneen Sheikh

VALENTINE'S DAY IN JAIL   197
Susan Musgrave

About the Authors   213

PREFACE
❦ ❦ ❦ ❦ ❦ ❦ ❦

Sex is everywhere, with its constant flaunting come-on and inalterable power to rivet our attention. On billboards and magazine pages, emanating from the radio, in the flickering glow of late-night television screens—always basic, too frequently offensive, never less than blatant. But one person's "tawdry" is easily another person's "liberating," and for better or worse, the infinite variety of human sexuality will always resist being legislated into a single standard of acceptibility.

What's really the problem—and one feels this after experiencing yet another crotch-clutching image—is that, for many of us, these representations of sex just aren't very sexy. Even figures caught in the supposed heat of passion on closer examination actually couldn't be colder. With *Slow Hand* and now with this second collection of new erotic writing by women, my idea was to supply what I've thought was missing: sexiness enhanced by intelligence, style, freshness, complexity, wit, and, best of all, surprise.

Whether *Fever*—its name inspired, of course, by another

equally compelling set of lyrics—offers the possibility of familiar sensual situations or fantastic ones, its stories are intended to provoke responses of curiosity and affirmation, to be satisfying as well as stimulating, to remind us of where we've been as much as where we're going. Like the stories in *Slow Hand*, they represent a mix of women who organized themselves into a diverse but cohesive group simply by the act of putting a submission in the mail to me.

Regret, reunion, flirtation, consummation, experimentation, ecstasy, intimacy, perversity, loss, and lust all play their part in these selections. There are private acts and public displays, choreographed seductions and spontaneous encounters, raunchiness counterpoised with elegance. Readers so inclined can even find a spot of reticence (see Marion Callen's "An Honest Transaction," which is deliciously, suspensefully sexy but modestly so).

Despite the fact that these eighteen stories have erotic intent in common, each one is utterly distinct in voice and mood. At the same time, it's gratifying for me to see that, when put together, they complement each other in ways I could never have imagined. I had so much fun picking them, and the authors themselves claim to have enjoyed their acts of creation so much, that I know that should be enough in itself. Still, every time I read, for example, Jenny Diski's rollickingly rude "Yarn" or Nancy Holder's joyous "Love in the Wax Museum," I catch a glimpse of another reflection I somehow didn't see before. And I don't think it's just because I feel a midwife's pride that I then wish to go back and read them again.

With every relationship, the chemistry is distinct, unpredictable; in the same way, these stories will effect unique relationships with each reader. Some you'll have instant crushes on, some you may reject, others you simply might need to get to know better. This may be the first book of erotic stories you've looked at, or it may be one of many—but what I hope is that you'll find yourself open not only to the "fever" of the title but to the special warmth shared by these writers who've opened themselves up for you.

FEVER

THE BREAK
❦❦❦❦❦❦❦

Toby Vallance

S he had died that spring. None of us expected it. We knew
she was ill, that she suffered and all that, but die? Beattie
couldn't die. Not ever. One didn't, you see, in those days, one
simply did not. Even the vicar was surprised. For all his baby-
faced solemnity he was a man of the world, our vicar; he'd seen
grief and relief and excitement and power and that special kind
of greed and need and *claiming* you get around death, but
never (he confided) had he seen people so shaken and so, what
were his words, so in love. We were all young, it must have been
that, and people weren't supposed to die, not yet. Anyway, here
were the cool, the hip, the unemotional, the usually collected of
London's Bohemia prostrating themselves on the muddy Norfolk earth: Roland, never before seen so much as to smile, crumpled completely and leakily sobbed, inconsolable even by the
arms of his former mistress, Fanny, now curled around his coat-
hanger shoulders; robust and forthright Prue fainted and was
led away by Joanna, her rival of years; and Peter, Beattie's
walker, seemed to throw himself after the shiny coffin as it was
lowered in, wiping his tears on its unrelenting wood. Beattie's
parents, who had lived through more of life, looked on with a
kind of bewildered resignation (dusting their cheeks with gloved
hands) at the scenes around the grave of their daughter. Arms
were wrapped around me whose owners I neither knew nor
cared for. They pulled me this way and pulled me away, holding

me in unwanted grips as part of me left and the earth thudded down on top of the wood.

All the same, there is a kind of highness following a death: There are things to do, people to notify, people to talk to, to discuss it with. One is suddenly important. Roland drove me to his studio for private drinks; Peter rang me daily for two weeks to find out how I was and cried when he heard my voice. Prue brought me white, invalid food from her shop. And Fanny, baffled into wearing something other than her usual black, took me shopping, telling me I should get out, or at least get changed. She confided through her tears that she couldn't imagine either of us, Beattie or I, without the other. To satisfy her need to find me perceptibly altered, or just so that she would leave me alone, I had my ears pierced: three holes punched through each lobe. Morning and night I turned the golden studs, twisting them until blood seeped out and then dabbing at them with sharp, surgical spirit until the flow stopped.

But what do I do when trouble comes along? I don't drink, or talk to people, or eat, or go shopping, or even, usually, get changed. Beattie did all that sort of thing, the woman stuff. I bolt.

I packed up the flat we had shared since college, gave the keys to the neighbor, told the office I needed sick leave, put Sofy in kennels, locked, and left. I left to drift, with the red bandana around my neck, until it all went away. By my going away. I mean, Beattie was home for me, and Beattie had gone and died.

Before I left I went up to the Norfolk graveyard. There was the neat incision in the grass and the trampled clods from our feet where her beautiful head would be. Pushing through the grass, lifting the clods just a little, were the gray-green snouts of daffodils and scillas, the rawer green of crocus buds. At last I cried; not so much, I imagined, from grief but more at the shocking, impertinent indecorousness of it all.

Borophus. Island of spring, of beauty. Persephone's isle. Set in an azure sea warmed by a stream from the Gulf, and the only place in the Med where you can swim in April. Down by the sea its smudged colors, its ochers and terra-cotta and olive greens, give it a kind of shimmer, a kind of blurred, fractional movement, like a heat haze.

"Or is it my eyes?" thought the lady in the large black hat.

Inland, deeper jungle greens of tropical overgrowth pour out of hidden mineral springs over its hills and valleys; perpetual ripeness streams from its secret sources. It is a place without seasons. An island of eternal youth.

She had been coming here three times a year for longer than she would admit to. She always brought books with her, from the spring, autumn, and summer lists, and always she brought a man.

But they were getting so young, she thought, while admiring his sculpted face even in its petulant frown. She had just picked up the phone; there had been the usual bribes, the usual threats, their *understanding*; he did what his agent said. And now there he was, scowling prettily into the sun, pretending not to read the book she had chosen for him, waggling his toes in irritation. The lady stared down at him, elegant and jaunty under her hat, and smiled:

"My best feature, my smile. Everyone says."

"She's bigger than me. I mean she's tall. She's vast. She reaches the sky. She towers. She blots out my light, is what I mean," said the smooth-limbed youth to himself. He pushed himself up onto one elbow and lifted his head from the drawing pad with learned insouciance. He didn't have to be here, he told himself; at any time he could be back in the city, in the world, with friends, and admired.

"I hate her," he thought, describing an angry line, "I'm going to have to hump and hump her and I hate her" (with another livid stroke) "and it's the humping and the hating that will give me pleasure. With her hat, her long white legs, that huge mouth, those eyes. I mean she pays me. I drive her. And then I have to hump and hate and hump and hate. Look at me, I can't even look at her; the sunlight crawling into every crack on that plastery face. But then she looks at me with thirsty eyes." The hair on his body was soft, not like fur, like men, but downy like an unformed animal's. He felt every wisp of it as he pushed away the pad, taking up a book instead, and thought, pressing on his swollen lower lip, "I'm going to have to hump her tonight."

I had made a terrible mistake. Everyone was happy here, fat and brown and oiled and grinning, lolling in the early sun as if there were all the time. Stupid of me: One packs one's junk. I could see that it was pretty: the sea, the warm soft sun that couldn't be warm enough for me (nothing too harsh about this island), and food and swimming and all the good things. My ears were starting to heal. But there were people—that rich family getting into a boat, with hampers, and sunshades and bikinis and wraps and a transistor. The elderly pair over there, he smoothing oil onto her rolling brown back. Those children, the heavenly twins, identically dressed as neat as neat can be, muddying their nanny clothes with sand and salt and castles and spades. I grazed my hand on a sharp rock when I took my first swim; it was all wrong for me. The people swarmed and splashed and *smiled* around me and sometimes they stared. That couple, for instance, she of the big hat that hides her face, and the slim man with her—much younger— who's staring at me now. A slight man, with a soft, angelic face. He smiled at me as if he knew me and I found I had smiled back at him. The hat leaned over him and I lost his face and then there he was again, like a sun over the horizon, glowing at me. I bit hard on my cut hand to clean out the wound, and looked away.

The book she'd given him—apparently this place was once Greek. Underneath the stalls, parasols, basket shops, cascading strings of gourds, boutiques, and in between the hotels and guest houses and trattorias, lay a civilization, a city: The square was an agora, that church a temple to Apollo, those paths not arbitrary at all but conforming to an ancient plan. The young man stared from his beach place toward the town, squinting until his eyes blurred and turned tawdry tourists into pagan Greeks, when—"A friend, don't I see a friend? A way out at least." There was a girl just arrived and pale as a librarian. She was walking away, aloof, distracted, a bit gawky, but adventurous too, he guessed from the absurd gypsy bandana at her throat. "A new game to play? Yes, I see a friend all right, a friend in need."

Wasn't she a little weary this year? She stretched her fine legs, elongated her spine, cattishly, sunning and languorous for the world to see. She paraded. But where was the thrill this time with her angry, sculpted young man?

"He could just as well have been chained to me, been on my lead—go there, come back, bring me a drink, my handbag, *oil* me"—this was the game they played of strain and stretch and pull away but never so hard that it hurt. She pushed him, she showed him, she told him repeatedly that she believed in him and he, what shall we say, *companioned* her? She thought of their obedient, tiring nights and yawned. When she looked down at him he scowled again and squinted into the sun, looking away over her shoulder. At last, she was pleased. He was raging more than ever, straining so prettily away. He no longer bored her, but began at last to excite her. He had never *interested* her. Some of his work, perhaps—those three meticulous still lifes. . . .

"Should I have sent him away? Crooked my slender white finger and called him back? Done something?" she was wondering when suddenly she noticed the girl as she walked quickly past, self-conscious and stiff-necked.

"Young enough to be my daughter," thought the lady, "if I weren't so well preserved."

From the coast you could see nothing but fat green hills. But as I walked inland up dusty roads the green became both separate and solid: The smell of the sea, the chatter and fresh breeze faded, giving way to a heavy, tropical silence. I followed a path into the jungle, hung over by sharp, shiny fronds and almost concealed from the sky. The air was dank, and under my feet the ground was creepily soft. Strong, wet leaves brushed against my face and arms; there was the noise of water dripping; the undergrowth rustled as I passed. I ran back into the light, down to the beach and the fresh sea air.

For days after that I didn't budge. The sun gets to you in the end; you can't help yourself. You take the first swim, beach yourself, warm yourself through and through, with the sand on your legs and back and elbows and your eyes closed and that peculiar dark glow under the lids. All around, the noises of children shouting, people walking, the splash of arms through water, leave you in splendid isolation. Then you swim again, beach again, all that; there's a rhythm. I'd hold my arms straight up, stretched out toward the sun, fan open my hands against its light and peer up through my feathered fingers at—

"Your scarf," said the angelic young man, holding out the red spotted kerchief to me. Then, as if embarrassed at his own presumption: "It was blowing away."

I propped myself up on my elbows, smiled up at him reassuringly, thanked him, and could think of nothing else to say. I was both glad of the approach and wished it were all over, so that I could drift and dream again and be nowhere. He was trying to land me.

"You wear it all the time," he persisted and then, caught out by himself again, "except when swimming." He ended with a shyish laugh.

How could I have forgotten the bandana, I wondered, tying it quickly round my neck? Only weeks have passed, how could I?

"It was a gift?" he asked, squatting down athletically on his heels. "From a, from him?" He gave a winning smile.

"From a friend," I said, with treacherous inadequacy, and clutched the ragged scarf to my throat.

"Ah," but he was unsure. I had corrected him; no lover, no him. In his language it should mean that I was available. "Ah, a friend," he echoed foolishly. I looked away.

Standing against the bar, elegant white legs crossed at the ankle, was that lady with the wide black hat. As I looked she turned and in that turn lifted up her face. I gasped. For it was Beattie. Beattie's mouth, Beattie smiling her old sardonic smile at me.

"Perhaps you would like," the man persisted and then, finding in himself a quite forgotten taste and kindness, "to be left alone?"

I remembered myself and apologized to him, for I had been miles away, somewhere else completely. Then I thanked him, glad, finally, of the company.

She watched them under the brim of her wide black hat—the sculpted, blinkered youth and some young pickup. She knew what he was doing. But it was the girl she fixed on, who held herself to herself, who would not give to him at all but huddled into some private place with spaces around her as one does, as she did herself, in unwelcome crowds. This girl, his little game, was fleshier, rubbery with youth, shining with it, but she had the same sleek hair, the coloring, the same isolation—the breath caught sharply in her throat. She held back her head and smiled up to the sun, in case tears rolled out.

Sometimes a strange place allows you to find yourself. The boatman greeted me in the mornings, the same waiter showed me to my table for meals and now there was this overfriendly young man. Familiarity was stalking me. I would have to leave.

I swam under the sea wall. The turquoise water supported me, but the clear depths dared me to dive further down. I dived, letting the sea take me. Through stinging eyes I saw a shifting sea floor, beckoning vegetable fingers. My lungs began to heave, my chest hurt, ears rang, my head was bursting. Something hard rubbed against me. Eventually I bobbed to the surface, breaking through the waters with a gasp and heaved clean air into my lungs.

"Thank God," came a voice above me, "I was worried."

A shape, dark against the sun, spoke to me; I was blinded and could see only an outline, the long pale legs, the voice with its slight accent. The voice I knew.

"Yes, I thought you'd never get here." There was a laugh in the voice now. I bobbed away under the legs. Long and firm I could begin to form them against the sun into more tangible shapes. A pale hand smoothed oil along the length of the thigh, caressed now one and now the other, up and down and up and down.

I swallowed water, choking down the salty clean sea taste. The hand moved on, up and down, the oil slicking the firm leg to a rounded sheen. The hand lingered, toyed, teased—I put mine onto the sea wall and could feel the warmth of the rock beneath me, the warmth of the bare foot beside me. The foot moved toward my hand, a toe touching my finger, lightly.

"You're bleeding again," said the voice. I looked up into the sun, blinded by the light, up the long, pale oiled legs.

He had begun to draw again. It was one of his most painstaking, one of his labors of love; in fact, it was a plan of the cool, harmonious order that he could now see underneath the violent foliage and cheap baubles of the island. When he looked up for a moment he saw the lady haul the young girl out of the sea as easily as if she were a child. She was doing it to spite him, he was sure of it, to twitch his chain. He turned angrily back to where his city had begun to loom beneath the terra-cotta and leaves. When he looked again they were in the café. She had ordered juice and sweet, colored jellies for the girl who ate and drank with a kind of breathless greed, like a child. The bandana was tied around one hand. The lady took nothing herself, just stared at the girl as her long white hand stroked and stroked her own empty glass.

When he looked down at the lines of his hidden city again

he found that his anger, his thwarted spite had gone and that he felt instead a kind of longing, an exquisite and gentle loneliness. He tensed his stomach, flattened his legs and dug himself more deeply into the sand. His body stirred in spite of himself.

I didn't really think I was dead. Only for a minute. Because she looked, she really did, she looked like Beattie. She stood over me, welcoming me, helping me out—

"I thought she had drowned. I thought I had lost her, this young stranger. I panicked. I swanned over—no, I ran, and searched the water, stood there until—and I counted, God, I counted minutes, until she bobbed up again. As she gasped the air so did I. I really thought I had lost her. I led her to the café, bright and light and anodyne, and our moment passed. But she stared at me—I caught her doing it when she thought I didn't notice. Perhaps I have a hair, a smudge, a mark—perhaps I look weird or old."

His obsession grew and filled the last few days. In the afternoons, having been fed by her with plums and dates and the sweet syrups of the island, he would go to the beach to draw. His city now teemed with people, young, ardent, untouched, all of them, and the men and women alike were sleek-haired and shining with youth. In the late afternoons he would walk barefooted into town like one of his pagans and drop into the cool of Apollo's temple or sit for hours in the shade of the agora, while the crowds dimmed around him.

In the evenings they would dine, she starkly elegant in black, clicking her painted fingers to bring waiters with bowls of spiced, creamy dips, dishes of tender local fruits, oiled and skinned and sliced open. She would tell him of other books to read, and places to visit, of pictures to see and to draw, and all the time she held him with her voracious black eyes. Sitting opposite and pinned by her look, he would shift so that he could see the girl in her corner, and smile at the lady, full of secret freedom. And then there were the nights.

On their last night she ordered French champagne. Maroon-suited waiters brought it grinningly. As she filled and refilled him (she took nothing for herself) her hand roved up and down her own empty glass and she fixed on him those burning black eyes. The young man looked away towards the corner by the door: The girl was not at her table that night. She had followed his gaze and now looked down at her painted fingers curling on the edge of the tablecloth. The gesture, full of a kind of shame, stripped her of years more surely than her paint had ever done. He took the bottle from her and let their hands touch when he filled her empty glass. Her eyes now flickered over the empty corner of the room, and her lips compressed into a line of resignation, the crimson stain leaving small pitiful runnels at their edges. She looked down again. As the waiters hovered at their elbows, he studied her: her face, whiter than ever, the creases and cracks of age, harder; the blackened eyes running a little into thicker streaks beneath the eyeline; the hat, the inevitable hat, perched to one side so that the sleek, tight hair peeped out underneath. The waiters had quieted down and formed a murmuring circle around the last of the diners.

The night lapped itself around me like a cat. I sat on the balcony with my robe half open. The wind was lower, the moon swelling in the indigo sky, the air sticky, balmy with a steady beating heat. Music drifted up from the square mixed with voices and chatter from the restaurant, fading to a single violin as the heat thickened and the night trembled around me. For the first time in weeks, was it months, could it be months, I had not thought of, had not thought back. I was drugged. The touch of the stranger had made me high. The air licked about my sunned, stretched limbs, my arms hung gently at my sides, my naked feet danced on the warm rose tiles. The lazy slap of the waves, the murmuring in the trees, the rustle—soft noises filled the air, my throat, my senses. "Where am I?"

❦ ❦ ❦

He led her to the room they had never shared. She said nothing, told him nothing. He guided her in, sat her down on the bed, then he lifted the black hat from her head, so that her hair hung stiffly about her white cheeks. He stared at her as if he'd never seen her before, biting back his full lower lip, looking at her so intensely that she could not meet his gaze. Then he reached for her hand and hauled her to her feet without a word. He took her into the bathroom and stood her in front of the mirror in a hard light, standing behind her with his hands on her shoulders. Then he began to run water and rinse out a face towel. Watching in the mirror, he began gently to wipe her face. First, he pressed the warm cloth over her mouth, wiping away all the crimson, smudging her chin and cheeks red for a moment and then a bruised, bloodless white. Then, he rubbed the white slakes of powder from her cheeks, leaving her pink and raw in the bright light of the bathroom. And then, moving so gently she could hardly feel him, he washed away the black from her eyes. The lady kept them shut; she was unable to look while the beauty she had so often devoured stripped her of her own. At last he stood behind her, lifted her pale chin, her naked head to the mirror, and commanded her to look.

"All my rage had lifted. I lay down beside her, feeling the heat from her body two inches away. She gasped when I touched her hand. Her eyes were closed tight like a child who would not be seen. I pored over her naked face. The face I'd so raged against and despised, that had held me, was now stripped—of its false whiteness, its blackened lids, and stains—for my greedy gaze. Blindly, her hand reached out for me, flattening itself on my belly. I began to shower that face with kisses while the tears welled under her reddened eyelids.

"Noises seeped out of both of us, muted and full of terror. She cried out when I stroked her lean hip beneath the silken skirt. I touched her pale, bruised face and then began to draw the dark wraps from her. I lifted and opened the warm silk things, putting them to my face before I dropped them, to inhale the scents still held by her empty clothes. Clumsily, she caught my hand and thrust it to her breast and then pulled my head down until my mouth covered her dark nipple, holding my head there. I buried myself in her bosom, enfolding myself, losing myself in its great heaviness. Tasting cool dark cream at first, I felt her change under my busy tongue and moist lips until she grew stiff for me.

"'Oh,' she cried softly, tears running freely down the scrubbed cheeks.

"'Oh,' I echoed, my mouth gaping, choking on, drinking in her giving breasts."

In the noise of the night, of the waves, the far-off fading music and murmuring of the trees, I heard "Oh," and a gasp of indrawn breath as near as by my ear, so near that I turned to it, expecting to find a person there. I turned toward the balcony of the next room and watched in the dark, for the door was a little open.

"Oh," I heard again, a man's voice, full and choking. "Oh, God."

The noises love makes: the soft meaningless cries that fill the air, filled, more to the point, my ears, my nose, my mouth. He cried out and I choked; I breathed in his cry. Her sobs, coming now, heaved my breast. There was an enervating pause before a great and terrible sigh as of the life leaving the body, the soul flying up. I could not help myself. I gasped. Abruptly, there was dead silence. I held my breath, high and thwarted, with every nerve straining, the warmth still playing on my stretched body like an instrument.

"She's out there. He poured himself into me, arching over me, quite lost, as I gaped beneath him. My welcoming mouth. Never before, never before—as the tears poured down and he poured inside me, never before had I felt that tugging, that sudden clutching, that quick inner squeezing—and I don't want to, no, stop, I don't want to be naked and lost as, God, as he is. But there is his panting and the drop of his sweat and his agonized cries and all the time my tears and my wet huge mouth—and I can't help it. The clutching and clenching goes right through me now, hurts me, taking me by the scruff as if I were a rag, shaking me.

"He had fallen beside me; we were tangled in juice and hairs and the salt smells of our night. Our fingers matched the tangle of our limbs. I hear the silence and our astonished breath. And then I hear hers—outside, she must be, but as near as he is; just as we finish I hear another sudden intake of breath, a gasp of shock. I *know* it is her.

"We both hear it. I sense from a stiffening beside me that he listens as well. Our breathing changes, is regular, quieter, listening. The noise on the balcony changes—also quieter, and there is the soft pad, less than a noise, of feet creeping towards us. She seeks to hear us; she *wants*. Our hands move together for the first time, twining fiercely around each other. He shifts his leg slightly against mine.

"There is another sound from outside, a chair is gently moved, breath awkwardly held, and then, in spite of itself, panting a little. He tenses briefly beside me. On the balcony the breathing is more regular now, deeper and heavier. There is again less than a noise, a sense, a kind of rubbing of the air, the whirr of cloth moving swiftly and rhythmically through the air. The chair leg scratches briefly against the tiles. But most of all there is the sound of breath as it changes, held now, let out, in spite of itself, heaving.

"His breathing changes and catches. We are all alive with it; the night is full of our discrete breaths. He looks down at me in the dark and reads my mind perfectly. My eyes have widened in acquiescence. Softly, he draws back the curtain covering the long window and eases the doors apart. Together we eye the shape in the reflecting glass—a musician playing, rapt and lost to everything except her music: The head is thrown back, the sleek hair falling free, the robe loose and flowing, legs straddling the chair, and hands, both hands coursing and roving—the stretched body working, busy, frantically playing.

"He's back. We burn up against each other, sides on sides, thighs on burning thighs, every nerve alight. The shape moves and changes, playing for us, faster and more frantic, feverish, the head thrown far back. We close our eyes, hear the sighs, the muffled gasps from out there. His hand begins to play upon my side, my white flank; my hand covers his, covers him. The firm belly, the smooth sides, those small hairs softened by his sweat, my tongue."

I had tilted my chair right back, my heels on the railings; I was taken wholly by the night, the sticky, dripping summer heat, as I dipped and dived. Dividing myself, head back, eyes closed to the night sky, my ears wide open for the answering sounds from next door. I *had* to do this; I *had* to perform.

I thought I was falling, that I was drowning again, and that I was lifted up by kind, strong hands, laid on a warm, hard place. My head remained thrown back and my eyes tight shut; hands, warm and kindly, replaced my own feverish playing; soft fingers unfolded me and held mine firmly down. My mouth was eased open, freed of the scarf I bit on, and a mouth pressed against it, stopping it; a mouth pressed against my other mouth, taking the sea out of me, bringing me into life again. A hard, smooth tongue pried me open and then at last it entered me. I was possessed. And all the time kind hands held me, and other mouths dipped over me with their firm kisses, their own salt, and I drank their other scalding tears.

The sun was already high in the sky. The square was busy with people—the bread buyers, flower sellers, chatterers, already about their tasks. "Peter," I wrote, "meet me. Collect Sofy and meet me. Take me home."

I saw that couple checking out of the hotel, the tall woman, the slender youth. He carried a small attaché case and her hat; he opened the car door for her and held her elbow briefly to guide her in. He said something to her and then slid easily into the front seat. Without hesitating for a second, as if attached by some invisible direct beam, she turned around and looked directly up into my eyes. I was held there until she got in behind him and I could watch their two heads, one sleek and dark, the other soft and fair, as he drove the car out of the square. I would sit for a few more minutes on the balcony before clearing up my things and checking out myself; my bandana, in a tight scrumpled ball, had fallen between the railings onto the adjacent balcony. I felt my naked throat.

"Later," I thought, "later."

———

My story is about loss and the recovery from loss. It charts a journey from grief and other entrapments to a sort of liberation and celebration of the senses. I hope that somewhere there's an island like Borophus.

MARIAN'S EARS

❦ ❦ ❦ ❦ ❦ ❦ ❦

Susan St. Aubin

W hen Joe Turner came into Hal's office cubicle and started
complaining about his ears, Hal could only see Marian's
ears, small and pink as shells, slightly peaked at the top like elf's
ears, a very different organ from Joe's fleshy, hairy protuber-
ances. Joe stuck his little finger in one ear and wiggled it
around.

"Plugged," he said, "completely plugged. What do you
think?"

Hal thought of Marian's pink shells. "See a doctor," he sug-
gested, shrugging at his computer screen while he scrolled up a
menu. Joe melted out of his vision into the next cubicle, his
voice fading to a mutter.

Marian was the only woman Hal knew who still had
unpierced ears. Even his mother had had gold studs nailed
through her earlobes in a department store one Saturday afternoon. His wife, Evelyn, had three holes in each ear, two in each
lobe and one on each side, where she wore two gold rings that
stuck out at angles from her head.

Hal first discovered the secret of Marian's ears when he
touched them after dinner one Sunday while they were sitting at
the card table at the foot of her bed in the center of her one-room
apartment. He reached both arms across the table and gently
stroked down from their peaked tips to their small lobes, connected to her jaw instead of hanging loose like most people's did.

She shivered, her hands flying up as though she wanted to push him away, but she stopped and breathed deeply as he moved his fingertips across the lobes onto her cheeks. He'd never seen such a reaction, and started to move his fingers back to her ears again.

"No," she said, putting her hands on his.

Later, in bed, physiology was turned upside down. Instead of reaching between her legs, his fingers went for her ears. She reached up, turned off the lamp beside the bed, and let him stroke the rims, the nearly fleshless lobes, the delicate peaks at the tips. With his tongue he explored one ear's orifice, trying to remember names for those inner convolutions. Labyrinth. Cochlea. Coiled shells.

Marian moaned beneath him, her pulsing ears warm. He bet himself they were red, the way they were when he embarrassed her or made her laugh. When he turned on the light, she sat up, crying out "no" as her hands jumped to her ears.

"You know I don't like the light on!" Her face was flushed. When he took her hands away from her ears, her hair fell over them. She was panting and her forehead was sweaty. He brushed her hair aside but her quick hands were on those ears before he could see a thing, so he kissed her on the mouth, turned off the light, and pulled her back down on the bed. She sighed as he traced the outer rim of her right ear, this time with his tongue, circling slowly into the labyrinth while his fingers stroked her other ear. Her breathing became deeper and faster in time with the rhythm of his tongue and fingers. He put a little finger in each of her ears, tickling the invisible hairs there until Marian gasped and shuddered, then sobbed, "Don't ever tell anyone this, I couldn't bear to have people know."

He paused. "Know what?" he asked, as though he hadn't noticed a thing.

At work he hid medical books about ears in his desk, furtively taking them out when no one was looking. Earlobes have few nerve endings, he read. That's why doctors take blood samples from children's ears, because they won't feel it. Hah, he thought, like baby boys don't feel a thing when their foreskins are peeled off. But when he touched his own ears, he found them strangely numb compared to his face.

She's a secret pervert, he thought. That's why this cool and doll-like girl excites me. Everyone's got some strange sexual button, and I've found hers.

At home in bed with Evelyn, Hal read about ears while she studied the books on French cooking the head chef at Chouette whose apprentice she was, had recommended. She licked her lips as she turned the pages, but those full, pink lips had temporarily lost their charm for him. He turned back to his own book and read that there are many myths about ears. Wrinkled earlobes, for example, have long been thought to indicate problems in the heart or circulatory system, but, of course, wrinkling of the skin is as common in old age as various heart problems.

Hal reached up to finger his earlobes, which felt perfectly smooth. Even though, as his book said, cause and effect cannot be presumed, he thought he'd take a closer look in the mirror sometime when Evelyn wasn't around to laugh at him. Connected lobes, he read, are a recessive trait in which the lobes, like Marian's, meet the jaw instead of hanging loose. He wondered if ear orgasms could be a recessive predilection, but there was no mention of sex.

He planned his next date with Marian on Friday. Evelyn worked at Chouette mostly on the weekends: Fridays, Saturdays, and Sundays were the big days; they were closed on Mondays and Tuesdays. Evelyn sometimes spent Friday night with her sister, who lived a block away from the restaurant. It gave them a chance to get caught up, she said. He reached over and stroked Evelyn's earlobe. Without all her rings, her ears looked delicate and damaged, slightly bruised around the holes. He wondered how much it hurt to have the holes done, if even now it was ever painful to wear earrings.

Evelyn dropped her book and lay back with her eyes closed.

He continued stroking, his smallest finger moving slowly to the secret and unseen part of her ear. He was more aroused than Evelyn, who breathed lightly, as though asleep. She moved one hand across his thigh to his hardening penis, while her other hand moved his fingers from her ear to her breast.

"Don't you like that?" he whispered.

"Like what?"

He flicked his tongue into her ear and whispered, "cochlea," loving the sound of the word and the sensation of entrapment that whispering it gave his tongue.

Evelyn laughed. "That tickles! What are you doing?"

"Some people's ears are very sensitive," he said.

He wanted to tell her. There was no reason why he shouldn't; they'd both had lovers before, but unimportant lovers they could laugh about together, like her friend George from New York with his pierced left nipple who tried to talk her into piercing her right nipple so they'd be mirror images. Hal was afraid that if Marian wasn't his secret, he'd be in danger of losing her. Evelyn's laugh could sometimes kill like a frost; she would be capable of making him think Marian's mysterious ears were silly.

She kissed him on the mouth, then slid her mouth down his body to kiss him where Marian never would. "I guess everyone's different," she murmured as her lips sucked his cock into the labyrinth of her mouth. He thought how the human body, especially the female body, was a series of labyrinths tunneling to an unknown center.

The next day at noon, he walked six blocks to the school where Marian taught and stood behind a tree just outside the chain link fence. In dark glasses, with the collar of his jacket turned up, he watched her play a circle game with a group of children. They all moved right, then left, singing a song whose words he couldn't catch because their voices were so high-pitched. One of the first signs of aging, he remembered, was a loss of hearing at higher decibels.

Marian's hair covered her ears except when the wind blew it back to reveal their tips, glowing red with the cold. He pulled his face further back into his collar, enjoying the role of voyeur. Once she looked in his direction but didn't seem to recognize him. Surely someone will call the police, he thought. Maybe Marian will when she goes back inside. A squad car will pull up and take me away at Marian's command. His heart beat faster. When no one came to get him after she took her class inside, he went back to work feeling light-headed with freedom. On his way into the office, he bought a bag of pork rinds from a machine in the lobby and ate them as he rode up the escalator.

Friday morning Evelyn kissed him, saying she'd be back early the next day.

"Early enough to get back in bed, if you're there," she whispered.

"I will be," he answered, glad he wouldn't miss Evelyn's Saturday morning seduction, glad Marian didn't like him to spend the night because she was afraid someone might see him leave in the morning—a neighbor or even her landlady.

Hal thought surely one of those watchful people would notice how the lights always went off for hours when he visited, even though no one left the apartment. He and Evelyn would laugh together about something like that, but when he mentioned it to Marian in an attempt to get her to leave just one light on, she didn't understand.

"We could be doing all sorts of things in the dark. We could be watching television in the dark. Having the lights on doesn't mean anything because you always want to do it with the lights on." She reached across him to switch off the lamp on his side of the bed.

Evelyn always liked the lights on and so did Hal because he wanted to see her vaginal lips turn a dark lipstick pink, her breasts rise and tighten and her face flush as dark pink as those inner lips when she came. Even though there was something exciting about scuffling around in the dark, he often wondered what Marian looked like in her secret inner parts, beyond the quick flash of pink lips and lavender interior before she pulled her legs together on the rare times they made love in daylight. There was more to life than ears, he thought.

Friday night after work he climbed the stairs to Marian's apartment, an image of her ears before him. Through the window he could see across the room into the former closet that was her kitchen. Everything seemed to be on a child's scale: miniature gas stove, sink, and counter, with cabinets packed beneath and above. An uncurtained square of window was in the center of the upper cupboards. She was grating cheese, her ears hidden by her hair, which was pulled over them in two loose pigtails. When she came to the door he lifted one to kiss the ear beneath it, but she ducked away and went back to the counter where she was arranging lasagna noodles in a baking dish between layers of cheese and sauce, like weaving a basket, he thought.

"I'm sure Evelyn makes this much better," she said. "I just use my mother's old recipe; it's probably not even really the way Italians do it."

"Evelyn doesn't cook Italian so far," he assured her. "Only French."

While her hands were occupied he pulled the ribbon holding one pigtail, then the other, loosening the silky light brown hair and smoothing it behind her ears in her usual style.

"No," she said, pulling her hair back over her pure, unadorned ears. "Not yet. Wait."

While the lasagna baked they sat side by side on her bed, his arm around her shoulders. They listened to the soft, unidentifiable music she liked, which, when he asked, always turned out to be something like Japanese flute concertos, or instrumental whale songs, or wind chimes played by musicians he'd never heard of. When he brought tapes of Talking Heads or Elvis Costello, she'd listen for a few minutes, then cover her ears.

Once she said, "This isn't very relaxing, is it?"

"Relaxation isn't the point," he answered, but when she looked blankly at him, he realized that, for her, it was.

He leaned his head on her shoulder, sniffing her ear through her hair, getting his nose right inside the vestibule, smelling a scent like dying roses, like rain, like dust. She pushed him away to go check the lasagna.

While they ate, she kept smoothing her hair over her ears with her free hand. Hal thought her hair looked like a helmet pulled down like that, or a nun's wimple. Later, in the dark, he hoped to penetrate that wall of silky hair to free Marian's ears.

"No," she hissed as his fingers felt for her ears. "It's too much, I can't take that much."

"That much what?" he asked.

She mumbled something that sounded like "pleasure."

"What?" he whispered. "What?"

"Nothing," she said. She guided his hand between her legs to her less certain arena of pleasure. He stroked and stroked with his fingers, then entered her, stroking from deep inside, and had his orgasm because he couldn't wait forever for something like that electric reaction she'd had when he touched her ears. He kept trying to sneak his fingers up to them to see what that zap would feel like inside her, but she kept pushing his hands away.

Late at night, walking down the stairs, he watched the clear, cold stars in the wet sea of the sky and thought, she'll stay the same, always hanging like that at the brink of the universe. It'll never be more than this. He sighed as he unlocked his car door, glad he still had Evelyn, his earthly love.

"Did you ever think of piercing your ears?" Hal asked Marian one winter afternoon when they were hiking. She stopped suddenly on the trail as though she'd seen a snake.

"Pierce?" she asked, turning around to face him. Her ears were hidden under the two navy blue mounds of her earmuffs.

"People do that." He laughed at her.

"I don't usually wear jewelry," she sniffed as she walked quickly on ahead.

They came to a meadow with new green grass already poking up beneath the dead grass of last summer. It was almost warm in the sun. They sat facing each other on two large rocks, their hands on their knees.

These hikes were a Sunday afternoon ritual because Evelyn was usually at Chouette from ten in the morning until midnight, doing brunch and dinner. He put his hand on Marian's knees while she looked at a distant ridge through her binoculars, then reached up and slowly removed her earmuffs. Her hair dropped over her ears as she lowered her binoculars to stare at him, the irises of her eyes quickly narrowing in the light.

"Not here," she whispered, turning and raising the binoculars to her eyes again.

"Where?" he whispered. "When?"

She pretended not to hear him.

Back at her apartment she made a vegetable soup, nervously consulting a book called *101 Quick Recipes* that looked old enough to have belonged to her mother. As Hal lay on the bed and watched her work, he imagined these were the simple recipes she was raised on, a contrast to Evelyn's mastery of thousands of sauces and ways to perform fellatio, none of them easy.

Marian frowned. "I'll bet Evelyn would never use *canned* stock," she said, adding chopped carrots, celery, and turnips, and then a can of tomatoes. She crushed dried basil and oregano between her fingers. He loved the smell of herbs on Evelyn's hands when she came home from Chouette, some as simple as sage or tarragon, and others he couldn't identify, not even when she named them.

"Fennel?" he'd ask. "Chervil?"

Marian washed her hands, drying them on a kitchen towel so immaculate it looked new, though he'd seen it often in the past year hanging beside her sink.

"Your soup smells wonderful. Come sit down here while it

cooks." When she crossed the room, he took her hands and sniffed the rose scent of her soap, then tried to pull her down to the bed, but she leaned toward the pot on the stove.

"It doesn't have meat in it," she apologized.

When he finally managed to pull her down beside him, she sat stiffly, smoothing back her hair with one hand, while he held the other.

"I don't eat meat half the time," he said. "Evelyn's studying eggs now, so we eat a lot of soufflés, and casserole things with cheese and vegetables. I don't miss meat."

He was staring ravenously at the ears that held back her hair. He was touched she'd bared her ears for him; he thought of telling her he missed them more than meat, but knew she wouldn't understand. He pulled her closer and circled the rims of her ears with his fingers. When she let her eyes shut, he watched the lids pulse and flicker with her breathing. He lowered his tongue to one ear, nudging aside his own finger, thinking she'd never notice the difference, but she opened her eyes at once.

"The soup! It's boiling, it's not supposed to boil!" She shot off the bed to turn it down.

The soup was done. "Overdone," she moaned as she ladled it into bowls.

Hal rolled off the bed to sit opposite Marian at the card table. For him the soup was perfect: the vegetables and noodles well done but not soggy, the broth clear. He even thought Evelyn might approve because she had an appreciation for simplicity as well as variety. He'd seen her open cans. He told Marian the soup was good, but lack of perfection made her sullen. She sipped, frowning, ignoring his slurps and murmurs of appreciation, so soon he was quiet, too.

She got up to put on a tape, something with flutes, and then sat down again. When a noodle, curled like an ear, floated to the surface of his broth, he sucked it up silently from his spoon, letting it slide around his tongue before he chewed and swallowed.

After dinner Marian did the dishes while he drowsed on the

bed, listening to the flutes. When Evelyn cooked he did the dishes because she told him chefs were above that, a division of labor that seemed fair to him. He usually did them early in the morning while he listened to the birds at the feeder just outside the window. He realized those flutes carrying on above the clink of the dishes in Marian's miniature sink were someone's idea of bird calls. All wrong, of course; real birds were never that melodiously annoying.

He opened his eyes when he heard the water gurgle out of the sink. Marian dried her hands, then moved through the room turning off lights until she stood beside him.

"Are you asleep?" she asked.

He could see her by the light of the winter moon shining through the high window of her closet kitchen. Her head was bent; the hair fell forward, occluding her ears. She sat on the bed beside him. He reached behind her hair to massage the rims of her ears.

"I have to ask you something," she whispered in his ear while moving his hands off hers. "I have to tell you your obsession with ears bothers me."

"My obsession?"

She lay on her back, arranging her hair over her ears. "It's not normal," she said.

"They're your ears," he answered, "so if you want to call them abnormal that's fine with me."

"It's not my ears," she said, "it's you, always touching them. If you'd just leave them alone, I'd be fine."

"But you like it." He sat up and turned on the light. "I can tell how much you like it. You *come* when I touch your ears."

"I do not." She sat up, her face pink.

He grabbed her hair to hold it off her glowing ears. "Ah hah! See these ears?"

"Hal, please! Turn out the light."

In the moonlight he pulled off her clothes, then stroked her breasts and belly down to her clit, which he took in his mouth and sucked like a nipple while one finger stroked inside her, feeling distant pulsations get stronger. The instant when he knew she'd say, as she often did, that's enough, I've had enough, he lifted his free hand to her ear, stroking from rim to lobe until she rocked beneath him like a boat on a rough ocean, waves lapping and pushing against the finger he still held inside her.

"No, oh, no!" she cried, then lay very still. "Why do you keep doing that with my ears?"

"It's sex," he answered. "I thought you'd like it, I thought that's what we were doing here."

"I don't like it like this," she said. "I don't like to go that far."

When he turned on the light her face was still as pink and swollen as he was sure her inner parts were, as well as her ears, now covered by her damp hair.

"I personally like going as far as I can." He was beginning to feel like a perverted missionary of sex, trying to explain himself to the unheathen. Right now he wanted to be in bed with Evelyn, on the road to eternity, holding her vibrator inside her and nibbling gently at her thighs just the way she wasn't afraid to tell him she liked. Evelyn's way was more ordinary, not quite the challenge Marian presented.

"Maybe I'm just not ready," Marian said.

"Ready for what?"

"I don't know. Men. A lover."

"Ears?" he asked. "You mean you're not ready for ears?"

"I don't see what ears have to do with anything," she said, covering hers with her hands.

He looked at her closely, but she wasn't laughing or lying.

"I guess it's your bad luck you met a man who appreciates ears."

His sarcasm went over her.

"I can't see being into just one thing, that's all," she said. "It's so narrow. What about my legs, my breasts, the things most men like? Why are you so exclusive? When I make love I want all my body parts included, and my mind. All of me."

He stopped listening and kissed her nose, her lips, her fingertips.

"That's nice," she murmured. "You can be so nice."

❦ ❦ ❦

He was glad to get home to Evelyn, who was sitting up in bed reading a book on Asian cooking. She wore a black cotton gown with cut out embroidered places all around the low neckline. He could see her flesh moving as she breathed.

"Branching out?" he asked. She never could stick to one thing for long; France to Vietnam seemed like a natural culinary progression.

She looked up. "Have you eaten? I brought back some spinach quiche if you want it."

"I ate." He stretched out on the bed beside her.

She returned her attention to her book, but stroked his hair with one hand until he was nearly asleep.

"Get under the covers," she whispered. She was wearing nothing now, the black gown in a heap beside the bed. He took her breasts in both hands as she kissed him and climbed on top. He liked being seduced for a change. She fit his cock into herself like a cork and began to ride him. His thumbs found her clit, pressing the way he knew she liked. She squeezed his earlobes between her fingers to match his rhythm. This was a sensation he scarcely noticed, like a fly buzzing. He grabbed her around the waist to pull her down harder while he rose up, coming. Every nerve in both their bodies centered between their legs in sparkling points of electricity. Evelyn fell forward on him, her hands on his senseless ears.

Next morning he lifted one of his medical texts to read in bed, carefully so he wouldn't wake Evelyn. In the dim light behind the shades, he read that there may be some truth to the old wives' tale that wrinkled earlobes mean a person is likely to develop heart trouble, because wrinkling of the skin in the extremities can be a sign of poor circulation. A weakening heart doesn't pump enough blood, so the skin withers.

He slid out of bed to go to the bathroom, leaving the open book on his pillow. In the mirror he inspected his ears: the lobes were large, fleshy, and wrinkled, especially the right ear, the side he slept on. When he turned on the light to have a closer look, he discovered even more lines. His ears were criss-crossed with white and red lines. He massaged his right lobe to improve the circulation, but when he dropped his hand his ear was still wrinkled. He thought of Marian's small, smooth, nearly fleshless lobes, and his heart lurched against his ribs. Was there anything at all to her except ears? He really couldn't see the rest of Marian in his mind. She was right: He was obsessed.

When he came back into the bedroom, Evelyn was paging through his book. She looked up, yawning, and asked, "So, are ears the doorway to the soul? The cochlear passage to the northwest corners of the heart?"

He sat down on the bed beside her.

"Well," he said, "I just noticed my ears are wrinkled. They say that might be an early sign of heart failure."

She laughed, turning the pages of the book. "Where? Where does it say anything like that? Anyway, you're thirty-five, so it should be normal to have a few wrinkles. Look—there's one at the corner of your mouth now. And look at your forehead."

She sat up and pointed. He slapped his forehead with mock horror. Soon they were both laughing.

"They're all bullshit anyway, those medical books," she told him. "What could ears possibly mean? Ears are nothing."

Evelyn could only say that because she didn't know Marian, and if Hal had his way, she never would. He was a man who could tell his girlfriend all about his wonderful wife, to whom he could say nothing about that girlfriend for fear of his own confusion. As he laughed harder he suspected that straight through to his weakening heart and his immortal soul, he was as insensitive as his ears.

It continues to amaze me that most people, sometimes even other writers, assume that fiction is fact, or, at the very least, based on real events. Often, what I write may be the truth in some philosophic sense, but it certainly isn't fact. Like most creative people, I'm a chronic liar. That's what's fun about writing—the moral and legal injunction to tell the truth can be relaxed. So, to answer the question I'm frequently asked, especially, it seems, about my erotic writing, the answer is no, none of this really happened. I must confess, I lied—and not only that, I had a great time doing it.

QUEER

Elizabeth Clarke

I admit I saw Anderson first. He served me a cup of coffee in Donut World. This place is a charming example of Only in America. Permanently sticky yellow Formica, waxy doughnuts under lights in a glass case, and a big sign on the wall: 30 MINUTE TIME LIMIT. NO LOITERING WITHOUT PURCHASE. Suddenly you've left San Francisco and stumbled into East Jesus, West Virginia. Free refills? My ass.

Someone had succeeded in mortally wounding the coffeemaker in the dressing room and I needed caffeine to see me though the ten P.M. to three A.M. shift. Donut World was practically across the street from the theater where I danced, the Cherry Pit. When I walked in, it was occupied by two cops scarfing crullers in a corner booth and a fiftyish hippie zoning out on the fluorescent lights. And Anderson.

Tufts of ragged black hair stuck out from under the paper Donut World hat and the yellow Donut World smock was unzipped to show a T-shirt featuring a skeletal mariachi band. There was a silver ring through his left nostril and another through his right eyebrow. More in his earlobes. He was leaning against the counter smoking a cigarette, tapping ringed fingers against the Formica.

Like Miranda said, retrospect always wears rose-tinted glasses. It's hard to remember, *really*, what you thought the first time you met someone who later became your lover. When they ask, you tell them your clit started throbbing instantly, of course.

Actually, I thought he was probably gay.

That was why my clit started throbbing. Aside from him just being gorgeous, with those big brown eyes. Faggots get me wet. Even when I'm attracted to straight boys, they're femmy little girly-boys. Boys with doe eyes, long delicate fingers, smooth skin that a few days without shaving only makes more tender and bitable. Much later I told him this and he said *he* thought I was probably a dyke.

He handed me my change. On the Donut World nametag, he had neatly lettered "Peasant." I hiked my backpack (full of wig and high heels and makeup) more comfortably on my shoulder and smiled at him. And I picked up my coffee and I went to work.

What did you expect? For me to fuck him on the counter?

It took three weeks of shy smiles and coffee before I even asked him his name. I had a feeling it wasn't really Peasant. And then it was another few days before I stopped in at Donut World after a six-hour late-night dance shift.

I had a severe case of wig-head and I hadn't bothered to take off my stage makeup. Just another Threat to Society on her way home from work. I was tired and I felt gnawed and ugly; my mouth was coated with sour fur. If Dante had wanted to portray an accurate vision of Purgatory, he would have had his sinners endlessly working a peep show at two in the morning on a Tuesday.

"Here." Anderson took one look and poured me a cup of coffee. "On the house." He looked slightly embarrassed at using a dumb-ass phrase like "on the house." "The profit margin on this is obscene."

We were the only two people in the place. Outside, crack-heads maintained shuffling curbside vigils. Cabs and police cars prowled the street. Alone together, Anderson and I smiled at each other across the counter. There was no warm bakery smell; it was more industrial-grade floor cleaner and stale cigarette smoke.

"Are you hungry? The muffins probably won't kill you."

"Thanks. I'm starving." I avoided chewing the gummed lipstick off my bottom lip. I was positive my breath was hideous. "Sit down with me?"

For half a second I waited for him to claw an escape tunnel through the linoleum. But he smiled. "Sure."

He helped himself to coffee and a jelly-filled and came around the counter, shucking the smock and hat and tossing them onto an empty chair as soon as he set down his bakery treats. This time his T-shirt had a picture of Mickey Mouse. He had a silver chain with a couple of fishing swivels and a Chinese coin, and four Fimo beads on a piece of what looked like dental floss.

We slid into one of the yellow booths. He lit a cigarette.

Awkward eye contact. I switched my gaze down into my cup. What I was thinking was, what do I want from this guy? And after that, what does this guy want from me?

I didn't know Anderson well enough yet to know that the only time he really got talkative was when he was stoned—which was unfortunate, since then all I wanted to do was watch "Star Trek," get my cunt eaten, and go to sleep. We must have sat there for an hour, making halting, shy smalltalk, trading stories about our jobs, our families, laughing more than things called for, the usual dancing around what we were both really thinking but weren't yet sure the other was thinking. Sometimes, despite its clumsiness, its awkwardness, its rich potential for mistakes, rejection, disaster, those hours or minutes (or months or years) when attraction moves from the potential to the actual, the brief space of time when things are still unspoken and unacted upon, when the air between you is heavily charged with the possibility of sex that *might not* happen . . . that's the time that often turns me on the most, and the time that I sometimes wish I could prolong. As my eyes met Anderson's with less hesitation and his stare grew more intense, my heart was already beating faster. Back when women were expected to Wait until they were married or at least engaged, I wonder if they could appreciate anticipation in quite the same way.

Here's a fun fact about straight boys. When I tell them I'm bisexual they (first of all) get a blistering hard-on and (second of all) think I want to hear every sexual thought they've ever had, or not, about other males, down to sleepover wrestling matches at age nine. Miranda said the same thing happened to her all the time. Don't get me wrong, I think boys with boys is hot, and my most recent issue of *Mandate* already has lube stains on it. But these guys think it's some kind of hip pickup, proving how cool and open-minded yet aggressively heterosexual they are. Snore.

When I mentioned my ex-girlfriend and the conversation turned to sexual matters (at last), Anderson said, "Yeah, I'm pretty much only interested in other queers whether they're men or women. It gets old having straight girls tell me they've thought about it and all but they just don't think they could handle eating pussy and besides what if the other girl was prettier than them."

"I usually get guys telling me they could fuck another guy, if they were horny enough, but not feel romantic toward them," I said.

We laughed and when we stopped laughing we looked at each other and there it was. You know the look.

The table was too wide for us to kiss, and it would have been awkward for one of us to get up and come around. But our hands met among the litter of cups and napkins, cold fingers knotting, our rings clicking together.

Our coffee was down to tepid dregs. "I need to close up," Anderson said. "How are you getting home?"

Should I invite him back to my place or suggest we go to his? And how do we get there, and does either of us have a pressing engagement before noon . . . I had all my supplies right by my bed; latex, lube, toys, but I also had a month's worth of laundry turning into a science project on the floor and two housemates, one of whom was my sister Patrice, always sadistically happy to do a morning bed check, plus she and Ron both got up at seven in the morning to go to school or work and could only eat breakfast to James Brown. Loud. On the other hand, I really needed a shower and men are terrible about having clean towels and an extra toothbrush.

He was probably making the same calculations. I picked at the rim of my cup. White Styrofoam with a yellow-and-red Donut World logo. Half-moons of lipstick. "This late I usually take a cab," I said.

"I'll close up," he said.

We went to my place.

I took off my makeup with baby oil while Anderson used the bathroom. I don't care about anyone seeing me with wet hair, no makeup, whatever, but the actually process of makeup removal, that incredibly attractive black oily smearing, is something I prefer to save until I know them a little better.

He came into the room and shut the door behind him. I could see him reflected in my mirror.

I dropped the oily Kleenex into the trash as I turned. "Just ignore the mess. I really need to do laundry." At least I wasn't scurrying around to straighten up. Are we just plain doomed to turn into our mothers?

"What mess?" He was still standing in the doorway.

I hesitated, decided there was no point in playing coy, and said, "I need to take a shower. Do you want to?"

"Sure." He stepped over a drift of Frederick's of Hollywood catalogues, porn magazines, unanswered mail, garter belts with sweat-crusted stockings clipped into them, to kneel at my feet, and he started unlacing my combat boots.

When he'd pulled off my boots and socks, me holding onto his shoulders for balance, he stood up and I kissed him. The first kiss: another area fraught with the potential for disappointment. I relaxed into Anderson's body with delight. His lips were generous. His jaw was rough with stubble. My face would be raw in the morning. My last few lovers had been women and I was surrounded by hard, thin boy body, boy smell of cigarettes and coffee and sweat.

I started to reach under my dress to pull off my leggings and Anderson took my hands. "I want to."

He pulled off the leggings, stood up and unzipped the dress, pulled it off over my head. The front clasp of my bra took him a while to figure out but he finally got it open. I put my arms around him, standing there, him dressed and me in my flowered underpants, goosepimpling from cold and lust, gnawing the tender curves of neck and shoulder and earlobe, while he squeezed my ass. I could feel him hard against me through his jeans. Briefly, I remembered kissing some boy goodnight with enough distance between our pelvises to build a skating rink, afraid to open my eyes and glance down—oh, my God, what if, you know, and I *see it?*—as if the looming monolith of an erection would burn me to ashes like Semele before Zeus in his full thunder god regalia.

We changed. I slid my palm across his butt and up his thigh to press against the swell; just letting him know I'd noticed. He jumped and I laughed. I pinched his nipple through the cotton of his T-shirt and found a piece of metal inserted through it.

Anderson went down on his knees to take off my underwear. "Very nice. I like the purple flowers." He smiled up at me, the thin nylon around my knees, and kissed my belly. The little blood left in my brain slammed downward.

I pulled him up. I unlaced his boots. I peeled off his socks. Pulled his T-shirt over his head, carefully not catching it on pierced nose or ears or eyebrow. I sucked on the barbell and the nipple containing it, ran fingernails down his back, complimented him on the intricate band rendered in black around his upper arm. He complimented me on the large purple orchid blooming between my shoulder blades. I unbuttoned his jeans.

Time and experience have made me much more relaxed around this moment, the final unveiling. When I'd pulled down his underwear I licked the insides of his thighs, complimented him on the tattoo of Calvin and Hobbes frolicking on his calf, kissed him from navel to pubic hair, before I put my hands on him, traced the tip of my tongue around his balls, up the shaft of his cock. He gripped my shoulder, the other hand gently rippling the close-shorn back of my head. A clear drop of pre-come glistened at the tip. I wanted to lick it off, taste him salty-sweet as a tear. Why couldn't I have been a slut in the seventies, when the worst thing around was penicillin-resistant gonorrhea? I got him the rest of the way out of his ripped black 501's and tossed his boxers across the room to nestle up with my dress. "Shower?"

"Right."

I got up, grabbed a towel off the doorknob and tossed it to him. He wrapped it around his waist, his hard-on making the usual amusing tent effect. I took the towel from the hook on the back of the door and wrapped it around my waist. "My housemates are asleep. We need to be quiet," I said.

"Right."

It was one of those Victorian-era apartments with separate bathroom and toilet. Also a claw-foot bathtub, which, as far as I was concerned, made up for the lack of heat, ugly carpeting, and obnoxious upstairs neighbors. We decided to take a bath instead.

I lit a couple of candles while the water ran, squirted baby oil into the tub. We waited for the tub to fill, mashed together against the sink, wrapped in our towels, blue for Anderson, Snoopy for me.

He kissed me again. Such an edible mouth. I sucked on his bottom lip and gnawed my way down his throat to the tender hollow at his collarbone.

"Lily," he said.

"Hm?" I was pinching his nipple, the one not pierced, while I chewed his neck.

"The tub's full."

I stopped to look over and confirm that this was so.

"Sorry to interrupt."

We got into the water, and his knees stuck up awkwardly. He looked taller, folded into the tub. I tilted my head back, watching the nests of shadows on the ceiling. My own skin was soft with oiled water and candle light. I smiled at him across water that was all arms and legs, distorted huge and wavery. He smiled at me.

I sighed, and scooped up a handful of water for my face.

He splashed water over his hair, raked it dripping from his forehead.

"Turn around and I'll wash your back."

It took some contortions. I planted him in the V of my legs, and took my time on his back, fingers and tongue on planes of bone and muscle, freckled shoulders, slight knobs of spine. I squeezed clear water from a sponge over his shoulders, down his back and chest. Then reached around, underwater, and found him still hard.

"That's not my back."

"Do you want me to stop?" My breasts were pressed to his back, warm, wet skin.

"Not particularly."

"I didn't think so."

I stroked him until he was gripping the sides of the tub, head back, mouth open. I stopped. "Do you want to go to my room?"

I lit candles on my windowsills, candles in colored glass jars, each one featuring a different saint. I tossed my flannel bathrobe and my vibrator and my copy of *Macho Sluts* off my futon and we nestled in, skin to skin, nipples hard from cold air after warm water, kissing, just barely grazing lower lips then sucking hard.

I reached down and cupped his balls and he growled into my mouth. Fingernails. His hands, mouth, dark hair falling across my breasts. We stayed that way for a while.

When it got hot under the blankets, Anderson sat up and threw everything off. Quick-moving candle shadows on his skin. He started rummaging through the stack of paraphernalia on the table by my bed. One glove stuck out of the box like fingered Kleenex. "Do you always use all this stuff?"

"Yeah." I raked my toenails up the inside of his thigh.

"What a good little Girl Scout you are," he said, holding up the bottle of lube to read the label.

"Yeah. I got a cookie for you." I spread my legs. "Put on a glove and see if you can find it."

He snapped the latex against his wrist, looking down at me,

and brushed light powdery fingers across my stomach. "You're gorgeous, Lily," he said.

"It's a little late for flattery," I said.

"Smartass." And he smacked me hard with his gloved hand, high up on my thigh, which made my toes clench and my cunt open in surprise.

"Ooh."

He smiled. "You're so wet . . ." He spread my lips and worked my clit with one lubed latexed finger. I was in full bloom. He leaned over me and filled his mouth with my breasts.

Say what you will about the poisonous habit of smoking. To me it says only one thing. It screams "oral fixation." Anderson sucked my nipples until I was dizzy, and no one with a Y chromosome, before or since, has eaten my pussy the way Anderson did. That was the way he phrased it—pulled his hand out of me and his voice rough in my ear, "Lily, let me eat your pussy," as if his life depended on it.

I pointed to the stack of supplies on the table. He pulled a strip of plastic wrap off of the roll. I watched it catch the candlelight as he put it between my thighs.

"I wish I could taste you," he said. The thin plastic crackled wetly.

"I know," I said.

But he was, like me, a pro at playing safe. I let him suck my clit for as long as I could stand it without coming, feeling layer after layer open and swell until I was nothing but a pulse, nothing but pounding blood. Then I hauled him up by the hair, his chin slick with saliva, wadded up the dam, and put him on his back.

I got a condom from the bedside table, out of the litter of matchbooks and ballpoint pens and tumbled stones. I've learned a few good tricks in the sex industry. Putting on a condom with my mouth, which I do on dildos at work, is a fairly simple one, but always a crowd pleaser. Anderson was duly impressed. He had a beautiful cock and I told him so. I see a couple hundred dicks a day and some of them would make you a vegetarian.

Anderson's wasn't the biggest I'd ever seen—and who cares—but far from disappointing and sculpted as perfectly as a Rodin bronze. I worked on him with my mouth, bit and kissed the insides of his thighs, sucked his balls, sucked his cock, my hand around the base, holding the condom in place and my fingers playing in his pubic hair.

"Good?" I asked, surfacing for air.

He nodded, somewhat out of breath.

"Hand me a glove and the lube."

He watched me pull the glove on. I touched his nipples, traced the line of dark hair down from his navel. Latex against skin. "Is this okay?" He nodded. Plenty of lube on my fingers and gently worked one, then two into him.

"Good?"

And it was good.

I took him in my mouth again and sucked slowly while I fucked his ass. Slow, careful, so I wouldn't hurt him. Such intimate contact, Anderson completely vulnerable to hands and teeth. His hands clenched, unclenched. His mouth was open. My tongue traced the tender ridge of his head. A third finger slid in without a struggle. He'd done this before.

"Lily—"

I stopped sucking him and looked up with my fingers still inside him. "Yes?"

"Get on top of me and fuck me."

I stripped the glove off; it joined the plastic wrap in the trashcan by the bed. On all fours I moved up the length of his body, breasts rubbing thighs, belly, chest. I bit his nipple softly and he yelped.

I rubbed the head of his cock between the wet, open inner petals, wanting him in me, enjoying teasing myself as much as I enjoyed teasing him. "Does that feel good? Hmm? Yes? Do you want that?"

"God—"

Anderson thrust his hips up, attempted to grab my ass and push me down onto him. I moved just out of range and pinned his wrists over his head. His look of frustration was damned amusing, considering how much bigger than me he was.

"Now don't you move."

He was getting incoherent. I was thoroughly enjoying myself. Again rubbing his cock against my clit, which was swollen like a grape. Just barely took in the head, quickly, enough to torture. My muscles were tense, clenched, waiting ready to come.

"What do you want?" I purred in his ear.

"I—God—Lily, fuck me."

That was what I wanted to hear. I slid down onto him, all of him inside me, perfect, tight around him, flowing like oil.

"God, you feel good. I want to stay like this forever." I kissed him, stuck my tongue catlike into his mouth.

"Okay."

We moved in slow motion, drawing it out. I didn't want to come; it was too good. Every motion huge, making me struggle for breath. Suspended. I lost any concept of time. His arms around me, his hands on my ass, his breath in my ear. We drifted in that place until I jerked myself back and sat up, still straddling him.

"Anderson."

"Uh?"

"Would this be a good time to ask what you're doing tomorrow after work?"

"Uh . . . this?"

"Good. Me too." I disengaged from him and rolled onto my stomach.

He took the clue. I got on my knees, elbows and chin in my Raggedy Ann pillow, and Anderson behind me. With one hand on my back he eased his cock to the mouth of my vagina and I rocked back, swallowing all of him, forcing breath out of him in a small surprised explosion.

Anderson grabbed my hips. "Uh-uh, girlie, now *you* hold still." He held my hips and fucked me, fucked me hard, sound of his tight boy belly slapping my ass, sound of rough breathing turning into a continuous groan, skin slapping skin, slamming all the way up to my cervix, almost hurting, please don't let him stop—

Supporting my weight on one elbow smashed into Raggedy Ann's face, I reached down to rub my clit and the sounds I was making doubled. Too late now to worry about the housemates.

"Yeah, come on, make yourself come, let me hear you . . ."

I was yelling now, clit huge and slippery, moving with Anderson, my ass in the air slamming back onto him as hard as I could, babbling an incoherent rosary. My muscles tightened, contracted, hovered for an agonizing heartbeat and then I was soaring. I couldn't have stopped it if I'd wanted to, face buried in the pillow, I mean really yelling, everything exploding into colors and stars and I came all the way from the soles of my feet. Dimly in the midst of it I was aware of Anderson coming, his fingers dug into either side of my ass. He collapsed, still inside me, across my back.

It was a while before we could move.

When he was capable, Anderson disposed of the condom and lay down beside me, facing me. Our sweat had begun to cool and we got under the covers.

"I don't think I've ever come together with somebody the first time."

"I hardly ever have at all." I burrowed my face into the curve of his collarbone.

Outside, the sky was streaked with pink. Two birds sang back and forth.

"I think I need a shower," I mumbled into Anderson's neck.

"I need a cigarette."

"I'm hungry."

He got up and got his pack of Camels out of his leather jacket (I watched his butt as he crossed the room and his quietly resting penis as he returned) and smoked sitting up in bed, using an unwashed coffee cup as an ashtray. I curled up on my side and watched him, the motion of his hands, the curls of smoke.

"Are you sleepy?" he asked.

"Not really."

"Me either."

"I wish we had a car. We could go up to Twin Peaks and watch the sunrise." I'd done that with a woman I dated when I first moved to the city. Morning never tasted so good, let me tell you.

"Too cold anyway." He inhaled, and knocked ash into the cup.

In the end we concluded that doing anything at all was too damn much trouble, and we went to sleep. I dreamed vaguely of music that, in the dream, had a very important and perfectly obvious meaning but that faded away and could not be recalled when I tried to translate it into words.

In my own writing, the line between "porn" and "erotica" is blurry, at best; it doesn't have a lot to do with whether or not or how many times I use the words "cunt" or "fuck" or whether or not the characters love each other. I generally write about people living in "voluntary exile" (my favorite self-serving term) from the societal mainstream, and I have some crazy notion about acting as a representative voice to let everyone else know that my ability to love and care and feel and think didn't leak out of my eyebrow piercing.

WEDDING NIGHT
❦ ❦ ❦ ❦ ❦ ❦

Francesca Ross

A woman was singing a lovely lilting song, a familiar melody with unfamiliar words. There was a cool cloth on his forehead, a cool hand on his cheek. And nothing hurt anymore. Brennan turned his head so his mouth brushed the palm touching him. He heard the woman's quick, indrawn breath, and her song broke off, and he knew a moment's sorrow. Then paradoxically rough fingers grazed his lips. A string-player, he thought, opening his mouth, tasting the callus at the tip of one finger before the hand withdrew to the safety of his chest.

"Open your eyes," she said. Her voice was stern but shimmered with a low note of laughter. "If you are well enough for that, you are well enough to look at us too. Minna," she called to someone else, and he heard the swish of silken fabric across the floor, and another hand, this one entirely soft, touched his cheek, drew the cloth from his forehead.

The soft one whispered a question in the dialect of the song. The reply was in the same dialect, an odd, sibilant blend of tones and syllables. Then he was alone again with the singer. "Minna will get the others," she told him, and he understood that, as he had understood her first remark. She was now speaking Dorran, the language common to the cities—not his language, but the primary one of the western principalities, the language he had spoken since he left his home fifteen years before. She spoke slowly, cautiously, fluent but uncertain. "Come now, sir, open your eyes. You'll want to see us before you decide."

"Before I decide?" His voice was rusty but still his own, and his eyes worked also. They showed him a half-lit room, a window open to a light evening breeze, three purple moons in a slight arc in the sky outside. I am very far from home, he realized, but that was nothing new, and this room was a more pleasant exile than he had known before.

"Before you decide to take us to wife."

He jerked his head to see her; the movement made him dizzy, but he took fistfuls of the coverlet and focused on the woman until the vertigo disappeared. She was sitting in a chair beside the bed, her hand still on his bare chest. She was a Dorran, he thought; she had the glossy dark curls, the slightly slanted eyes, the winged brows of that warrior race—and so, like him, she was very far from home. Take her to wife. No. Take us to wife.

Then the door opened and the room echoed with women. The candlelight flickered over their light, flowing garments, their fair, untrussed hair, their smooth, ivory faces. Two whispered at the door; a third, taller than they, with the strong stern bearing of a captain, came up behind the singer.

"These are my sister-wives. Celie." The singer tilted her head toward the tall one. "Minna." That was the soft one, near the foot of the bed, one of the whisperers, bending her head shyly. She was tiny, ethereal, blonde, angelic. "And Dacie." The other blonde whisperer wasn't so shy; she gave him a smile so brilliant he had to close his eyes. "And I am Rica."

He had traveled long, voyaged far before this. He had fought off mountain-worshipers and barbarians, escaped cannibals and head-traders. But he must have lost some fight he didn't remember—"Am I in the endworld?"

Rica laughed as she translated this to the others. The two younger women giggled, but Celie, the elder, called to them sharply and they quieted. Rica said, her voice still quavering with laughter, "No, quiello." Quiello—it was a lover's word. Did she know that, this Dorran girl, so far from home? "This is Tyne."

An island kingdom, remote in a remote ocean. "Your ship foundered yestere'en on the rocks on the north cape. Do you remember?"

Suddenly he remembered—a long voyage, the stirrings of mutiny, the gale winds, the sight of land ahead. He turned his head and stared out into the darkness, the moons swimming into a single misty arc while he gathered his voice to ask, "The others?"

"We found none." Rica made a quiet request, and the soft one, the one in silks, Minna, left. There was silence then, except for the women's soft breathing and his own, more harsh. Rica's hand stroked his chest, her fingers each in its own position, a musician's pattern. He closed his eyes hard, concentrating on that, hearing the chords she was shaping even as she must be hearing them too, shaping another traditional lulling melody he remembered from his childhood.

Minna came back; Rica's hand left him. "We found this on the shore near your hand. It is yours, I think."

He opened his eyes. She was standing now, holding what was left of his guitar, the body caved in, the strings dangling. His words choked in his throat, and he held out his hand. She laid the guitar on his chest, and he took hold of its neck, rubbing his thumb on the rough strings, his fingers along the slick varnish, the jagged edge of the break. "It's broken," he whispered.

"You can fix it. I can help you."

For a moment he let the grief grab him, strangle him. The guitar destroyed. Sixty men dead. All the music stilled.

Celie spoke finally, a cool voice, the voice of calm, and though he understood none of the words, he let it calm him. To Rica, however, it was a command of some sort, a call to order. She took his hand from the guitar, gave the instrument back to Minna, and said, "Can you sit up? Dacie, come."

With the help of the two women, he sat up, propped on pillows, more in control of himself now that he could hold his head up. To escape the memory of the broken guitar, the broken ship, he said, "What did you mean, before? About—about taking you to wife."

"We lost our husband. A year ago. We must have another." Rica sat down again, smoothed the coverlet over him, took his hand. Her strange slanted eyes were alight in the dimness. "We thought you might—you are very far from your land, you know. We do not attempt the sea, and ships come seldom. Yours was the first in two years. If you must stay here, we thought—we thought you might stay with us. As husband."

"But I—" Then the reality of his situation broke over him. His shipmates were lost, all of them, in a single night. But he could not think of that; it would drive him mad, and he couldn't go mad. He was six months' voyage from the rest of the world, lost and alone on this rocky island. He might never be able to leave, to return to his home—

She was offering him another home, if her words, so unthinkable, were true. That was what she meant, that he could live here, in this cliff-house. It was a saving thought, oh, this offer she made, a shelter from the storm. He could rest here, in this house of women, if in truth they wanted him . . . Then he thought of that broken guitar, the lost ship. He had two professions, and they were both lost to him now. Hot shame coursed through him. "I couldn't support you. And there are four of you. You would need four men, not one."

"Oh, I'd forgotten. You haven't the same custom, in the West, do you? We have one husband for several wives here. It is best."

"Best?" He pressed his head back against the pillows, his gaze intent on her, searching for some key to all this in her exotic, familiar face. "Why best?"

"We have so few men. More baby girls are born, many more. We don't know why. It is not the same in the West, is it?"

"No." There had been twelve children in his family, twelve who lived, anyway, seven boys and five girls. He was the final, drawing his first breath as his mother, exhausted, drew her last. It was women, grown women, who were rare in his land. "More women than men?"

"So we must have several women to bear children from each man. And the men—they are not long-lived."

Her long lashes swept down to hide her expression, but he knew. She was thinking of that husband, the one they lost. Something hot rose in him. He wondered if this was jealousy.

"You are strong. You survived the shipwreck; you are awake now and your mind is quick." She smiled at him. "Even as you slept you sang ballads. Dorran marches, Fadeen love songs. You are a good man."

"How do you know?" He leaned toward her, almost persuaded by the certainty in her voice.

"You are a musician." Her hand sought his, found the telltale roughness on his fingers. Her other hand cupped his cheek, her thumb sliding over his mouth, and she smiled. "And very beautiful. Beauty and music are goodnesses. We would be fortunate to have those in a husband." When he started to protest, she covered his lips with her thumb. "You needn't think of supporting us. We have our own work, a family concern. You will be our husband, give us love, stand father to the three children we have, and give us other children. That is all you need do. We know you can do that. We know that you are entire—and entirely healthy."

"How do you know that?"

She smiled, and slipped her hand down his chest under the coverlet. For the first time he realized he was naked. Her hand, rough and gentle, brushed the line of hair down his belly, and to his dismay he found that was enough to stir him. He was a young man, and he had long been without a woman, and there were women, beautiful women, all around him.

"But—four wives. It is wrong." The edicts of a long-abandoned faith pricked him, but then, along with that, came the quickening. Four wives . . .

"It is our way here. We should not survive otherwise. We share our home, and our husband's bed."

"All at once?"

The words were out before he could call them back. Rica drew away, and he was sorry. Then she laughed, glancing back at her sister-wives but apparently deciding not to translate that. "One at a time, you wicked boy. A night for each, and then each again other nights."

He knew the barest bit of disappointment, then the vision she described opened for him, and he fell back against the pillows, knowing this must be a dream, a dying man's dream before death.

But her hand on his belly was real, rough here and smooth there, and so was his anguish when it withdrew and she rose at Celie's voice. Celie called to the others, and the women gathered near the door, holding hands, talking in low voices, though he wouldn't have understood them anyway. Then Rica detached herself from the rest, and came back toward the bed, and the others left, Dacie lingering to flash him another radiant smile before closing the door behind her.

"Can you try to get up?"

It was too late now to plead modesty. He swung his bare legs over the side of the bed, and using her shoulder as a crutch, he stood. He was predictably light-headed, but he gripped her shoulder hard until the dizziness went away. He heard her stifled gasp, and immediately released her. "I am sorry. I didn't mean to hurt you."

"No, no, I did not regard it. Come, walk with me to the window. It is too dark to see the water, but you will hear it."

At the window he took great swallows of the cool sea air, and as she must have known, the familiarness calmed him. He was very near the sea, near enough to hear the steady ebb and flow, the crash of the waves against the rocks, the calls of the swooping seabirds. And he was well enough, only a slight ringing in his ears—concussion, probably—and an ache in his chest to remind him of the shipwreck and what was lost to him now forever.

Forever. He would likely never again see his home.

He dropped down onto the cold stone sill, less weary now than waiting. Rica was watching him, waiting also, and he returned her gaze, studying her wild, lovely face. She was as foreign as he in this land of Tyne, and she had made it her home, this warrior girl.

"You are Dorran, aren't you? How came you here?"

She must know how expressive her dark eyes were, for her long lashes swept down again, casting shadows on her cheeks. "My mother brought me years ago, when I was a girl. Then she died. Celie's family took me in." There was a wealth of secrets hidden under that sweep of lashes, in those dark exotic eyes. But when she looked up at him, her expression was teasing, tantalizing. "I was chosen, of us all, to persuade you to stay. Will you let me try?"

She did not touch him then, but he had felt her caress before and felt it again, a memory brushing his loins, and the alienness, the uncertainty, the grief ebbed away. "You may try."

But she slid away from his embrace, a slender elusive form leaving him in the dimness. "Wait there," she said, and he was alone again, entirely bereft in the cool night air.

She returned, her hair tumbled over some new, flowing gown, gossamer like the candlelight—a nightdress, made for seduction. But she was not yet to be his. She brought with her a varnished tub dragged by two girls, serving girls to judge by their sober dress and deferential air. They were plain compared to the blonde and dark sister-wives, and he wondered if the foreign Rica would have shared their fate had she not such quicksilver beauty. One of the girls glanced up at him as she pushed the tub into the corner, her eyes wide, a gasp hovering on her lips. But a sharp word from Rica had her scurrying out after the other one, out into the hall that lay behind that thick, sheltering door.

"They have never seen a man like this, you see," Rica said, and he felt her admiration warm on him. "And you are so lovely a man . . ."

The girls were back with jugs of steaming water; he was to bathe, he realized, and was glad of it, running his hand through his hair, stiff with saltwater. He must make himself ready to be her lover, worthy to be her lover, if that was what she wanted of him.

But Rica did not leave him alone, as he expected. She helped him climb into the water, knelt beside the tub, took the sponge from his hand. "Just rest," she murmured, a hand on his chest.

So he lay back, all sybarite now, breathing in the fragrance of her perfume, of the flowers she had scattered in the water. He understood none of this, why he was here, why he had survived, why these women wanted him. But he had ever been a fatalist, and accepted this comfort as he had all his life accepted sorrow, with stoicism, with hope.

As she drew the sponge in a lazy circuit over his body, Rica sang softly that slow, sweet song from their childhoods. He sang with her, but in his own language, as he had heard his father sing it so long ago. She fell silent, and then, to his amazement, she began to echo his words, hesitant over the gentle rhythms of the ancient Eirenn tongue, as if they came from deepest memory.

Their voices joined in the quiet night, hers a throaty contralto, his deeper and fuller, and the joining seemed to him so aching with promise, with desire, with something so close to joy that the song faltered as longing closed his throat.

In his anguish she became brisk, scooping up water in her cupped hands and letting it pour over his head, caressing the tension from his temples and jaw, tangling her soapy fingers in his hair. "Such lovely red curls," she murmured. "Who are your people? Not Dorran."

"Eirenn."

It was a small country, on the western edge of the west, poor and rocky and obscure. But she nodded. "Your music, of course. We had a troubadour, when I was a child. He taught me that song. Oh, I knew the Dorran words. But he taught me the Eirenn verses. I had forgotten, till you sang them."

Only the elite Dorran families had Eirenn troubadours, who held themselves high and their talent priceless. "Who are you, Dorran?" She had the grace of a princess, even on her knees beside him, even serving him.

She only shook her head, took his hand, pulled him to his

feet. He took the heavy, woolly towel and wrapped it around his waist, bemused by the half-revealed secrets of this woman. She left him there, but returned almost immediately with a tray of food, and he knew a sharp, sudden hunger that drove out any other thoughts.

They sat cross-legged on the bed, the tray in front of them, and though he protested she insisted on feeding him by hand. "This is what we do for our husband," she told him, nudging his mouth open with an anglaberry. As soon as he swallowed it, she kissed him, her tongue tracing his lips and slipping inside, sweet as the berry it chased.

There was bread and cream and kisses, and bites of savories and the tug of her teeth on his lip. There were goblets of wine and the cup of her silk-covered breast warm in his hand. There was a sleek slide of chocolate down his throat, and the sleek slide of her legs over his: a meal so sensuous, so sating, that he thought he could never eat again without her hand at his lips.

But then, a neat chatelaine, she gathered all the crumbs and empty glasses and linens onto the tray and put it outside the door. He rose from the bed, meeting her in the middle of the room, his impatient hands slipping through the fastenings on her loose robe to the slender waist underneath. She let him revel in the satiny texture of her skin, the sweet curve of her hip, for just a minute. Then she detached his hands and stepped back. "We Tynan women are taught to please our men. Let me show you. It is the only way I know to make love."

He was almost mindless with frustration, but grudgingly he nodded, and she turned slightly to undo her gown. She let it slip from her shoulders; she was naked underneath, golden in the candlelight. By sheer force of will, he kept his arms at his sides as she came to him, warm and silken against him. She stood on tiptoe to kiss him, and then, generous, she let him kiss her, his tongue sliding across her full lower lip, tasting the sweetness of the wine they had shared, the sweetness of her. His arousal rose, pressing against her thighs; she moaned softly, deep in her throat, and closed her eyes as he kissed her neck, the hollow of her throat, the valley between her breasts. When his hands slid over her waist, down her hips, cupping her derriere, she came aware again. "No," she murmured. "Let me. *My* pleasure is pleasing you."

He had no time to object, for she was slipping down his body, her breasts brushing against his belly, his thighs. She went to her knees before him, her head bent, her dark hair spilling over her face. She laid her cheek against his erection, and his breath caught in his throat. He was all hard, searching desire, a question in need of an answer, and he found it in her lips, tentative, sweet, in her delicious murmuring moan, in the teasing tug of her mouth slipping over and back, back and forth.

When he could bear it no longer, he withdrew from her, slid down her body, knelt with her, stifled her protest with a kiss, tasted himself on her tongue. He pulled away, breathless. "I am not used to this, to being loved so. Let me, now. Let me love you. I know how to do that."

Her answer was a sigh, a lingering kiss, a hand that crept round his back and pulled him closer. He cupped her derriere in both hands, lifting her slightly so that he could slide between her thighs, his erection pulsing against the soft damp heat there. He slid back and forth, across but not in, and she gripped her thighs tight around him, her dark, intense eyes softening, hazing, as the sensation flowed from him to her, and all through her. Her head fell back; he kissed her throat, traced with his tongue the clear sweep of her jaw, the delicate bow of her mouth, echoing the gentle thrust and ebb of his arousal against hers.

"Please," she whispered against his mouth, and he laid her down gently on the rough carpet, covering her against the chill with his body. With a sense of waiting, a half-held breath, he entered her, paused there to listen to her quickened breathing, to his own, joining there until he could no longer hear himself apart from her. She closed her eyes, waiting, waiting, and finally they began to move together, in point, in counterpoint, in harmony again.

A symphonic swelling into a hush, then breaking free a stringed melody, a single, ever-changing note soaring against the silence, up and up aching, intense, sweet like the curve of her breast, the curve of her cheek, like the cling of her mouth on his, of her body on his.

And then, almost too late, the note broke, dissolved, a shatter, a shimmer of sound, and he broke with it, with her, dissolving into her, into the elusive hidden essence of her song.

Gradually the hush receded, left him there listening again, hearing her quiet breath, his own, separate again amid the night noises. What joy to lie there, still entangled with her, to feel her stirring sensuously under him, to imagine this always . . . two lost souls, cast up on this shore, finding home.

"Do you know," she whispered, her tongue flicking at his ear, "why I was chosen to persuade you?"

"Because you are the best."

"Oh, no." She laughed, a rippling breath on his neck. "Oh, no. I came here so late, I was never properly trained. See what I did with you, slip off into my own pleasure, when I should think only of yours—"

Somewhere here was an answer to a question he had never known to ask. "It is the same, isn't it? The pleasure, the joy? It is both ours."

She glanced up at him, a slanted look through those shadowy lashes. "We are neither of us Tynan, or we would not think that. No. I was chosen, quiello, not because I am the best. Because I am the worst. The clumsiest, the laziest, the most distracted. The least adept at the arts of love."

Then she spoke aloud the thought that half-formed in his mind. "Imagine what the others are like."

He couldn't help himself. He loved her madly, entirely, but he couldn't help himself. He thought of Minna, the little fair beauty, all demure delicacy, of Dacie with her bold radiance, of the serene Celie. One by one by one, and then Rica again.

There had been women in his life before, intermittent loving, an occasional spell of peace, a few moments of sweet passion and tenderness. But these were never enough, always just an interlude, a transitory occurrence ever longed for and soon forgotten. He had wandered the world an orphan, alone in life as he had been alone at birth, and he had imagined that solitude was his destiny, and music his only solace. But now he was offered another destiny, one that was his for the believing. He had only to say yes, and this was his: the trust, the meaning, the women, the loving. Rica.

"I will always love you best," he whispered.

She pressed her fingers against his lips, closed her eyes tight, slowed her breathing until she could speak. "This is my home. Yours too, if you will take it. And this is our way, to share. You must not choose, or prefer, do you see? Or we will not know peace."

She opened her eyes; they glowed dark and brilliant and fierce. "So you must never say that, never." Then, softly, "Except to me, in the dark. Never, never to another." Then fierce again. "Say it now."

And he did, laughing, taking her in his arms, sitting up with her in his lap, cradling her like a babe, singing it softly like a love song. "I will always love you best. Always, always, always best. Always always always you."

As the working mother of two small children, I've often declared, "I need a wife!" So far, no one's volunteered. When a science fiction writer friend let me read a story about "her" universe—a place where each woman is allowed more than one husband—the prospect of two or more male egos just didn't appeal. "What I'd prefer," I told her, "is an extra wife or two." "Wedding Night" was the result of this exchange.

AN HONEST TRANSACTION
❧❧❧❧❧❧❧

Marion Callen

At 7:30 A.M. on May 14, Mavis Fletcher returned to bed to sip her first cup of Earl Grey tea. With a frown that was half concentration, half disapproval, she surveyed, through the open bedroom door, the small suite of rooms that was her sole capital asset. "This will not do. Not any longer. I need space and elegance and a view of a well-kept garden. I need tall trees and birdsong. I have let things go for too long."

She made a brief entry in her diary. "53rd Birthday. Four cards; one from John and Nancy, one from Mr. Myers, two from the girls at work. Decided to give a month's notice and pursue my destiny."

She swung out of bed and made a tour of her tiny, tidy kingdom as though a removal van were already at the door and she about to step delicately into a waiting taxi. She returned to her diary and made a list: "Phase 1—Reconnoiter.

A) Buy *The Lady*
B) Prepare a c.v.
C) Find an agency to handle short-term lease of flat (preferably to single, professional woman)
D) Purchase interview outfit."

As an afterthought, she added, "and 3 sets of matching underwear (lingerie, not M & S)."

🌹 🌹 🌹

She boiled and ate a celebratory egg and went to work. The shock of her announcement gave the manager such acute dyspepsia that he swallowed half a box of antacid tablets before lunchtime and had to cancel his late afternoon round of golf. In spite of his agitation, Mavis was serene in her purpose and composed all the letters her employer had not the heart to tackle before typing out an immaculate curriculum vitae. Her skills in organization and administration were beautifully balanced by evening classes in Cordon Bleu Cookery, Jams and Preserves, First Aid (certificated), Choral Singing, Flower Arranging and Assorted Crafts. Leaving the office at five o'clock with ten photocopies in her bag she felt well-satisfied. Even if she had known when Father was alive that one day she would be applying for a post as housekeeper, she could not have chosen a more suitable cluster of interests to develop, and Mr. Myers's despondency would not prevent him from supplying an admirable reference.

Forty-eight days and three interviews later, Mavis was unpacking two modest-sized suitcases in the first-floor bedroom of a large country vicarage. As she moved about, she watched her reflection in the long mirror of the wardrobe, the triple mirror of the dressing table, and the oval mirror over the handsome, bow-fronted, mahogany chest of drawers. Not bad at all. An agreeable face; neat, compact figure inside a well-fitting dress; deft, economical movements and the haircut in the West End had been worth every penny. Setting the last personal item, her new, softly chiming alarm clock, on the bedside table, she pushed open the casement window to admire the tranquil view: well-tended lawn and borders, mature trees full of songbirds, a small orchard, and the stooped back of the twice-weekly gardener in the vegetable plot. She could see enough ripening soft fruit to make summer puddings galore; gooseberry crumbles, strawberry shortbread, raspberry pavlovas, and a shelf full of vermilion and claret-colored jams to last into the winter. From her first sight of the Reverend Michael's spare frame as he waited for her in the lane outside the railway halt, propped against his aging Riley, she knew that he had not been properly fed since his wife's demise ten months earlier.

But she would change all that. Gathering speed, her imagination conjured up a beautiful, tan-flanked, golden-eyed cow browsing in the meadow beyond the garden wall and herself, in an apron and floppy cotton hat, sitting on a three-legged stool to milk it night and morning. Fresh, frothy milk to churn into butter; cream for the scones at afternoon tea; a row of soft cheeses on plaited straw mats—she realized she was extremely hungry and that, if she did not stop daydreaming and go down to take stock of the immense kitchen with its walk-in pantry and cold store with marble shelves, her first attempt at producing a meal would be an overdue disaster. And she must remember to rein in her appetite also, or the trim figure she had been admiring would outstrip its new outfits.

By ten-thirty, Mavis was exhausted. The journey to Suffolk with its three changes of train, the preparing of supper in a different kitchen and listening to the history of the parish narrated by a widower who was as starved of conversation as he was of good cooking left her with little energy for her diary. She wrote, "The way to a man's heart . . ." and immediately fell asleep.

"Phase 2—Infiltration" started with the laundry, which Mavis hung out each morning. In between clumps of short, gray socks and solid, ribbed-cotton male undergarments she planted her flower-sprigged camisoles and French knickers. White shirt alternated with pastel blouse; dark trousers with cream, eight-gored skirt. "Summer is a-cumen in," hummed Mavis, hearing a cuckoo in the wood at the bottom of the valley. She stood back to take pleasure in the billowing line full of washing; the way a lacy, dove-gray brassiere entwined and danced around the out-flung arm of a manly shirt. And if the vicar should happen to glance up from his letter writing to the bishop, at the desk in the study window behind her, might not he be thinking that she, too, made a pleasing picture as she stood with the wicker laundry basket tucked against her hip and her apron pulled tight around the waist undistorted by childbearing and over her generous bosom?

Other domestic conjoinings took place. Their Wellingtons stood side by side in the back porch, outdoor coats hung from adjacent pegs, and their two black umbrellas were so alike that each frequently took the other's by mistake. The Reverend Michael, now urging her to call him "just Michael, please," had apologized for what he called the lack of en-suite facilities for her, but the intimacy of a shared bathroom suited Mavis's purpose. On the window ledge her row of matching floral toiletries confronted his modest duo of shaving mug and talcum, their flannels overlapped on the bath rack, and two bath towels, one dark blue, the other fluffy pink, nestled up to each other on the narrow heated rail. On a Sunday evening four weeks after her arrival, Mavis made another cryptic entry in her diary, a catch phrase remembered from her youth: "Softlee, softlee, catchee monkee." Phase 3—Settlement was about to begin.

On her next afternoon off, Mavis borrowed a bicycle and pedaled to the public library in the small market town four miles to the west. She spent two profitable hours in the reference section and emerged with several pages of handwritten notes: a well-rehearsed list of the names of major crime writers and outlines of the plots of their chief successes. A detour to the bookshop to buy the latest paperback P. D. James, five minutes in the haberdasher's next door to collect the darning materials that were the ostensible reason for her trip, and she was ready to cycle home, singing alternately "Praise to the Holiest" and "All things bright and beautiful" as she dipped and soared along the country lanes.

After a light Saturday night supper of poached salmon, new potatoes with mint, and a well-turned green salad, followed by a crème brulée, the two sat in companionable silence, Michael reading through his notes for the next day's sermon, Mavis turning the pages of the new *Radio Times*.

"Oh!" She gave a little hoot of delighted astonishment.

"Sunday evening! Another Dorothy Sayers on the television. Starting at nine P.M., so Evensong will be well over. *And* it's filmed on location in Suffolk. Won't that be a treat?"

She waited. Michael scratched his ear with the pencil end and looked at the mutual pile of fish bones on the serving dish. He said, thoughtfully, "That old black-and-white portable in your sitting room won't do justice to the scenery. I think you should join me downstairs. I hadn't realized you shared my passion for detective stories."

"Thank you," replied Mavis, "I should like that. And, come the winter, it should save a little on the heating costs." Immediately she regretted the last comment. Wishing to appear frugal, she feared she had been presumptuous.

But she had not and, thereafter, evenings were shared in the large, comfortable sitting room with French windows leading to the terrace and a view of the terra-cotta urns filled with geraniums and trailing lobelia and of the heron that occasionally visited the fish pond. Mavis experienced many a frisson of excitement as, without looking up from her book or her sewing, she sensed the vicar's eyes turn with ever-increasing frequency in her direction, traveling slowly from her ankles to her hips and breasts. He sometimes opened his mouth as if to speak and then sighed and said nothing. One evening he sat down briefly on the arm of her chair to look at the *Radio Times* she was holding, and she smelled the attractive odor of washed shirt and clean male body. Before going to bed, she made a brief entry in her now rarely touched diary. Influenced by a recent rereading of *Tale of Two Cities,* she wrote, "The Storming of the Bastille cannot be far away."

And she was right. The very next evening, after an exhausting supper of lasagna, followed by fresh fruit salad and homemade chocolate eclairs, Michael dozed off in his armchair. Mavis sat in the deepening twilight, unwilling to disturb him by switching on the lights and enjoying the rare opportunity to gaze openly

at her vicar, who was, one could say, almost handsome and certainly what her mother called "a fine figure of a man."

Suddenly, he sat bolt upright, opened his eyes, and said,
"Sarah?" Without his glasses and still half-asleep, he had mis-
taken her for his wife. He rose, took a step forward, tripped over
the book that he had laid beside his feet, and fell heavily onto
the carpet. Instantly she was on her knees, helping him to sit up.
Naturally, she drew his head to her bosom and naturally stroked
his neck and made little soothing noises.

"There, there, my dear. Where does it hurt?"

"I think it's my ankle, my right ankle," he said. "I do apolo-
gize."

"Just sit where you are," said Mavis, "I have witch hazel and
a bandage in my room. I'll be with you in one minute."

When she returned with a bowl of water, a towel, and her
first-aid kit, he had pulled himself up into the armchair and was
lying back with his eyes closed, looking pale. She set a low stool
before him and rested his slippered foot on her thigh. And if, in
the course of the sock removal, the foot bathing, and the tender
application of a cool bandage to the twisted ankle, her breasts
brushed the tips of his toes or his heel slipped down toward her
groin, neither of them appeared to notice it. However, by the
time she had finished, the vicar had a slight flush in his cheeks
and a brightness in his eye, and she detected a tiny sigh of regret
when she replaced the injured foot beside its healthy partner.

"That feels good," said Michael, not sure to what he was
referring. "My father's father was a shoemaker," she said, to ease
his embarrassment. "He taught us all to take care of our feet. I
think I should bathe the other one, or you will be lopsided."

"That would be . . . nice," he said, struggling for a suitable
adjective.

"Good," said Mavis, thankful that she had decided to put
on the suspender belt and stockings for an experimental wearing.

Naturally, it was impossible to keep her knees pinned together
as she smoothed talcum powder between his toes, or to prevent

her skirt from riding up over her thighs. Naturally he could not resist slipping a hand into the enticing divide between her breasts, or easing the buttons through the button-holes of her charming V-necked blouse. Summer clothing is easily removed, and a chaise longue makes an excellent impromptu substitute for a bed, although they did move to the bedroom later, when they had discussed details such as the length of the engagement and who would officiate at the wedding ceremony.

While Mavis collected a few essentials from her room, Michael stretched out comfortably on his back in the roomy double space and addressed his dead wife, somewhere beyond the foot of the bed. "Your plan was an inspiration, Sarah," he said softly. "You knew the stipend would not run to a housekeeper's salary indefinitely." And he turned over to wait for his new fiancée.

With this story, I wished to widen our current perceptions of the erotic. Like most of the characters I find myself writing about, Mavis is neither gifted nor glamorous—at least, not in the conventional sense. She has, however, reached a moment in her life when change is imperative.

LILITH
❦❦❦❦❦❦

Francine Falk

A stick of sandalwood incense smoldered in a bronze burner, its filament of sweetly pungent smoke curling and shifting in a soft breeze that now and then wafted in from the open bedroom window. A fragrance like sex, thought Mona. Lying on the bed, she inhaled deeply and sighed, stretching her long, thin legs. She was nude, nude and waiting for a phone call—for words that would waft her to a temporary heaven the way the breeze . . .

Her languid thoughts were interrupted by the jangling of the phone; before the second ring, she eagerly reached for the receiver, cradling it between her ear and a hollow in the pillow.

"Were you waiting for me?" asked a husky female voice.

"Yes," answered Mona, and when she heard the tension in her own voice—the telltale note of desire—she blushed. "Yes," she repeated, the warmth of her embarrassment increasing her ardor.

"I knew you would be. I love it that you lie there naked—primed—waiting for my call. You are naked, aren't you, my sweet?"

Mona's chuckle was like the throb of a cello. "Buck naked, ma petite." She delighted in their use of silly, extravagant endearments.

"Good," cooed her unseen friend. "Mona—even your name is sensuous. Describe your body to me in detail. Gaze at it, scrutinize it closely. I want you to get turned on by the sight, as though you were someone else. Do that for me, Mona. Make me see it."

"I can't. I'd feel so—I don't know—narcissistic."

"Why must we always equate self-appreciation with narcissism?" The voice had taken on an assertive, pontificating tone. "I think women need to focus more attention on themselves— in every way, and without a sense of guilt; it's guilt that trips us up every time. We need to erase it from our lives, we need to reclaim ourselves and our right to happiness and . . ."

Mona shifted on the bed, stretched her legs, and let loose a massive sigh. "Is this going to turn into a sociopolitical lecture or are you going to . . ." She paused, searching for words to clearly yet elegantly state the activity they engaged in almost every afternoon.

The friend whom she had never met laughed a velvet laugh. "Or am I going to . . . what?"

". . . do your stuff."

"I love it when you're blunt. You're turning me on, you know."

"I'm glad," said Mona, warmly. "What about you—are you naked?"

"Yes—except for a long string of pearls."

"A nice touch. Do me a favor."

"Anything, puss. I'll do anything you want. I have no shame. I'm your slut, your slave."

It was a playful abasement but heady nonetheless, and Mona squirmed. Finally, she was able to collect herself enough to issue a request. "What I would like is for you to take the pearls and drag them slowly along your crotch."

"As you wish." There was a pause.

Glancing absently about the room, Mona found that her attention kept returning to the oval-framed picture that hung opposite her four-poster bed; it was a Victorian fashion plate showing two delicate, doll-like women hidden under layers of frilly, bell-shaped skirts and crinolines. They seemed to be watching her—sly, knowing expressions on their otherwise prim faces. Mona stuck out her tongue at them and averted her eyes.

"The beads feel smooth and bumpy. Oh, yes," murmured the voice. There was a long, lush sigh. "I'm holding an end of the necklace in each hand as I glide it along my lower regions— my knees bent in a most obscene position. Can you picture it?"

"Yes—I can almost feel it, in fact." Of its own accord, Mona's hand drifted down and wedged itself against her slippery, satin folds—her thumb softly and rhythmically mashing against a clit that had become an alert and throbbing nub. "Mmm," she murmured, "tell me more."

"Now and then, a bead or two lodges in my quim and ass. I pull them out—slowly. It's an exquisite sensation." The words flowed like syrup, the speaker sounding drugged with ecstasy, as Mona began to savor the pulses of heat now flowing through her own body.

"You're tempting me to get up and go hunt for *my* pearls, but I'm feeling much too lazy. I'll just use my hands." And as she said this, two fingers slid into her hungry channel, then skimmed down her perineum to probe at the tightness of her twitching anus. They were avid explorers, those fingers— wicked, determined. "I'm hot and slimy," Mona informed her friend. "Mmmm, what you do to me."

There was a chuckle on the other end. "We're animals, aren't we?"

"Like two bulls in heat," she agreed.

"An apt metaphor—though the gender's wrong. Tell me what you're doing to yourself, my horny lady."

"What do you want me to do?" asked Mona. "Just name it."

"I can't. The phone lines would melt."

"Let me describe myself, then, as best I can—even at the risk of sounding narcissistic. You see what you've done to me— I'm no longer the modest and demure young woman I was at the start of this exchange."

"Good," said her lover.

"Well, first off, I note that my nipples are about the size and color of pencil erasers. And I sport a mammoth muff—a noticeable contrast to my narrow hips and coltish legs."

"The body of a pubescent tomboy. I'm drooling."

"I'm twenty-seven," said Mona. "That's postpubescent, I would say."

"What I would love more than anything right now is to probe you with my tongue."

Mona shivered.

"Tell me what you're doing this very second."

"Right now, I'm batting at my clit."

"So am I," said her friend. "Let me hear you come. I'm ready."

This request was all Mona needed to be catapulted into heaven. A yelp, a moan—and as her invisible lover climaxed with her, the sounds were echoed in the receiver that still lay pressed against her ear.

"My god," said the voice, "I came like the end of the world."

"It was an apocalypse for me as well."

"Tomorrow?" breathed her friend.

"Yes. Oh, no—wait, I can't. The painters are coming tomorrow. Damn. Make it Friday."

"Friday, then. Sweet dreams, my Mona."

"Wait—before you hang up—tell me your name. Please. It's not fair that for all these weeks you've known my name but I don't know yours." It was a plea Mona had made several times before.

"I told you, I don't like my name. Anyway, I prefer it this way. We can feel secure and totally uninhibited—totally. Besides, you once said yourself that it's extremely titillating—the strangeness, the anonymity."

"Yes, I know, and I agree, but, well, fair is fair. You're one up on me."

"All right—how about a compromise. *You* name me. Any name you like."

Mona pulled at a loose thread on the bedspread while considering the matter. "It's not the same, you know."

"It's the best I can do. Believe me, I have a really hideous name. I'd prefer you didn't know it."

"Poor baby." Mona wound the thread around her finger and yanked, grateful that the spread did not unravel. "Well, how about Lilith, then? I like the legendary sound of it; it seems to suit you."

"Lilith," said the woman, testing it. "It's lovely. Lilith it is."

"Bye, Lilith."

"Bye-bye, Mona. We'll be in touch." She giggled.

"Wait a second."

"What?"

"What we do—is that what they mean by 'oral sex'?"

"Very funny. Bye, now."

"Bye."

Reluctantly, Mona scooted off the bed and began to gather up her discarded clothing—jeans, wrinkled blouse, scuffed loafers, thick socks; while doing so, she briefly experienced the strange feeling that she was picking up the worn, mismatched pieces of herself. Since leaving her teaching job to pursue a writing career, a course that so far was proving unsuccessful, she had often felt that way—disused, even scruffy.

The Victorian ladies on the wall seemed to mock her. They, at least, fit their place and time and even now were suited to the quaint decor surrounding them. Mona, on the other hand, felt that she was neither fish nor flesh nor good red herring.

The words "double life" flashed into her consciousness. She studiously ignored them, and went about tidying the bed— replumping the pillows, pulling the white chenille spread taut so that no one could ever guess what glorious self-abandon had taken place there.

The sweet delirium had begun innocently enough. It was not deliberate on either of their parts; it had simply happened, which made it seem all the more magical to Mona.

In an effort to launch an informal poetry workshop, she had

posted notices on the bulletin boards at the local colleges, and among the calls that trickled in was one from a friendly, vibrant-sounding woman with whom she had struck up an immediate rapport—the kind of instant camaraderie she hadn't experienced since high school.

Within minutes, they found themselves joking, laughing, philosophizing, griping. That simple request for information stretched into a gab fest lasting for over two hours, and after they had hung up, Mona went about with a sense of exhilaration that persisted throughout the remainder of the day. Later she realized she'd failed to get the woman's name.

The very next day they were on the phone again, reveling in the pleasure of newfound affinity. The conversation turned to the topic of sex—their turn-ons, turn-offs—until gradually, in what seemed a natural development, they found themselves making verbal love to one another. This time Mona remembered to ask the woman's name, but by then she would not reveal it. Nor her phone number. And, not surprisingly, she never appeared at the workshops.

"You have me at a definite disadvantage," Mona had complained.

"I know, my sweet. But I'm a coward. Maybe someday."

So far, that "someday" had not arrived. The unseen Lilith was still in the control seat, so to speak; Mona could only wait for the calls; she could not initiate them. At times, she rather enjoyed that aspect of the situation, but more often she felt hurt and vexed by the imbalance. And "Lilith" remained a beloved stranger, a phantom she could neither see nor touch.

She folded the towel and returned it to the bottom drawer of the nightstand. The "fuck-towel," Norman called it. Mona stared at the scrolled mahogany drawer for a moment while absently fingering a zit that was forming on her chin. Such an earthy, practical man—an ordinary Joe. She had called him that once and he had gotten pretty steamed; in fact, he had sulked for two whole days.

For the hundredth time Mona wondered how he'd react

were he to learn of her afternoon delights. Outrage or titillation? Poor Norman. What he would probably feel was desolation. He would think he'd failed her sexually or at least romantically. He must never know, she decided. Never.

That evening for supper she fixed spaghetti and meatballs, his favorite. Later, she lay on the four-poster bed, the towel underneath her, while he plunged his rampant cylinder of flesh in and out, in and out, like a machine. She smiled limply, and when his face crinkled and he grunted, she emitted an authentic-sounding moan, and he kissed her lips, then rolled over and quickly fell asleep. The ladies on the wall appeared to sneer. They knew her secrets.

Friday morning, hours before the anticipated phone call, Mona became a prey to certain longings; her soft cleft throbbed and grew moist; her face was warm; she was feeling restless and distracted.

But she didn't masturbate. Not alone—that would be cheating. It really would seem that way, she thought—like infidelity.

Odd. She realized suddenly that she seldom felt that she was cheating on Norman. Funny.

"It'll have to be a quickie," said Lilith in a silken drawl. "My brother just called to tell me he'll be here in about a half-hour. He has a paper that's due out tomorrow and he wants to use my computer."

Mona pouted, scratched at a large mosquito bite on her knee, wrapped the coiled phone cord around her finger.

"Mona?"

"Yes, I'm here. I hate feeling rushed."

"Consider it a challenge, honey-love. You start."

"Tell me about yourself."

There was a pause. "I'm tall and slender. My breasts . . ."

"That's not what I mean. Tell me, you know, what you do, or fill me in on your past or something. Tell me about yourself."

"I can't." Mona heard the drag in the woman's voice. Sadness? Exasperation?

"I think I'm in love with you." Mona found that she was holding her breath, and she expelled it with a quivering sound.

"You know that I'm married."

"Yes, I do know that."

"We have to keep it this way," explained Lilith, in the pleasant but firm tone of a headmistress. "And it's not just because it's more exciting. It's safer, for both of us. I don't think either of us wants this to get out of hand. I mean, we don't want to screw up our lives over this or hurt anyone, now, do we?"

"I don't care anymore." Mona sat up in bed, excitement creeping into her voice. She gestured with her free hand. "I want to soar. You're the one who's always talking about freedom and eliminating guilt and how women should feel they have the right to happiness and fulfillment."

"Now you're lecturing me. That's a switch. I deserve it, though, I suppose." Her voice sank. "I'm a hypocrite and a coward."

"No, you're not," said Mona earnestly. "You're, well, it's understandable, I guess."

"Listen," said Lilith, "I better get going. Ron'll be here soon. I'll call you."

"When?"

"Soon. Tomorrow, if I can."

After they hung up it occurred to Mona that Lilith had not really responded to her declaration of love. She felt her stomach tighten.

She glanced around, nor really seeing anything. The heavy, acrid smell of paint hung in the room. Incense and open windows had failed to dispel it.

Rapt, Mona sat on the edge of her bed, staring at the sleek beige phone, willing it to ring. She was attempting to summon Lilith telepathically, if she could—commanding her with the force of her thoughts to call.

It wasn't working. Three weeks had gone by since the last brief exchange. "I shouldn't have pressed her," thought Mona, berating herself. Her anguish was lavish, all-consuming. Slumping, she took a deep breath and gazed out the window at the green park across the street. There was no breeze, and the motionless, closely spaced trees had an artificial look. Somewhere in the white, neutral sky a pale sun was lurking.

She was very sweet to Norman that evening—solicitous, charming, attentive. He responded in kind. At one point, he even made her laugh. He was really a good man, she thought. And he loved her so.

"You can't have everything," she thought. She was sure Lilith would agree, despite all her assertions to the contrary. Maybe that was why she'd decided to end the affair—she was being mature and realistic.

The next day, the sun was out in full force; the sky was a piercing blue; the trees rustled. Mona was sitting on a bench in the park, watching a robin that was hopping and strutting about with a small worm dangling from its beak. The bird suddenly flew off, and as she raised her eyes to follow its flight, she spotted the figure of a woman who was standing motionless some distance away. Mona received the distinct impression that the woman had been watching her for some time.

She squinted, trying to discern her features, but the woman was standing in the shadow of a large oak, making it difficult to see her clearly. With a start, Mona realized suddenly who the woman was, and she slowly rose and took a few steps forward. The woman remained stationary and continued to watch her steadily and without expression.

She had a handsome, regal face with dark, liquid eyes, chiseled lips, black brows. Although fairly young, she emanated a serenity and self-assurance that verged on hauteur. The eyes were sultry, the body lean, statuesque.

Mona approached within five feet of her and still the woman didn't move. For several moments they stared at each other, locked in a wordless and profound communication. Then the woman turned suddenly and strode off, as though feeling some dreadful enchantment. Mona refrained from calling out; she loved her enough to respect her uncertainty, her fear of complete surrender.

The next afternoon the phone began ringing gaily, insistently, and Mona scurried up the stairs to the bedroom. She knew who was calling.

"I'm sorry if I worried you," said Lilith. "I had to take a break and sort things out."

"Tell me all about it." Mona felt suspended, no clear thought or emotion stirring in her; she merely waited.

"I want us back the way we were. Maybe someday I'll have the courage for more than that. Take me back, Mona. I missed us. I do love you. I'm sure about that much, at least."

"That was you I saw in the park, wasn't it?"

"I don't know what you mean." There was mirth in her voice.

"Go ahead and tease me if you want," said Mona, "but I know it was you, even though you'll never admit to it. You're quite beautiful, by the way."

"Thank you. So are you."

"Oh, really?" said Mona with an exultant laugh. "And *how* do you know that?"

"I can tell by your voice and manner. I'm very sensitive, you know."

"And very stubborn," added Mona.

"And sexy?"

"Very sexy."

"I know. So are you. Make love to me."

Mona nestled lower into the pillows and exhaled a rapturous sigh. "Softly press two fingers against your secret folds and pretend that they're my lips . . ."

"Yes, my butterfly—anything you want."

And as Mona continued with her elaborate and delicately

lewd instructions, she could hear and feel the mounting passion of Lilith; and as she fondled her own warm flesh, seeping its excess of pleasure, she saw the face of the woman in the park— an image of hope and desire that she knew would remain with her forever.

For many women—at least for those who, like myself, are somewhat inhibited—the idea of anonymous sex is very freeing. Although the affair between the two women in the story involves the safest of safe sex—no physical contact—both find it thrilling. I also wanted to explore just what constitutes infidelity. Do desire, fantasy, and verbal love play alone, even if they culminate in climax, count as cheating?

SHOES
❦ ❦ ❦ ❦ ❦ ❦ ❦

Lawanda Powell

Girlfriend, I don't believe in spendin no whole lotta money on no shoes. And even if I did, that ain't no reason to keep 'em locked up. So what am I doin with this here box? See, I got to explain how it is with me and Russell.

I had been knowin him for a long time. Always did like him. Not like that. I just liked to keep his company. Russell had somethin about him that drawed me to him. He one of these men that like women. I mean, really like 'em, not just for foolin with, but to be friends with and joke around and laugh with. Russell and me went out lots of times and spent the whole night laughin bout one thang and then anotha. Couldn't remember the next day bout what, just that we had a good time.

Well, one night I was up to Marguerite's. You know that place where Gilbert's band plays. Gilbert was wailin on his sax and, girl, we was ballin. Everybody was all dressed up. I had on my purple dress with the gold threads and the turquoise flowers. You know, the one with the ruffles around the hem and the back out. Lookin good. All the mens was posin around like peacocks and all the women was flouncin round like peahens tryin to be noticed.

You know I thought I was too cute to be standin around with the rest of those heffas. I mean those mens' heads was big enough without me addin to they adoration. So I took to standin by myself at the bar facin the door so I could see whoever was comin in. That's how I happened to see Russell.

Now, in all the time I spent with him, I never thought of Russell in any way more than as a friend. So you know I was not ready for what happened next. And while I know why I stay with him, for the life of me, I cain't figure out what made me get started. I mean he ain't much to look at, bald and short, but that night, I'm here to tell you, that man was fine!!

It was hot outside and he had his jacket slung over his shoulder when he walked in so I could see everythang he had. His shirt was fittin him real close, and I could see every muscle in his chest. When he turned around, I could see how his pants cupped his behind. And, right off, I knew just how it would feel if it was my hands on his naked behind 'stead of his draws. Just thinkin about it gave me a thrill that started in my coochee and spread up and out so far he must have felt it too. Cause he looked up, and, girl, our eyes met, and right then we both knew that we was gon' get it on.

Now, don't get me wrong, we didn't just like that run off and do it. We worked up to it. First he had to pretend he didn't see me. And so did I. But you know I knew where he was every minute of the time. I saw him talkin to Rosalee and the way she was rubbin his thigh. I saw how that huzzy Greta Mae was lettin her titties brush up on him tryin to pretend she didn't know it was happenin. All the women was flockin to him. It was like he was a chocolate ice cream cone and they all wanted a lick. That's all right, I said to myself. They was just warmin him up for me.

He finally worked his way round to me and asked me to dance. The band was playin somethin whiney and slow and we pulled up real close to each other and started grindin. Chile, I hadn't done no grindin since I was in high school. I had forgot how good it felt. He had his thigh rubbin between my legs, rubbin and rubbin in time to the music. I could feel his thang get hard and his breath hot on my neck. Breath hot and soundin like he had asthma or somethin. I like that. Listenin to a man breathe hard and knowin he's doin it 'cause of the way I make him feel. Makes me hot.

His hands was strokin the middle of my bare back and I was holdin tight onto his shoulders tryin to keep myself from grabbin his behind and everythang else 'cause after all I was in public and I don't do that stuff where folks can see me. Girl, that man was gettin to me.

Now, that's how we got started. And we gon' stay together, too. Cause we know just what the other one likes. Russell know how to touch me. He got hands that know when to be rough and when to be soft. He knows I like him to grab my behind real firm and make it move so the stroke is right. He know how to touch my nipples just so, makin me want to scream out his name. But I don't, 'cause his mouth, his lips sweet like candy, is over mine, and for me to scream out, he'd have to move 'em. So I moan. Only real low, so I can hear him breathe. I love to hear him breathe.

And I know what he likes. Russell likes me to wear shoes. Not just any shoes. He likes me to wear mules. You know, those shoes with the toe out, and no straps, and four-inch heels. I remember how I found out. He gave me some money and told me to buy a pair of shoes. I went out and bought this pair of black pumps I had been eyein for about a month. When he saw 'em, he was mad. He grabbed me up, took me to the store, picked up a pair of mules and told me that the next time he sent me to buy some shoes these were what I was supposed to come back with. Now, sometimes he sends me and sometimes he comes home with a pair. I got 'em in every color. You can look over there in the closet and see 'em if you want to.

Anyway, we bought those shoes, went home, and he showed me what to do. I got all dressed up, shoes and all. And then I stripped til I didn't have on nothin but those shoes. Russell watched the whole time, his thang gettin stiff as a baseball bat and him breathin heavy. That was some of the best lovin I ever had.

Now, any time I see him with a pair, I know what to expect. I know we gon' do us some real good lovin, that he gon' last a real long time. I put on those shoes and nothin else. Parade around, throwin my hips everywhichway while Russell lays on the bed watchin me. All the time I watch him out the corner of my eye, likin to see his thang jumpin up and down and hearin him breathe.

But you didn't ask me bout all that. You want to know about this here pair of shoes and this lockbox. I already said I don't pay no money for no shoes, but one Easter I saw this pretty pair of white slingback pumps with the toe out that was just what I needed to go with my new suit. They cost way more than I usually pay, but they was so pretty, I bought 'em anyway. Come the day I wanted to wear 'em, I couldn't find 'em nowhere. Somethin told me to check the closet where we keep my special shoes, and there they were. No longer fit to wear to except in the privacy of my bedroom. That man had cut the straps off!!

So now when I buy toe-out, slingback pumps, I lock 'em up in this here box. That way, girlfriend, I keeps my shoes and my lovin in good shape.

The incident of the cut shoe straps is true: It happened to someone else. I first heard it in a hotel room where a group of women were discussing men's preferences in sex. We laughed at all the stories and, for this one, had to be picked up off the floor. But the more I thought about how we laughed, the more I thought about how vulnerable we are when we reveal our sexual preferences and how hurt and humiliated our partners would be if they knew how we'd laughed. Then I started thinking about the power there is in knowing what pleases our partners. What a turn-on, this power! Yet I also had to wonder how much of our sexual behavior is engineered solely to maintain this power and its feeling.

A SLOW FREIGHT

Phaedra Greenwood

When I fell out of a twenty-one-year marriage back into the singles meat market, I made three rules for myself: No one-night stands, no married men, and if I'm going to go to bed with some guy, he at least has to love me. The last part was trickier than it seemed.

It was summer in North Carolina. The radio said the heat index was going up to 105. I worked in the dark room all morning and then felt so sleepy I lay down for a nap. I woke up longing to be outside lying in the grass with Sam, looking into his cat-green eyes. He hadn't called or sent me a letter all week. He had told me he'd be busy this weekend. Maybe he even had a date. The first time he'd taken my hand, I'd gently pulled away. "I'm fifty and you're thirty-three," I reminded him. "So why even start?"

A couple of days later I got a letter saying, "I'm not a hit-and-run artist, but you're wise to protect yourself by setting limits rather than diving in head first with your eyes closed as you have in the past. But about the difference in our ages, you must resist the urge to 'protect' me from myself, as you tried to do the other night. I felt humiliated and diminished by it. We're both adults. This is the only ground rule I insist on as we open these emotional negotiations. Someday I would like to have a wife and family. My wife will probably be closer to my age than you are, but that's a long way off. What I am ready for now is an emotional, growing relationship with a woman."

I wrote back, apologizing, but said I thought almost any woman would prefer that a man move slowly so they could both savor each step. I included an article about human courtship that showed how we tend to follow a pattern as prescribed as the dance of mating birds. I was surprised and gratified when he started using these steps on *me*, sending me flowers and poetry. I loved having a friend to hike with, someone who needed the quiet forest paths as much as I did. But the closer we got, the more Sam's cheek twitched up in a nervous squint. Then he withdrew.

Now I was halfway out the door when the phone rang. Sam's voice resonated with a deeper note, and I resonated with it. "I have to see you."

"Okay."

"I wasn't going to do this," he said.

"Me neither."

"We have to stay out in public so things won't get out of hand."

"Okay." His AIDS test was negative, but I had to wait for my six-month test until September. We arranged to meet in the parking lot at the art museum in half an hour.

I took a quick shower, patted myself dry, and rubbed some lotion on my arms. Fifty years old, and my body still felt good, but I noticed the fine wrinkles on the backs of my hands and a couple of age spots. No makeup today, I decided. We've been dating for three months. If he's really my friend, it's time for him to see me as I am. I slid into my shorts and a tank top. All my bras were in the wash—the hell with it.

I raced over there. I was fifteen minutes early. I climbed the green mound of the hill where I could view the whole parking lot. In the distance I heard the sharp wail of a train as it sped by. In two months I'd be on one headed west. And not have tasted Sam? I didn't want to get locked into another long-term relationship, but I was curious about where this might go. I wanted to give it a full breadth.

At last he pulled his Toyota into a space below. He got out and locked it. The sun struck the gold wire of his glasses as he squinted in the direction of the museum. That squint went right to my heart; sometimes he seemed like an old man. He was tall and walked stoop-shouldered. There's your Lancelot, I thought, following him along the crest of the hill. At last he looked up. "Terry?"

I waved and skipped down the slope into his arms. He laughed and hugged me, then gave me a letter he'd just written. I flopped down on the grass to read it and in a second he was lying beside me.

The letter said, "Terry, you are so funny, strange, magnetic, and erotic. I have to have you. Let's be pals. Let's walk in the woods. Let's be artists. Let's get it on. Your pal, Sam."

"Have to, eh?" I laughed. "What about my test?"

"There are lots of other things we can do. We don't want to skip any steps, right? Restraint heightens the passion. I just read that."

He took off his glasses. Without them his face looked wider, more boyish; when he smiled, two dimples appeared. He braced his foot against the bottom of mine and kissed me. "Sometimes I draw back," he said, wiping his mouth, "because your mouth is too wet. You want it moist—enough to make a good seal."

"How you go on."

People were walking by, glancing at us surreptitiously. He swung one leg over me and kissed me into the ground. I was coming unglued. "I want to get on top of you," he said.

"Not here."

"Can I look down your shirt?"

"All right." I sat up. He pulled my top out with one finger and peered at my breasts.

"I can't see without my glasses." I snorted.

"I'd like to give it to you, just the way you want it," he said, breathing in my ear. "Fall asleep, wake up, do it again. Fall asleep, wake up. Do it again."

"Can you *do* that?" I asked, surprised.

"I don't know. But I have a very vivid imagination. You don't realize how inexperienced I am. The last date I had was a year ago. She slid down on my couch as we were kissing. I was thinking, Oh, now I'm supposed to feel her breasts? Okay. I guess. I hardly knew her. Just when I was beginning to relax and think I might be able to perform, she jumped up and said she had to go shopping."

"How humiliating."

"My shrink says I'm afraid of women."

"Sex is less scary when you feel some affection."

"I don't really know what love is."

"Neither do I."

"But I read somewhere that people need to be touched about twelve times a day. Let's go to the park where we can feel each other up."

"Not your apartment?"

"I'm not ready for that. We might do something wild."

We drove to the park. The landscape was heat-blasted; a gray haze hung above the highway. We strolled down a path to a picnic table and paused to admire a huge oak tree, the muscular roots, the spread of the branches. Cyclists spun by on the path and disappeared into the woods. I sat on the tabletop and he stood in front of me.

"May I touch your breasts?" he whispered.

"Okaaay."

He leaned toward me and slowly massaged my breasts. "Were they once less floppy?"

"Sure. Bigger, too. Wish I had the body I had at thirty-three. I'd wow you. I was really beautiful."

"You're really beautiful right now. I like how your breasts fit in my hands—like perfectly shaped fruits. Can I spread your legs apart?"

"You're so outrageous!"

He took my ankles and spread my legs. "Can I kiss your crotch?"

I shivered. "Okay."

He glanced around, then bent over and thrust his head between my legs. I felt the pressure of his mouth on my pubic bone. My pants were wet.

We got up and wandered down the path that led to the river. The woods were dry and still. I watched a trickle of sweat start from under his hairline and run into the folds of his neck. I wanted to lick it. At last we bumbled down the hill and saw Maple Creek sparkling through the trees. We paused to listen to the woodthrush as it dropped liquid notes, one by one, into the leafy coolness. In this loop of the river the water was so still and clear you could see all the way to the bottom. The clay banks made the whole river look red. Young maple trees arched over the water, lime-green leaves reflected against the burnt sienna bottom, their spiky shadows clearly outlined on the sand. "Wish I'd brought my camera!"

"Do you see those little fish in the shadow of that rock?" he said. He was standing so close I could feel the heat radiating off his skin, smell his sweat. I took off my shoes, while he stood on the bank, his face pink with the heat, slapping at a horsefly. I waded into the water, hesitated, then launched myself flat out. I rolled onto my back and paddled a few strokes. Suddenly, my whole body felt refreshed. "God, this is nice!" My nipples swelled against my tank top. Sam knelt and unlaced his boots. He waded in, sat down, sighed, and closed his eyes. I paddled up beside him and leaned back on my hands, silky water soothing my shoulders. His eyelids were a delicate lavender. His body hair came in three colors: red, black, and blond. Every red hair of his stubbled cheek glowed in the sun, but when he turned his face into the shadow, the blond ones stood out. The folds of his blue shirt were molded to his shoulder.

He opened his eyes and turned his mouth to mine. "Try this," he said. With the tip of his tongue, he pressed something into my mouth. Sweet and sour. I took it out and looked at it. A Jolly Rancher. We shared the candy back and forth, tongue to tongue, until it was gone and we were both out of breath.

It took forever to get back to the car. Fireflies winked phosphorous yellow in the blackness between the trees. The car door was still warm from the sun. I leaned back against it. He made a sucking noise with tongue and teeth. "Wanton woman." He fell in slow-motion against me, pressing me with the full weight of his chest and thighs and soft belly, taking my whole mouth in his. The top of my head was buzzing. I panted and pressed back.

"You're so delicious!"

"Have we skipped anything? What's next?" He led my hand rather forcefully to the bulge in his pants. I caressed it through the fabric.

"This is building trust," I said, "taking the scare out of it. But you'd better be careful. I'm relentless when aroused."

A pair of headlights caught us and we sprang apart. "Well," he said, folding his arms, "what do you think of the economy?"

"It sucks." We guffawed.

"I'm beginning to have real feelings for you," he said.

"I hope so!"

"I'm so lecherous."

"That's healthy."

"It takes such a long time to get to know someone," he said. "What is love, anyway?"

"A warm feeling in your chest."

"Just that?"

"Yes. No."

"Are you hoping if I go to bed with you, I'll fall in love?" he said.

"No. I'm hoping someday Miss Wonderful will parachute into your life. Meanwhile . . ."

"I want us to stay connected, no matter what happens," he said.

I ran my fingers down the valley of his spine and up under his shirt. His skin was cool, silky. I couldn't get enough of him. "We're good together," I said, stroking his arm. He nodded.

"I'm sorry you had so little touching in your marriage. I'd like to take you home, take off all your clothes, give you a full massage and then make love to you." I burrowed my nose into his furry neck.

"Let's."

"I'm embarrassed."

"About what?"

"The train. It runs right behind my apartment."

"I've always had a thing about trains," I said. "Take me home. I just want to hold you. I don't care if we make it or not."

He put on Santana, lit a candle, then gently undressed me. My arms were stiff at my sides, bolstering my breasts. In the candlelight the stretch marks won't show. But what about the hysterectomy scar? Oh well . . .

"Where do you get off having such an outrageous body at your age?" he said. I gave him a faint grin.

"I dance. And roller skate." I lay face down on his bed and he gave me the massage, just exactly the way I wanted it, pressing into my neck and the sore places around my shoulderblades with strong thumbs, slowly loosening my muscles, his total attention in his hands. He massaged me from my scalp down to the arches of my feet till my whole body tingled. His hands were so large that together they spanned my back. His palms were hot and molded to my curves as they slid around and around, up and down my arms, across my bottom, down my legs.

He flopped down beside me and looked into my eyes. "That's it."

"Aren't we going to make love?"

"Something's not connecting . . ." He was still wearing his jockeys. I ran my fingers gently over the lump that just fit my hand. It stirred like a sleeping animal. I reached inside his shorts and brushed the back of my hand across his belly. I tugged at the elastic.

"Why don't you take these off?" He grinned, embarrassed.

"Can I leave my socks on?" I nodded. The hair that curled up out of his groin was reddish gold in the candlelight. I moved down and kissed his expanding flesh. I licked the blue rivers of veins. His penis pulsed and lifted toward my mouth, seeking heat. The tip was the shape of a ginger leaf and the tiny wrinkles fled beneath my tongue until it shone red and silky. I closed my mouth over the whole shaft, gently sucked and flitted my tongue over the cap until he let out an "ahhhh!" I caught his liquid in the palm of my hand. His toes twitched, he sank down on me and lay still, but I was panting and wet.

In the distance a long wail rose and rose. "It's the cry of the wild train," he said. "About to come right through the kitchen."

"Waaah . . . wa . . . wa . . . waaaaahhhhh . . ." The wavering note flattened, fanned, and broke into two notes, one high and one low, echoing back and forth between the buildings and trees.

"Nothing like a slow freight," he said, pinning me with his heavy thigh. "My turn." He kissed my breasts and my belly and opened my legs. "I did learn something in college," he said. His agile fingers explored my crevices. His tongue circled my nipple and his long finger slid into me.

Now came a deep rumble as the train hurtled toward us, a surge of power, tons of rolling metal, a bell clanging, a squeaking of wood and banging of metal. I felt the engine throbbing in my chest like another heartbeat. Then the click-pause, click-pause, click-pause, of the wheels vibrating through me. "My god!" It went on and on and on.

"Take your time," he said. "I'm with you. I'm enjoying this." I trembled and rocked under his relentless hand, lifting my hips to meet him, till I cried out and came.

In a swirl of air, the train was gone and the woods settled slowly back into stillness. His eyelashes brushed my cheek. One eye looked into mine.

"I don't know which I love more," he said, "you or the Norfolk Southern."

I laughed and kissed his neck. "Neither do I."

I have always loved trains, the dark journey that takes us out of ourselves into worlds we never imagined. Like Millay, "There isn't a train I wouldn't take, no matter where it's going."

THE NIGHT MARE

Susan Dooley

Her father picked up the quill and made the entry in the family bible. "Hannah m. William Eaton, May 14, 1692." Marry in May / rue the day. But Will had insisted. Now her father was reaching for her hand, giving her over to the stout, middle-aged man whose sudden, relieved smile showed the brown stumps of teeth that marred his mouth.

"She has to marry someone," her mother had argued when her father had protested the union. Hannah had agreed. She had to marry someone.

Will tugged at her hand, pulling her toward the door, not seeing the cup of cider her father held out. Ill luck. Ill-mannered. Ill. Hannah fought a fog of dizziness and jerked her hand away. Surprised, Will turned, and then he saw the cup. He drank it down quickly, his mind on the rising wail of a child. A second shrill voice had joined the first. Five months since Anne had died. Five months of listening to his children cry. He wanted his new wife at home.

That morning Hannah's father had driven the farm cart to Will's house and unloaded Hannah's spinning wheel and the dovetailed chest he had made to hold her linens. They stood now where he had left them, pushed against one wall of the low-ceilinged room. The house was smaller than the one where Hannah had grown up. There was only this room, with the bed in the corner, a table and stools, and a loft where the children slept.

As they stepped through the door, three-year-old Natty asleep in her arms, and Lem, five, riding on his father's back, she saw a bunch of wild roses in a jug on the table. She was touched that Will had bothered, but it was Abby who danced in front of them, pointing, "See! See what I got thee."

It was seven-year-old Abby who helped her boil the beans and the salt pork for dinner, while Will sat outside. It was Abby who, when dinner was done, pushed her brothers up the ladder to the loft. Will had gone outside again, leaving Hannah alone to open the chest and take out her nightdress, to climb into the big bed. Hannah lay with her eyes closed, listening to the deep twang of the frogs in the pond. Fiddle frogs. Joining them, playing its sweetness through her mind, was the memory of Thomas's flute.

They had lain like this in her parents' house, the bundling board making a small wall between them, the heavy quilt shutting out the cold and wrapping them together with their whispered plans.

She heard the door open, heard the soft huff of Will's breath as he blew out the candles, and felt the heave of the bed as he settled beside her. Hannah felt his hand touch her leg through the heavy linen of her nightdress. Then he was pulling the cloth up around her waist, shoving at the bulk of it, pushing it aside as he rubbed his hand up her leg, across her stomach, until it rested on her breast, closing, opening, squeezing tight, letting go. He was like a cat kneading a quilt, Hannah thought, rigid under his touch. He had begun to make quick gasps, and with his other hand he pulled at one of her legs, opening her up, spreading her apart. Hannah pulled her legs back together, but now Will was on top of her, using his legs and his knees to hold her open, poking at her with his hardness. He was beating against her, thudding up against bone and unyielding flesh, trying to force his way inside. He found the opening and she felt herself give way with a rip of pain and a dragging of flesh as he pushed himself in and out, beating, beating, beating until he moaned and shuddered and brought himself to a stop. She felt the full weight of him, sinking down on her, burying her in the softness of the bed, making it difficult for her to breathe. She bucked her hips, trying to make him move. Then she wiggled sideways, inching her way out from under him. As she escaped he gave a great breath that slid into a small, whinnying snore.

Hannah wanted to get up and wash away the stickiness between her legs, but she was afraid to move. By closing her eyes and keeping her hands at her side she could avoid contact with Will's unfamiliar shape. She could pretend that the warmth and the weight next to her was Thomas. Thomas come back.

His eyes were gray as the slick, slatey sea, laughing at her when he bent over to stroke her cheek. The first time he had touched her. She was thirteen, gathering shore greens for supper. He was sitting on a rock, mending his net with long wooden needles. He had come from England to live with his uncle, he said, and offered to show her a patch where the wild blackberries had just come ripe. They had eaten all that they picked, and he had laughed at the way her lips had turned purple from the juice. It was when her skirt had gotten caught in the brambles that he had first touched her, lifting a hand to cup her chin, tracing a rough finger along the line of her cheek, lightly, mockingly touching her purple mouth.

Abby pushed the treadle of the spinning wheel with her toe, touched a finger to the wheel, setting it in motion. At seven she should have learned to spin, but for months her mother had lain sick in bed. Now Hannah dragged the wheel outdoors under the elm tree that shadowed the yard and sent Abby inside for the stool. Holding the young girl on her lap, Hannah guided her foot to the wheel, held the small hands inside her own as she showed Abby how to take the greasy fleece, comb the fibers so that they lay in one direction, and then feed them into the gulping mouth of the ravenous wheel. The child spun out a long, thick lump of yarn, looked at the fine thread that was wound around Hannah's spindle, and began to cry. "It takes time to learn," said Hannah, and then remembered what her own mother had done when, at five, Hannah had first been set at the wheel. "We will save this, Abby, as my mother saved mine. Would it please thee to see the first thread that I ever spun?"

Abby nodded. Hannah found the crude, lumpy rope at the bottom of her chest, under the linens, lying next to the flute Thomas had left behind.

The flute played in her dream that night and brought Thomas with it. It was the first time she had seen him since he had gone away. "I'm sorry," she said, looking into his gray eyes. "I never meant for thee to go." He smiled. "I never meant to," he said. Hannah was glad he was back, glad that awful night was forgiven. She had been fifteen and her father had accepted that she and Thomas would wed. When Thomas came on the winter evenings, the two were left alone in the big room where the fire threw shadows on the wall. They were allowed to lie together in the bed, warming each other under the quilt, as long as the board lay between them. Thomas had become adept at unbuttoning her bodice from his side of the board, at rubbing the nipples on her breasts between his thumb and forefinger until they grew hard and Hannah felt the pleasurable heat spread between her legs. That night, when her parents began to snore in the next room, Thomas had wickedly moved the board.

"We are on our honor, Thomas," Hannah had reminded him, but he had ignored her, sliding his hand under her dress, under the heavy petticoat and up her leg until his palm rested on the rounded mound of hair. He stopped his rubbing when Hannah protested, but he kept his hand there, warming her with a flush of desire. "Sin," she had hissed at him, but he had begun again, rubbing the heel of his hand gently against her, bringing her a surge of pleasure. His mouth had moved to her breast and for the first time he had taken the nipple between his lips, licking the hardness with his tongue. Hannah wanted him to keep touching her forever but, instead, she had sent him away.

"We pledged our word," she had said, making him leave the warmth of the bed. She never thought he would go home by boat. The wind was too high. Hannah pitied Thomas the long, cold walk along the shore, but she thought of the danger to their souls and she could not let him stay.

It was late afternoon of the following day when his uncle came. The canoe had washed ashore. Thomas had not come home. Turning her back on all of them, she had rested her head on the chimney piece. Level with her eyes was Thomas's flute, lying where he had left it.

The weather had turned warm and dry. Will had gone off to Apple Island with the other men to fish for cod. He would be gone several weeks while they pulled the nets and hung the fish to dry, storing them in barrels for the winter.

Lem was playing with Natty in the tall grass, making the baby giggle by blowing puffs of seedy dandelions up into the air. Abby had dragged the bag of seed corn from the cowshed and now Hannah was showing her how to plant. Wrinkling her nose, Hannah picked up one of the dead fish they had found on the beach and buried it, firming the soil on top and pushing the shriveled yellow corn seeds into the center of the mounded earth. She took a handful of red-speckled beans out of her apron pocket, and, using her thumb, pushed them one at a time into the dirt around the mound. "When the vines come up, they'll climb the corn," she explained to the watching child. Hannah felt happier with Will gone, teaching Abby, picking up Natty when he cried and feeling his soft, sobbing breath tickle the nape of her neck.

Evenings were long in June's lingering light, and after the children had climbed up to the loft, Hannah took her knitting outside. The lilacs had begun to bloom. Their sweet scent reminded her of how Thomas had once come to call, his arms so overburdened with the purple blooms they spilled out behind him in a fragrant trail. From that night on, as soon as the children were in bed, Hannah hid herself in sleep.

Thomas was riding a mare with a coat so black it was patched with blue. How strange, thought Hannah. Thomas had never owned a horse. Seeing her surprise, he laughed, caught hold of her, and swung her up behind him. Hannah tried to tell him that she had thought he was dead, but the horse stamped and fidgeted and Thomas didn't hear. Hannah gave up trying to talk and wrapped her arms around his waist, rubbing her cheek against his back and pressing hard against him, feeling the warmth of him through his shirt. Thomas kicked hard, and the mare jumped. Hannah tightened her hold, but the mare did not jolt back to land. She kept flying higher and higher, soaring over the tops of the spruce trees, out over the rocky shore, up and up until she finally brought her hoofs down among the scattered stars.

When they landed, they were on a strip of wet, dark sand curled with silver where the waves rolled in. Thomas slid to the ground and began to play his flute. "You left it behind," Hannah said, amazed that he should still have it. But Thomas shook his head and smiled at her. Holding it up to his mouth, he blew a few false notes and then began to play a soft, rollicking song, dancing toward Hannah, his feet shooting sprays of sand onto her skirt. She laughed at him, grabbing up her skirt and giving it a shake, sliding off the horse and letting her own dance keep pace with his. Hands at her side, she danced in front of Thomas, moving faster and faster with the music until she looked down and realized that she had danced the buttons off her bodice. Her breasts were bouncing bare under Thomas's delighted eyes. Hannah danced forward, letting her breasts come within inches of Thomas's chest, then she darted back, her feet kicking up mussel shells and tangles of rockweed. Her bodice had slipped down off her shoulders, leaving her naked to the waist, and she shivered with pleasure as the sea breeze touched her skin. "It is wicked," she told Thomas, but he shook his head. His clothes had come loose, too, and she saw him grow hard as they danced. He danced closer, teasing her, letting his cock brush her skirt.

Her skirt was gone. She and Thomas were naked, their feet stamping prints in the sand. Then they were lying together as they used to do, and he had come into her, not like Will, hard and hurtful, but gently pushing pleasure into the place between her legs. He put both his hands around her buttocks, holding her tight against him as he rolled over on the sand. "Sit up," he said, and she sat astride him, looking into the dark mist of his eyes. "Like a horse," she said, rocking herself atop him, feeling a sweep of warmth. "I am riding thee like a horse."

She woke hard, dropped back onto the bed from a far height. The cock was crowing, and the geese were making a shrill complaint. She felt heavy and stunned all that day, her mind slipping back to the beach where she and Thomas had lain. It began to rain shortly before supper, and she used the weather as an excuse to send the children to bed. She pulled the quilt over her own head and closed her eyes, seeking sleep.

She stayed in bed for a week, dreaming and languorous, ignoring Abby's frightened questions, irritated when Natty tried to climb into bed next to her and cuddle inside her arms. With her eyes closed, she held onto the night, held onto Thomas who was somewhere nearby, waiting for the descent of darkness. When Abby had fed the children and they had climbed up to the loft, Hannah would feel the floorboards shake. The mare would trot into the room and Thomas would reach down his hand, pulling back the covers and pulling her up out of bed. "I have two mounts," he teased her, the second night he came. "I ride my mare and I ride my mistress Hannah." Later he had had her kneel on the silver sand and had come into her from behind, fluttering his fingers over the nipples of her breasts as he drew himself in and out. Hannah was happy to please him, to have her desire bring him back from the waves that had washed him away.

❦   ❦   ❦

On Saturday, Abby gave up trying to rouse Hannah. She walked the road until she found the house where she had seen her father wed. When she returned, she brought Hannah's mother with her. Tea of raspberry leaves and tea of vervain. Her mother stayed by her side, making Hannah sip the warm drinks. That night it was her mother's body that bulked in the bed next to hers.

On Sunday they all went to the meetinghouse, Lem and Abby walking solemnly ahead, Natty trying to wiggle away from her arms. There were people Hannah had never seen before. If she had not been so sleepy she would have wondered at the unfamiliar crowd, at the murmur of voices that should have been stilled in prayer.

"Satan is among us!" The words came as a bellow of rage. The Reverend Winthrop stood in front of the congregation, his words shocking them into silence. The rumors from Salem were true.

Later, when Hannah tried to remember what he had said, all she could recall was that if you flung a witch into water, she would not sink. That there was an ointment that enabled them to fly through the night. Smallage, wolfbane. She couldn't remember what else. And then, "With a strange and sudden music, they fell into a magical dance, full of preposterous change."

Hannah was afraid to sleep. Not Thomas, but an incubus. Satan had seized her soul and she was sick with shame at the pleasures she had felt. That night, she did not climb into the big bed. She took her stool outside and kept herself awake by praying in the dank night air.

For three nights Hannah sat outside. She slept only in the light of day, while Abby sat nearby practicing at the wheel and Natty curled inside the curve of her arm. She tried to shame herself by thinking of Tituba, the slave-witch. Flying through the night, as she had done. Dancing to the devil's tune, as she had done. She thought of the loss of Thomas and it hurt to breathe.

She slept. Abby, frightened of what was happening to Hannah, did not wake her. She fed Natty and Lem beans and biscuits from last night's supper and helped them up the ladder to bed. Alone, exhausted from her nightly vigils, Hannah drifted deeper and deeper into sleep. It was not the noise of the horse's hoofs that woke her this time but Thomas's hands, pushing against her shoulders, rocking her gently awake. She opened her eyes and saw his face. He looked so sad. "How can thou doubt me, Hannah? Do thou not recall? 'If two be one, as surely thou and I, / How stayest thou there, whilst I in heaven lye?'"

"In Ipswich, not in heaven," Hannah corrected, remembering the poem and sure now that it was Thomas before her, repeating the lines he had used to bid her farewell. She was light with joy at his return, giddy at the mistake that had led her to think him the devil. They rode this night to the blackberry patch where they had first met, and he placed the juicy pips one by one upon her tongue. Then he kissed the sticky sweetness of her mouth, letting his tongue travel along the edge of her lips, licking her clean. When he pulled back, she leaned toward him, letting her own tongue etch the outline of his mouth, a tool to retain forever the image of his lips. With her mouth on his, tongues touching, they breathed their souls to one. If he were to pull away, thought Hannah, my life would run with him, draining away on the ground. With their mouths still touching, they slipped slowly down to where soft green moss made a springy cushion of the earth.

Thomas touched the top button on her bodice and her dress disappeared. Hannah felt his mouth smile against hers. He was proud of his trick. She smiled back, and pressed her forefinger against the front of his shirt, making his clothes vanish as well. What a clever pair we are, thought Hannah, as he rubbed his nakedness against her. The wind of the ride had loosened her hair and Thomas delicately brushed the strands away from her eyes. He traced her mouth, then let his fingers memorize her breasts, her stomach, the soft place where her thighs came together in a mound of silky hair. His fingers drifted past the opening, teasing her with their nearness, but he continued down the length of her until his finger stroked the sole of her foot.

Then, slowly, he was moving his hand up her calf, warming the soft skin of her inner thigh, letting his fingers find a home in the place between her legs. Hannah was edgy with pleasure by the time he came to her. She closed her eyes, still seeing his face floating in the darkness of her desire as he loosed his life inside her.

There were things one could do. A knife laid under the foot of the bed. A horseshoe over the door. Satan banished, or would it be Thomas she kept at bay?

Will would come back and lie between her and the night mare. There would be no more danger. No more delight.

Hannah dreaded the day of Will's return. Still more, she dreaded the day when she might feel life quicken inside her, might feel the kick of a small, cloven hoof.

When the children had gone to sleep, Hannah walked down to the shore where, earlier that week, she had seen a canoe. The wind had begun to rise and she had to use the paddle as a pole, pushing away from the rocks. Wind and tide tied her to shore, and her shoulders ached with the effort to push out to sea. Then the wind dropped and the tide turned. She was free. As she began to paddle, she heard a faint whickering. She had known Thomas would find her, the night mare dancing toward her on the darkened water.

"Let us sleep in thine arms, and awake in thy kingdom," she whispered to God or to Thomas as she felt herself lifted out of the boat and folded into the familiar warmth of his body. Safe now, she let her hands find their way beneath his shirt, her lips breathing life into the nape of his neck. Thomas turned and smiled. He held up one hand to show her he still had the flute whose soft, sweet notes Hannah could faintly hear, drifting across the water.

———————

I wanted to write about guilt and found it hard to do so in a contemporary setting. How do you write about the way love can break down your boundaries when sexual satisfaction is considered a right and eating dessert a sin?

G.T.T. (GONE TO TEXAS)

❧❧❧❧❧❧❧

L. M. Lippman

She does not admit it now, but Cameron came to Texas for a man. With a man, her college boyfriend. It seemed to solve so much, on that gray March afternoon, when Paul announced he had one of those teaching jobs that wasn't really a teaching job. If she went with him, she wouldn't have to think about what she might do, or who she might be, or if she should be with him at all. Those questions could be postponed, just a little while longer. Cameron saw her life as a cloth to be laid out for a picnic on a beautiful but windy day. Having a place to live it, San Antonio, would anchor the first corner. The others would follow.

"It's like the Peace Corps but in a public school!" Paul had told Cameron excitedly, and she tried not to listen to the part of her mind off in the corner, evaluating him. It was a part of her mind that seemed to be getting louder recently. It was hard to imagine they would last, in any city. Still, as spring stalled out somewhere south of Boston, Cameron found herself checking the San Antonio temperatures in the *Globe*'s weather tables. Seventy degrees, 80 degrees and, just once, a high of 87 degrees. To Cameron, who was pale and thin, with blood pressure so low she fell into near-swoons if she stood up too quickly, it had an undeniable appeal. She found herself eager to hear Paul's impressions after he visited his school in April, during some city-wide revel known simply as Fiesta. She found that a wonderful conceit—a party so big it was simply called Party. Paul told her people ate turkey legs in the streets, waving them around as if they were Latino versions of Henry the VIII. There were four parades—three through the streets, one on the shallow river that wound through downtown. Better yet, the entire city smelled like La Choza, their favorite cheap restaurant.

"Fiesta is bigger than Mardi Gras," he told her, sounding faintly like a brochure for the Chamber of Commerce. Bigger, better, grander, hotter—Paul's vocabulary had already been corrupted by Texas, Cameron noted. Still, she was pleased when he rolled a dyed egg toward her across the Formica table. They were in their kitchen, the warmest room because it had only one outside wall, which faced on a narrow courtyard. Here, Cameron could prop her always cold feet on the radiator and keep her back to the space heater, while Paul brought her cup after cup of hot tea.

"They call them *cascarones*," he said, as she examined the egg, dyed an uneven blue, its tip shaved off and replaced by a thin piece of pink tissue. Then, to her dismay, he took the egg from her and smashed it against her head, just above her left ear. Tiny pieces of confetti—blue, pink, turquoise, red, gold, silver— scattered through her hair and spilled across the table. She liked the effect but was annoyed he had broken her egg.

"You can't save it," Paul said, laughing at her. "The whole point of a *cascarón* is breaking it."

He had brought her salsa, too. Mild, medium, hot. It was important, Paul said, that they learn to eat the hottest kind. They didn't want to be gringos or, worse, *bolillos*—white bread. Cameron noticed his "r" rolled like a runaway train; he hit the double "l" diphthong like someone biting off a piece of beef jerky. Her own Spanish was far more fluent, yet prim and contained. She considered it in bad taste to speak a foreign language too familiarly.

Paul poured a sample of each salsa into their Four Corner snack trays, found in an overpriced consignment shop they loved. They had been able to afford the gilt-edged squares only because Utah was chipped and Arizona was missing. Paul handed Cameron a tortilla chip—this, too, from San Antonio, he told her, one of its many fine local tortilla factories—and she whisked it through each sample, her sinuses clearing for the first time in weeks. Paul's forehead began to sweat on medium and the hot made him wheeze, inhaling a chip's sharp corner. Cameron had to pound him on the back to dislodge it. She had known they would not last. Now she found herself wondering how long Paul would last on his own. In San Antonio, in teaching, in any place that was not Boston and college. She could not buttress him. She suspected no single person, or place, ever could.

He gave San Antonio six months, not even the entire school year. For him, it was over before she got there. Paul flew down in early August. Cameron followed ten weeks later, arriving just before Halloween in the ancient Toyota whose ownership was no longer clear, and found him surprisingly pale and fragile. Haunted. In fitting Gothic style, there was even a streak of gray in his left sideburn.

"You look . . . distinguished," she said, after considering and rejecting several other adjectives.

Paul muttered that the city was unlivable, more like an outpost of Mexico than the U.S. of A. He actually said "the U.S. of A," as if he were one of those military types who retired to San Antonio, the kind of people who called talk radio shows. He said he was stuck with an ESL class—English as a Second Language—that was twice as much work, because you had to translate everything, which was ridiculous, immersion was obviously the way to go, hadn't anyone here heard of "Hunger of Memory"? The phones went out when it rained, he said, and innocent-looking streets filled with water, sweeping people away. So why did they call them low-water crossings? Weren't they high-water crossings? And these red bumps on his arm, he asked her, was that heat rash?

Cameron, unsure how to respond to this rush of words after four days and almost forty hours on the road, simply said:

"What about that all-night taco stand you told me about?" That produced another rush, about how the classic Mexican diet was really very healthy, but Texas had perverted it, with too much cheese and sour cream. He had especially harsh words for avocados—"All fat, even if it is a monosaturate!"—but he finally took her to Taco Cabana.

On the patio there, a *tostada compuesta* and *carne guisada* taco in front of her, Cameron lifted her thin shoulders, enjoying the harmless breeze eddying around her. She was warm, her food was hot. Across the street, a mechanized billboard spilled forth a neverending circle of white bread slices. Butterkrust. She felt very white herself, almost larval, surrounded by so many wonderful hues of brown skin. But no one seemed to hold it against her. She would buy a Guatemalan belt, the woven kind she had seen back East. And she wanted one of those T-shirts with the tinted photographs of old cowgirls. As for cowboy boots, she was already wearing a pair, purchased on a detour through a town called Rosebud. She stretched out her legs, admiring the dove-gray boots, with white and navy insets. She felt like one of those outlaws in the nineteenth century who scrawled "G.T.T." on the door—Gone To Texas—and disappeared into their new lives. Or the men who flocked to the Alamo to fight and die, although they had no real stake in the future of Texas. That was it—she was Davy Crockett.

As Cameron fell in love with San Antonio, Paul's hatred of it grew. Whatever had spooked him in August stayed with him throughout the sweet, mild winter, a time of achingly blue skies and balmy temperatures. When spring break came, he announced he needed to take a little trip alone. To Nepal. For Cameron, the hardest part was trying not to be too happy. She was fond of him, in the way that one feels affection for any significant part of your life that is about to end. Graduation had brought out the same nostalgic twinge—and the same firm desire to see it all done. She helped him pack, checked to see if he needed any booster shots, didn't quibble when she saw him take T-shirts and soft, worn polos she knew were hers. They said goodbye at the airport, surrounded by rich Mexicans carrying bags from weekend shopping sprees at Saks and Marshall Fields. Cameron tried not to rush the farewell. They even kissed, for old time's sake. Then she drove to a nearby taco stand, one that served beer. When a plane flew overhead, she lifted her Pearl Light in salute, and watched, telling herself it was her past vanishing on the Northeast horizon, although she could not know if it were Paul's plane. Paul ended up in Nepal and a distant corner of Cameron's memory, where he existed solely as someone she called "my college boyfriend." San Antonio was hers now, hers alone.

She quickly forgot Paul had found the perfect apartment, just one big room on the top floor of an old mansion, with stained glass windows facing east and west, French doors to the south, and a tiny deck on the north. And she seldom recalled it was he who had seen the ad that led to her job, working at a small foundation that underwrote folk art exhibits and local artists. History had always been particularly malleable here, she knew. Some of the best stories were true—Colonel Travis drawing a line with his saber, daring the Alamo defenders to cross it, separating the men from the boys. Some, like the legend of Emily Morgan, the beautiful slave who made Santa Anna late for San Jacinto, appeared to have little basis in fact. It made no difference, Texans stood by them all. Cameron especially admired the Daughters of the Republic of Texas, the keepers of the Alamo, who steadfastly withstood any attempt to disrupt their myths.

It was an old city, at once wilder and stuffier than any place she had known back East. The Anglos still ruled, especially the old German families. The city's aristocrats were so sure of themselves that they crowned each other during Fiesta. Then the daughters of the finest families traveled through the city on flatbed trailers, so the citizenry could admire the embroidered-and-beaded trains on their $10,000 court costumes. And at the "coronation," the girls bowed to the King of the Order of the Alamo by sticking one leg out directly behind them, then pressing their foreheads to the floor. Most needed an escort's hand to rise again, but an occasional princess or duchess, her thigh muscles tightened by years of horseback riding or soccer, rose of her own accord, drawing an ovation from the audience in the municipal auditorium. Cameron went, just to see this, then practiced the curtsy at home, giving up after she toppled over and bruised her forehead. She would never be a duchess.

At work, the Vaca Naranja Foundation, she served at the pleasure of a board of retired duchesses. She was a go-between, the buffer between them and the artists they patronized. Yes, patronized was the perfect word. The president of the board, a banker's wife who had endowed the foundation and named it, more or less, for the University of Texas mascot, liked to tell Cameron: "I think those Day of the Dead figures are just precious." Or, "Do you think you could tell that woman who makes the puppets to put a little more pink in their costumes? I think that would look *darling*." Cameron claimed she forwarded the requests, but they always seemed to get lost in translation.

It was hard enough just to get the Latina artists to take the pitifully small amounts of money offered. She would sit across from, say, Beatriz Villarreal, trying to convince her that the $350 stipend was free and clear, a way for her to buy paste for the *papier-mâché* monsters she made under the pecan tree in her backyard. Or she would drive all the way to Hondo, just to sneak up to Josefina Cisneros's mailbox and leave a certified check to cover the costs of the paint she used on her bleach-bottle versions of various saints. It was a wonderful life. Then August came, and she began to understand what might have dimmed Paul's pleasure in San Antonio.

It was hot, of course, and had been hot since April. The city, like a slow-baking oven, gathered more and more heat with each week. Cameron was stoic at first, almost smug, telling people it was no different from the humid summers back East. She was even rather proud of not having a working air conditioner in her car. At day's end, when the seat belt left a wet sash along her clothing, she felt as if she had been decorated for bravery in the world's oldest battle, the struggle against the elements. Then August began and soon she was stripped of her medals.

In August, San Antonio was hotter still, a seeming impossibility. Meanwhile, the city's interiors seemed to get colder and colder, as if it were written somewhere that inside and outside must be equally inhospitable. Even the air conditioner in her apartment could not be controlled; no matter how she fiddled with the little dials, it roared forth with a blast of too-cold air. She was reduced to wearing socks to bed. And that was before August.

In the daytime, she wore even more clothing. Slips, cardigans, pantyhose, things she had left behind in grade school. But you needed them indoors here. Then she would step outside, and her pores would seal beneath her nylons as if she were the gilded woman in *Goldfinger*. Or perhaps it was more like some cheesy science fiction movie, where one lived beneath a bubble dome and was cautioned never to enter the Forbidden Zone that lay beyond, so beautiful and enticing. She moved quickly through the outdoors, from home to car to work and back again. She felt as if she were scuttling through some war-torn city where gunfire might erupt. She carried the necessary supplies—dark glasses, diet soda, an elastic band to whisk the hair off her neck—and kept her head low.

And there was no end in sight, no cool breeze promising an imminent change, no hope that Labor Day was anything but a Monday. This was August's true cruelty here. People went to the Coast, to wade in the flat, warm waters of the Gulf and drive on the tar-flecked beaches. Cameron, used to the Atlantic, could not bear to look at it, much less swim in it. Nearer by, people drove to New Braunfels and rented inner tubes for floating down the icy Gruene River. The river froze one's backside, while the sun baked the front. Or they drove to Austin to swim at Barton Springs, a quarry that was never above 63 degrees. People sat on the lawn until it was unbearable, then surrendered to the frigid water. There was no modulation here, Cameron noted in disgust, just extremes. August stretched out before her, taking up September and, she feared, the early part of October. She felt like a runner who had trained for a ten-kilometer race only to find it was ten miles. Her only relief came in Mexican restaurants and *taquerías,* where hot food and iced tea, or cold beer and margaritas, combined to make her feel neither hot nor cold, but like Goldilocks at Little Bear's plate, just right.

She sensed it was her golden locks—really more of an ashy blonde—that drew Jesse to her. Or perhaps it was her appetite. She felt him before she saw him, sneaking up behind her in Los Arcos, where she was eating the no. 12 dinner. Two chicken enchiladas, a crispy taco, a gordita, beans, rice, and a basket of flour tortillas. It was the meal she ate everywhere, and everywhere it was served with the same warning: **"Don'touchthe-plateisveryhot."** Yet the person who served it often carried it in bare hands, suggesting the plate was not so hot after all. Cameron, noticing they gave her mild salsa, suspected they thought she was a lightweight. She ate more to compensate, wiping the plate clean with a lard-light tortilla. This is what she was doing when Jesse crept up behind her.

"*Cálmate, la flaquita rubia,*" he said, touching her elbow. Tex-Mex for: Calm down, skinny blonde. Cameron turned, let her narrow eyes take him in. Slender, with the long, tight muscles of a marathon runner, the profile of an Aztec, and skin the color of flan. Brown eyes, of course, and black hair, with color so true that light couldn't penetrate. His Spanish had a precise, fussy edge, as if he were mocking her, or himself. He wore jeans and a clean, white T-shirt, stretched tight across his chest. He could have been a lowrider, a *vato.* Or he could have been one of those new-and-improved Mexicans, who want to grow up to be JFK or the mayor of San Antonio. Impossible to tell, and not important. If Cameron wasn't sure she liked him, she knew she liked the way he looked.

"I'll show you someplace where you can eat your fill." He put money on the table, more than enough to pay her bill, and Cameron, knowing only what his fingertips felt like, followed him from the restaurant. She still had a tiny crescent of beans on her left cheek, a refried dimple.

She followed him as if he were Juan Seguin, sent from the Alamo in the dark of night to bring help for the 180 or so who remained there. She followed him as if he were Zapata and she, a Mexican farmer ready for a revolution. She followed him for the simple promise of a bigger, better taco, and it seemed to her the history of Texas, of the world, of time, was based on nothing more than the desire for more.

He led her through the streets of the West Side, supposedly a dangerous place. They walked past piles of rubber tires, past *botánicas* and *farmacías,* through Alazan-Apache Courts. Even the housing projects sounded exotic here, Cameron thought.

They found a festival. There was always a festival in San Antonio. Fiesta, the one that had so charmed Paul, started the season, but another followed every weekend, increasingly obscure in origin and purpose. By August, they didn't even bother to name them anymore. The disc jockeys on the Spanish radio stations simply said: "*Venga al Mercado, para más cerveza y comida.*" ("Come to El Mercado—or the park, or the convention center, or the River Walk—for more beer and food.")

Smoke from a hundred grills hung over Eureste Park. An accordion dueled with a saxophone. In front of a makeshift stage, people danced the polka and the merengue. No one seemed to notice it was at least 95 degrees, even at eight o'clock. By daring to move, to dance, they staved off the heat, beers clutched in their hands, sloshing over their feet.

Jesse guided her through the crowds with his fist in the small of her back, hard enough for her to imagine a bruise starting on her knobby spine. "Our Lady of Sorrows," he said, and it seemed mystical, thrilling, ominous. Then she realized he was simply referring to the church booth whose tacos he preferred.

A girl with skinny legs and a round belly leaned across the plywood counter until it bowed dangerously. "TACO, TACO, TACO, TACO!" she bellowed. "Make your own! No skimpin' on the fixins'! Guacamole *and* borracho beans!" She was a good advertisement; she looked like she had eaten a few tacos in her time.

Cameron held a tortilla on her fingertips, large as a Frisbee. She spooned in skirt steak, grilled green onions, *pico de gallo,* guacamole, and still it stretched out, larger and whiter than ever. She added a little bit more of everything, folded it in half, took a bite, and the guacamole overflowed down her shirt, leaving a yellow-green stain. Jesse licked the overflow from her chin and neck, and eagerly she licked him back, although there was nothing to taste on him, not yet. It was the hottest part of the day, but Jesse pressed a bottle of beer against her neck, and she felt as if she were standing in a stiff breeze somewhere along the Atlantic coast. Braced, cooled, refreshed.

Cameron thought of the poster that hung in her boss's office at Vaca Naranja: *El noche cuando viene el hombre con las patas del gallo.* The night when the man with the chicken feet came. If a woman danced with that man, she belonged to the devil. Cameron looked down at Jesse's feet but saw only black Chuck Taylors. Paul had worn those, too, and if she knew anything about Paul, it was that he wasn't the devil.

She thought they might dance, although she had no idea how to approximate the moves she saw. And she felt plain among the women, dressed and made-up, so obviously anticipating the Saturday night they were having. Cameron wore a baggy T-shirt and baggier shorts; her hair stuck out of the back of her head in a straggly ponytail. She wanted to tell them she understood their culture, that she had a degree in Central American studies, that she understood their accented Spanish, so unlike anything she had ever heard in a classroom. She wanted to announce that she could, with a little warning, look pretty good herself. She wanted to put on some mascara and lipstick. But Jesse—had he told her his name, or did she simply bestow it upon him—had other plans. As suddenly as he had brought her here, he took her away, past the *farmacías* and the *botánicas,* past the pile of tires, through Alazan-Apache Courts, ending up at a dark green Lexus, its steering wheel locked with The Club.

She guessed that they were stealing the car and, somewhat dreamily, accepted it as inevitable. She was more surprised when Jesse produced a key, opened the door, and removed the red metal bar from the wheel. "Where do you live?" he asked, and that was more surprising still, for she thought he was, if not the man with the chicken feet, if not the devil, then someone equally dangerous and omniscient. She told him how to get to her apartment. It was the last thing she would have to tell him.

In her apartment, where there were no walls, just area leading to area, it was easy to go from the front door to the bed, with only a few detours in between. But Jesse didn't hurry. While Cameron lay on her soft mattress, staring at the ceiling and trying to remember if she were drinking or dreaming, he found a cognac bottle and two jelly glasses and pulled a chair up to the bed. For a long time, he seemed content just to look at her.

"Show me your stomach," he said, in English or Spanish, she was no longer sure what language they were speaking. At any rate, she did as he asked, pulling her shirt up and shorts down, baring the very white expanse of her belly.

"It still goes in," he said, marveling. He walked over to the bed and held his hands over it as if it were a fire that would warm him. "All that food, and it still goes *in*."

Feeling cold, exposed, she tried to move beneath the covers, but he caught her by the ankle. He snaked his hand up the wide leg of her shorts, and held her there, testing her, taking her pulse. His palm was the perfect temperature, like a bottle of milk tested on your mother's wrist. She felt something she had forgotten: the sensation of being warm, yet not hot, of being cool, yet not cold. She was wet, but she wasn't sweating. He squeezed and she felt her own steady pulse, her blood rushing toward that one point.

Next to the bed, in the window, the air conditioner roared. She could hear it, but she no longer felt the cold blasts of air that had driven her mad all summer, driving her beneath the blankets, only to surface again at three A.M., sweaty and disoriented. The air was still now, but not stagnant, more like the first breeze she had ever felt here. Cameron saw the Butterkrust billboard in her mind, but now it was her body falling forward on the plate, then circling around again.

Her shirt came off, but she did not flinch. He hovered over her, her own bubble, protecting her. He kept his hand between her legs, then fastened his mouth on her breast. Everything was the same perfect temperature, there was no variation. She felt as if she were suspended in amber liquid, ready to be fossilized for whatever future archaeologist wished to excavate her. She felt like a fly dipped in honey. Her muscles worked without her, taking her nowhere. Her legs slapped against his hips, her arms circled his neck. When had his clothes come off? When had the rest of hers? Except for her white crew socks, she was quite naked.

He showed himself to her with a shy pride. "It's like a churro, isn't it?" he said, and the light brown length of him did remind her of the pastries sold at Mexican bakeries. She ran her tongue along it, expecting to taste bits of sugar still clinging to him, but found a different sweetness, more like molasses cookies, or butterscotch brownies.

He began to push inside her, and this felt better still, just a shade warmer than his hands and mouth. Then he stopped abruptly, pulling back, and she heard her own cry, a banshee wail, echoing around them. Her legs boxed his hips as if she were boxing his ears. Bad boy. Bad boy.

But all he wanted to do was remove her socks. She waited, sure this part of her must still be cold, that blood could never reach those distant extremities. He would be disgusted, he would be repelled, and she would be left alone, too cold and too hot, all at once. It was only when he pressed his lips against the arch that she realized her feet were no longer cold. Nor was her nose, nor her fingertips. She felt like a lizard on a rock, or the Cameron who once sat in a Boston kitchen, drinking cup after cup of tea. Warmth became heat, but so gradually that it felt good, natural. And they could face the heat, without air conditioning or icy water or an inner tube to float them down the river. He took her temperature, finding it just a degree hotter with each thrust, until she felt as if she had finally equaled the record high of the day, of the month, of the summer.

She crawled on top of him, determined to make him sweat, indifferent to her too-full belly. She should be ill, she knew, or at least stupefied from her day of overindulgence and extremes. Yet all she noticed was the perfection of the climate—the mechanized breeze washing over them, their mouths swollen as if they had been sucking the salted rims of margaritas all day. Hip to hip, thigh to thigh, they smacked together, and she waited for the hideous tearing sound that comes when perspiring bodies collided in the heat. It never came, they moved easily as two dolphins, twins floating in their mother's belly. From this perspective, she saw how similar their bodies were. Straight, tall, slim. His legs were as long as hers; his ribs winked at her through brown skin. She wanted to get closer still, allowing no space, no air, no breeze, nothing between them. She wrapped herself around as tightly as she could, allowing no movement at all. And it was in the stillness that she felt it, a long rippling sensation that she wanted him to feel, too. She placed his hand back where it had started, so he could feel the pulse again. Stronger, steadier. Hot. And the world settled back into its separate spheres. It was August again.

"A Latin lover," she thought, as the chill crept in. Viva Zapata. Or was she thinking of Santa Anna, so besotted with sex that he showed up late for the battle of San Jacinto, guaranteeing Texas's victory? Time was back in focus, but she could no longer remember her history. The future suddenly seemed near and sharp, and the present was all too fleeting. She could feel August slipping away from her, see the fall's first blue norther massed on the horizon. Shivering, Cameron tucked her feet beneath Jesse, as if he were a radiator she once knew. The mechanized breath of the air conditioner raised goosebumps on her back. It was not that different, after all, from floating down the icy

Gruene River or diving into a quarry. Surviving a San Antonio summer, it seemed, was just a matter of finding which extreme worked best for you.

I hate heat. I hate adjectives like "steamy" and "sultry," which remind me of swamps. But more than this, I hate air conditioning. Only cheap motel rooms, which feel, already, as if they have no connection to the outside world, are improved by air conditioning—but that's another story.

CLIMACTERIC
❦❦❦❦❦❦

I. Buguise

I've been avoiding him for the past three months. Taking the tube at a different time. Waiting till nine-thirty when I know he's already left. Not buying the newspaper on the corner. Not taking the rubbish out. Making sure my husband gets the kids on the school bus. He might walk past. I can't bear the thought of running into him. I can't bear the thought of not running into him. Especially in the morning. That's the hardest time.

It worked. For three months I haven't thought of him. I went to the office. I made dinner. I slept with my husband—never pretending he was someone else. I coped. Well, sort of. And, then yesterday I saw him again. Oh, God. I was coming out the door and he was standing on the pavement, talking to the postman. I walked toward them. It was difficult. I sucked my stomach muscles in. Stood up straight. Dropped my shoulders. Sucked my cheeks in. Held my chin up. Tried to make my double chin disappear. Tried to make myself not look fifty-five years old. It doesn't work. I feel so ugly. So ravaged by time. No one will notice me. No one wants me. My legs were wobbling and my face was trying to organize its friendly-muscles expression. Christ, I'm a walking timebomb. But I made it. The postman smiled and walked off. We were alone. I looked him in the eyes. I always do that. That's the hardest part. His eyes are really the only remarkable feature he has. The rest is just regular middle-aged, probably paunchy, middle-class man. Why does this happen?

He stares back. Very few men can do that. Most of them look away.

"Hi," I say, trying to look composed, feeling shattered. My mind is a pressure cooker.

"Where have you been?" he asks as he walks toward me, starting to come closer. Oh, God. Is he going to embrace me? Why? Does he really miss me when I'm not around? Is this all in my mind? He's looking at me. Not through me. But right at me. I pull back. I stiffen. He holds back. He senses my tension. He must. It's so obvious. He's nervous. No, it's not just my imagination. I'm not making this up. He must feel something. Why else would he notice I haven't been around? He must have missed me. That's clear. Is he scared of contact? Maybe just as scared as I am? Does he want contact? Just as much as I do? I can't talk. I know I have my vague, blank look on. I try not to slouch. I don't want my double chin to appear.

"Where have you been?" he asks again.

"Hiding out. Hiding and working. Working really hard. What's new with you?"

"Nothing. Same as ever."

Don't ask him where he's been. Pretend you haven't noticed the absence. Does he know I avoid him so that I can put some order in my life? Does he know I'm obsessed with him? I know I'm about to ramble. I know I'm about to start saying things that won't make sense. I better leave. That's it. That's all there is to it. Be casual. Be normal. Look him in the eye and say bye. Get out of here. Hurry.

"Bye. See you later." I go back inside, crawl into bed with my husband.

And now I have another conversation, another posture for my fantasies. I'll spend the next few weeks playing with these words, with his meaning behind these words, with his movements. I won't be able to concentrate on anything else. I'll resent any intrusion into my thoughts. I'll be bitchy and mean to my husband, to the kids. My work will suffer. The people I work with will find me distracted and uncertain. No decisions will be made. Oh sure, decisions will be made but only insofar as they don't distract from my thoughts and his comings and goings. He'll be sitting on my head directing my every movement. I'll be out on the street all the time now. I'll be looking for him. I'll consider everything I say and do and hope he approves of my thoughts and actions. I can't stop thinking about him again. I sit in front of the telly. The news is on. I can't concentrate. Is he watching the nine o'clock or the ten o'clock news? I better watch both. I don't want to miss any of his experiences. Did he watch the program on ferrets? Did he read the article on Hemingway? Does he like Hemingway? Does he like the films better than the novels? Does he go to the movies? Did he see *Damage*? Did he think about me when he saw Jeremy Irons fucking his brains out? I couldn't stop thinking about him. My crotch was zooming off into clitoral fling land. Christ. I don't even know if he goes to the movies.

It's not as though my life is lacking in luster. It's even exciting most of the time. I have everything I want. Even more. Lots of travel. Great house. Great kids. Loving husband. I even have great sex. It's just that I want him. No. I don't. I want him to want me.

When I'm not working, I'm thinking about him. No. I'm thinking about him when I work. I think about him all the time. How I can meet him, what we will say, what our first kiss will be like, how we will get in bed, how we will get out of bed. I'm obsessed with what kind of sex he likes. Is he slow? Is he gentle? What does he smell like? Does he sweat? Is he selfish? Does he care about the woman he's with? Does he want to satisfy her? Oh, God. I don't mean her. I mean me. Does he want to satisfy me? Does he like to kiss? I mean, does he really enjoy it? Not just do it to get to another stage? What position does he favor? I don't care. I don't care. I just want him. I've got lots of scenarios in my mind. They often get tangled up so that the end product doesn't make much sense.

And then today we meet again on the street, this time near where we both work. Two days in a row. I can't stand it. Yeah.

We even work near each other. I didn't do that on purpose. I had my job first. It's lunchtime.

I walk down Crumble Street. See him approaching. I pretend I don't see him. Either he's pretending he doesn't see me or he really doesn't see me. I've got to do something quickly or my chance will be lost. What can I say? Say something intelligent, slightly sarcastic. Sarcasm is the best. It will make me sound nonchalant yet knowing. I look up and say "Hi. What are you doing here?" So much for brilliance. That was pretty trite.

"Joanna!" he exclaims. He seems pleased to see me. Is it just a pleased-nice-to-see-an-acquaintance face or is it a finally-we-meet-and-end-up-in-bed face? I don't know. I'm concentrating on staring into his eyes. I don't want anything to ruin this. Do I make the first move? Is that too forward? Can two people, male and female, meet on the street and have lunch? Is it allowed? Will he think ill of me? Does he want this as much as I do? Does he ever fantasize about me? Maybe he's shy and he can't make the first move. He's not shy. Don't be silly. I've got nothing to lose.

"What are you doing here?" he says. Do I read friend in his eyes? Is it maybe even lust? Is he nervous? God. I'm so nervous I can't think? Didn't I just ask him what he was doing here? Why is he asking me the same question and not answering mine? Is this a good sign? Is he just as nervous as I am? Or is he just being polite? Oh, God. Quick, answer him. Don't let him move. Don't let him get away.

Putting on a bored expression, I say, "Getting out of the office and getting something to eat. I'm famished." Maybe my expression was too bored. Now, do I ask him to eat with me? Oh, no, I can't put the words eat and me in the same sentence. I'd faint with pain and embarrassment. I can't say dine. That isn't me. I make fun of people who say dine. What do I say? I know. I know. I can say, "Do you want to have lunch?" No. What if he says no. I couldn't bear it. My hands are shaking. Can he see it? He isn't shaking. He's totally composed. He doesn't know what is going through my brain. I'm just fantasizing. He just thinks of me as an acquaintance. He has no idea. So there's no problem. I can ask him because he won't think it forward or rude. No, no, I'll wait for him to say something. Ask him. Control yourself and ask him. Get the words out. It's OK. He's only human. No, he isn't. That's the problem. I see him as superhuman. No, he isn't. There's nothing special about him. He eats, drinks, and sleeps like everyone else. I know. Imagine him snoring or worrying about prostrate cancer. That will make it easier. He probably has hemorrhoids. That should help. Just visualize him sitting on the toilet and it will be easier. OK. Go.

"I like this street. There's this cheap Indian restaurant over there. I go there whenever I want to run away from work and relax," I reply. I know he likes Indian food. He told me that before. Oh, shit. I've told him I eat here before and he has never said, "Let's meet there. It's right by my office." So. He doesn't want to eat with me. Oh, God. There are those two words in the same sentence again. He doesn't want to spend time with me. He only thinks of me as a dumpy, slightly ditsy middle-aged crone. I don't know what to say now. He hasn't said anything. He hasn't put his hand on my shoulder and steered me toward the restaurant. He's going to go away. I know it. What can I say to make him stay longer? To make this accidental meeting something special? Something we will both remember. Don't say anything corny. Don't mess it up. Keep looking him in the eyes. It's getting harder. It's his eyes. I know. Pretend they aren't staring back. Pretend he has a stye. Oh, don't be stupid. He doesn't have a stye.

It isn't going to work. I'm sure he doesn't have hemorrhoids. And he probably doesn't snore. My legs are wobbling again. Not my legs, really. But my crotch. Oh, my God. I just felt his hand on my breast. I can't stand it. I've got to sit down. I've got to lie down. I've got to hold him. Those lips. Oh, no. I can't look at his lips. His lips are more sensual than his eyes. I never thought about that before. Now there're two things I have to focus on looking at and not looking at. Thinking about them, looking at them.

I lie down. He lies next to me. Suddenly we have no clothes on. We are drowning in a pool of feathers. His body is firm. Not flabby. Not the body of a middle-aged man. We are holding each other. Not tightly. Just gently. We are rocking. Touching each other. Softly. Everywhere. Our lips meet. They touch softly and then harder. We can't stop kissing. I can't open my eyes. I can't breathe. He rubs his leg against mine. I breathe in his smell. It is the smell of sex. Clean and newly born, fresh, scrubbed. I taste toothpaste. I feel muscles, strong and knowledgeable. I hear moans. I sit up. I climb on top of him. Put him inside me. Easily. He slips in easily. I sigh. I move up and down, over and over. I open my eyes. His are closed. Well, really half-closed. His tongue moves gently over his own teeth. I want that tongue in my mouth, not his. I want his taste in my mouth. I lean down and place my lips on his. Our mouths meet again. I don't want to let go. I want to feel this forever. I see apple orchards and sun and hear rushing streams from my youth. From the sex I used to know. From the past I want to relive. I am young and supple again. I have no ties. Total freedom. Lust and innocent pleasure. Moaning, he comes inside me. I can feel him spilling out of me. It is warm and clean. Again, there is the fresh, scrubbed scent of birth. I'm pleased and satisfied. But, I want more. I want to devour him. I want to be devoured. I don't want this to stop.

"Where's this restaurant?" I hear his words through a fog and a tunnel. Are they coming from him? I can't answer him. I don't know what he's talking about. What restaurant?

"Is it the one on the corner?" he asks, still looking into my eyes. His mouth is moving. I can't see his tongue. I don't feel his hand on my heart.

"Yeah. Yeah. The one over there on the other side of the street, next to the lighting shop. They have a lunch special. As much as you can eat for five pounds. Quite good." Well, is he coming or isn't he? Doesn't he understand this is my way of inviting him? Doesn't he realize we've just made love? Doesn't he know the colors and smells and sights are so much more vibrant now? Can't he feel the electric current running from my thoughts through his veins? How much longer can I live with this?

"We'll have to go there sometime," he says.

When, when? Now. Right now. Let's go now. We can make love under the table. On top of the table. Against the door. Anywhere. I don't care. I'll do anything. Just come inside me. I'll climb on top of you. You can slide in. No one will know. I don't care where. Let's just do it.

"Yeah. I need a good curry to get me through the day every once in a while," I say.

"Enjoy your meal," he says as he walks off in the other direction. I stand there alone. Does he know I'm not moving? He's not looking back. He's forgotten me. I no longer exist. I can't leave this spot. We made love here. He lay inside me. He came inside me. I was free. There was no pressure, no pain. How can he just walk off and leave me? Did he mean it when he said, "We must go there sometime"? Was he just being friendly? Did he mean just the two of us? Is he still thinking about me?

This story is part of an ongoing set of narratives. I find myself especially drawn to women whose dramas involve growing old, unwanted, and unloved.

WHERE THE CYPRESS
PAINTS THE SKY

Laurel Gross

The land stretches flat and brown as a piece of toast, then lifts into peaks overlooking the sea.

She is thinking how Dali painted the landscape of his native Catalonia as the contours of a woman—the tan mounds of burnt hills the breasts, the valley between them extending into flatness until a slight rise of belly, and then the lowlands, pressed between the thighs.

But maneuvering her rented Fiat further along a scratch of red earth, not in Dali's Spain but in Greece, she is seeing the face of a man she once knew on this island. For a moment, she can feel his presence, hot on the seat next to her. But it is only the sun.

A little edge of earth is all that separates her from a spill into the sea, a reminder of how quickly the end can come. The way things turn out is not always up to you, it takes luck too . . . even as a child she knew that, skipping over the cracks in sidewalks, just in case . . .

The grip of the stick shift feels unnatural. She's never gotten used to it, all the adjustments you have to make in a manually driven car. The automatic is what she craves. Automatic—that was how it was when she met the man whose imagined presence still seems so real to her. The way she fell for him was instantaneous.

Fall.

It is a long way down to the sea. Others have slipped from paths just like this. The twisted carcasses of metal sprout foliage in neglected meadows and cliffsides. But she is cautious, wary, careful. A planner. She makes lists. Lists are her salvation. She makes a mental one now, running down an inventory of the stuff she has lugged across the sea and crammed into the tiny Fiat—her Nikons, their wardrobe of lenses, tripods, film, flashes.

She is well equipped, prepared for anything.

Anything—except the old feelings that rush up at her as fast as hairpin turns in the road. It is amazing how much you can feel . . . for a dead man.

The landscape has triggered feelings she'd thought were buried. But they are fresh as plowed earth.

The earth that here is red as an open wound.

Again she sees how close to the edge she is. Her hand wavers. He used to do the driving along these foreign roads.

It's a relief to see the path widen, the tall cypresses signaling that she is on the right road. There must be a dozen of them. Giant feathered arrows pointing to the sky. Or fingers in prayer: supple, swayed, steepled.

He had taught her to see like that. One thing always changing into another. Trees . . . arrows . . . fingers.

The drop to the sea vanishes. Secure enough to lean her head out of the window, she swallows the fresh scent of lemon from the groves stretching out in a field with no boundaries. On the other side, the tangled tops of olive trees scrub the sky like brushes.

A paved drive leads to a cool white villa. Sleek to the ground, everything about it reads privacy, and a discreet plaque identifies the place as "a distinguished hotel of the world."

Outside, a young man shields his eyes from the noon glare. He looks like a dark paper cutout against the white. A sailor on the lookout for land. Getting closer, perhaps he is not quite so young. But he is a good number of years younger than she.

She is one year shy of forty, and feeling older.

He motions for her to leave the car right there. She pulls up, cuts the engine, and almost steps out before realizing that she isn't wearing shoes.

A heel pokes out from under the passenger seat. The rubber floor is grainy with sand. She scrapes the straggler out. The other comes easily. But, swollen from the heat, her feet resist the leather. Suddenly she's Cinderella's ugly sister anxiously stuffing a clumsy foot into a rejecting shoe.

The Greek is still there. Something self-possessed and gracious about him suggests he is not the bellman.

The gravel rearranges itself underfoot as the spiky heels dig in. They're so impractical on this terrain, making it hard to retrieve your land legs. And yet it feels sexy the way they break the arch, forcing you to hold your belly in when you walk.

"*Kaliméra,*" says the Greek, reaching for her hand.

She had forgotten how beautiful a language it was. It had been a long time since she'd heard it spoken like this on its own turf—an utterly different species from the harsh voices shouting food orders in Greek diners.

"You may call me Stathis. I am the proprietor here."

His hair curls tight around the head like one of the statues in a museum. He is fair for a Greek.

"Claire Winter," she says.

"Yes, I know. I recognize you from your photograph."

What photograph?

The portrait on the back of her book on Alaska, he says. A guest had sent it after hearing him confide that he had "always wanted to see snow." So it seemed "fortuitous, like an omen" when her letter arrived saying that she was coming to photograph his island for a book on Greece.

And so he is definitely not the bellman, this receiver of gifts, but the owner of the island's best hotel.

It occurs to her that this Stathis had been waiting for her all along. Does he wait outside for all of the guests?

But she is a curiosity. Someone to greet.

And she has made snow real to him.

He leads her into shade. A white hall sparkles with the colorful chips of mosaics. The floor like a picture shattered and put back together. Blue sea swirls, and a dolphin encircled in the center by a ring of shells. The room, evoking a royal residence from an earlier time.

"Perhaps you have time for lunch before you start?"

Is he inviting me? she thinks. She's not sure, but he might be. Then again, maybe not. But Greeks are friendly, hospitable, there's no harm in it. "Yes," she says. "After I've stored my gear away. I can't live without my cameras."

"Your cameras? Oh, yes. Of course." He gives her such an endearing smile, she suspects he almost pities her for being so intimately attached to so much baggage. She almost expects him to say, "Life without love, or children? Impossible. But cameras?"

She may be stereotyping him. He is so Greek, so handsome. She looks away. It's one thing to stare through the camera, but doing the same thing with your eyes alone reveals too much.

She doesn't usually react to people this way. But these islands, they can work on you in strange ways. You can come with the best intentions, to work, for instance, but soon you are staring out to sea . . .

Even the dedicated loner will be wishing there was someone standing beside him, someone whose eyes will follow as he points out something on the horizon.

She thinks, I've been here five minutes, and I'm almost forgetting my cameras.

But her host has not. "We'll put your things in my office. They'll be safe there. Nobody can get in there but me," he says.

His hands are like roots. Brown and firm against the white tablecloth. His fingers lean toward hers.

"You've been to Greece before?"

"A long time ago." She doesn't volunteer more.

"You will know, then, what you wish to photograph?"

"I have some ideas. But I'll look around, see what strikes me."

"So you can be—how do you say—spontaneous?"

"Spontaneity's highly overrated."

She gets the feeling the stranger senses more about her than she admits. She would give anything to be able to live in the moment instead of being fed by memory or anticipation, but that is a talent that eludes her. Surprisingly, the idea that the hotelier may have some insight doesn't make her feel uncomfortable.

Instead of contributing further to conversation, he swishes the wine in its glass. The sun glows through it, stamping a ruby reflection on the damask.

Spontaneity. She'd given in to impulse. Once. It had been the most joyful and the most treacherous time of her life. It was just like Theodorakis had said. One thing's always capable of changing into another. Joy and pain, how closely they were linked. How one flowed back into the other.

First, his exquisite presence expanding to fill her like a fertile womb, and then, all that transformed into torturous absence when he returned to his family and his wife.

Life is fluid, he'd say. Like the clay he molded. He hated it when it was time to set anything to bronze. "By then—it's a dead thing," he'd say, his fingertips still throbbing to mold the clay. To destroy and build again.

That's why he'd never go to museums or galleries to see his sculptures. "It's a funeral," he'd say.

How many times she'd found him inspecting some "finished" object that, despite its beauty, didn't please him. In an instant, he'd pummel its features back to pulp.

But she doesn't share any of this with the stranger who now challenges her solitude from across the table. Stathis refills her wine glass without being asked, as if he has known her for a long time and is sure she will drink it.

She lifts the hard edge of the cup to her mouth. It feels like some kind of assent. She doesn't usually drink in the afternoon, especially when she's planning to work. But this is so pleasant, and she hasn't been near the sea in a long time.

The sea, which has always been seductive, the way it reaches out to you with its sounds and enfolding layers of greens and blues.

The terrace where they've been dining overlooks the water like the deck of a ship. It's mystical, the way Greece can be, and she half expects a mermaid to jump up and greet them. But then she is reminded how fickle the sea can be. How it can change at any moment and swallow up great ships, devouring those who love it most. The Greeks know its double-edged nature so well they put a message on their money warning about it.

Her companion softly calls something to the waiter, and a plate of fruits and pastries appears. Yet still they sit in silence.

A famous radio host once told her, don't feel you have to fill the empty space with words. There has to be room to breathe. "Sometimes the best part comes in the silence." Instinctively, she follows that advice now.

The honey from the pastries sticks to her fingers. She licks them like a child. Stathis pulls on one of his curls. It springs back into place. A nervous gesture? Or a flirtation? He delicately peels an apple, cuts the pulp into thin slices. Bites one of the half-moon shapes he has neatly arranged like a series of mirror images on the plate. She can almost taste the juice.

How many times in your life are you aware of the sound of your own breathing? Of another person's? These things preoccupy her.

These, punctuated by a crossfire of bird cries. The soft step of the waiter. The chime of a china plate. The pines shuffling their needles.

She watches him take some slivers of cheese and arrange them on their plates as if they were the petals of a pale flower.

"You eat like an artist," she says. The words ring so strong in the quiet that she imagines she hears them twice—once for real, and then again as an echo.

But they do not offend. "Growing up in a house full of

chaos, you learn to appreciate order," he says. There's an edge in his voice, but he softens it. "My mother was something of a decorator, so I suppose that could've rubbed off. I wouldn't call it art."

"And your father?"

"What people call 'a great man.' Rich, famous—but difficult to share. It was a rare moment we spent alone. I spent half my life craving his attention. The rest trying to be different. As a result, I couldn't be more reliable or more responsive to children and animals. But in some ways, we were a lot alike."

"Like how?"

"We both couldn't eat potatoes without ketchup."

"Everybody likes ketchup on their fries."

"Only in America."

He places his fork down gently, so it doesn't ring against the rim of the dish. Such genteel, impeccable manners—his father must have been a brute.

It's funny how one thing breeds another, how people yearn for what they don't have. People who endure long winters dream of Greece and the sun, while Greeks count snowflakes in their sleep.

"What about you?"

"What about me?"

"Your family."

"I'm not married."

"I meant your parents."

"Like anybody else's."

Stathis is too polite to press. She's grateful, although he would probably understand. Like his, her father was elusive.

A man with money for opera tickets but not for rent, he went on trips alone. Looking for work, he said, but he never once came back employed. His postcards could have been icons, the way she prayed over them, scrutinizing the glossy images and bland messages for hidden meanings, while her mother sought solace in sleep.

But she doesn't invite that conversation. Instead they watch the waiter scrape crumbs from the tablecloth onto the edge of a broad silver spade. The job is accomplished with amazing grace.

"Would you like anything else?" Stathis asks.

Only to sit here in this spot and do nothing.

Instead, she politely says, "No, thank you," in a Greek voice she had forgotten she had. "*Ohi, efharistó.*"

Words from another life.

"So you know some Greek?"

"Only a little."

He looks at her as if he suspects she knows more. But again, he doesn't push. "Shall I show you your room, then?" he says.

She nods and follows.

Her eyes shoot around the room like a camera. Wherever she goes, she needs to know exactly where she is in relation to what's around. This, she sees quickly, is a splendid room. The sea makes itself available through a wall of glass. Such a wide-angled, inspiring view that, even with the best equipment, and on a good day, it would be tough to capture it in a photograph.

The double bed is cloaked in a canopy of pale netting hanging down from its slender posts like a veil. A bed made for dreaming.

"Is it satisfactory?" he asks, putting his hands in his pockets, disturbing the smooth line of his tan trousers.

With his hotelier's instinct, she suspects he must already know the answer. But she is moved to say something in Greek, anyway, about how special the place feels. Yet the vocabulary is lost to her. She nods and moves toward the window, with its floor-to-ceiling exposure of the sea. Edging the terrace on the other side of the glass, purple clematis clings to the bushes of plump pink azaleas, making it seem as if the plant bears two fruits.

The transparent panel of the terrace door glides aside easily. The sea fizzes like seltzer poured into a glass. Something irresistible about it. The way it laps toward you, and then away.

Theodorakis—not seen through the camera now but in the

bare eye of memory. Theodorakis in his mountain studio, his thick hands glazed with damp clay. He lifts a finger to rub his face, leaving an ashen scar on the jaw. Color in the blue of the sky through the wide white archway carved out of a wall in this high place, where he works under a cathedral ceiling until sunset.

"You've been hurt," Stathis says.

She is almost startled to hear him speak, as if he and not Theodorakis is the figment of her imagining. But he is standing so close, this Stathis, that she can almost feel the scratch of his starched shirt on her bare arm.

"I'm all right," she says, reflexively searching her arm for scrapes.

"Not that. In the past. Someone hurt you, very badly?"

She should be repelled by such intimations from a stranger, but she is not offended by this beautiful man, standing with her so near to the sea.

He puts his hand on her shoulder. She doesn't shake it off.

It feels natural, as if she's known the touch before.

There is a thin sheet of air between them. He does nothing to enlarge it. Does he sense the acceptance in her?

And then, she knows the answer, because his hand is pressing the point where the straps of the sundress cross the back. She leans toward him. Not a decision, really. More like an involuntary movement. A plant to light.

And then, the soft, moist flesh of his cheek—smooth as a boy's who has never needed to shave—is hard against hers. The skin of a wild fruit. Her lips are pressed against it.

And then her mouth opens, his tongue assaults the softness, and she feels the loosening of the joints. Especially in the gut, and downward, there's a fierce rushing of blood . . .

The inside of his mouth . . . amazingly, it suits her taste, and there is a sweetness to his scent, especially around the warm expanse of his throat, that tells her she is lost.

Scent is key to sexual attraction. You can't go to bed with someone whose smell repels you. Everything follows from there.

Theodorakis was exactly right—the smell and flavor of an exotic, refreshing fruit, sweet but not cloying. And now this boylike man delves into her, and the scent, the taste, is right. The brain says don't give in to impulse. But her breasts are packed against his chest and he is growing larger between her legs, crushing out any air remaining between them.

She hasn't felt this urgency for anyone—not since Theodorakis. Theodorakis again. Nostalgia, not for David, with whom she's just ended a nine-year marriage, but for the ghost of a man she hasn't seen in ten—no, twelve—years.

Did David ever sense the intrusion? Somehow, this acquaintance of just a few hours does. Grasping her head by the cheekbones, Stathis demands an inspection of her eyes. He reminds her of herself looking through the camera. The object that, no matter what beneficence of light and position, eludes her capture.

"Are you sure that you want to?" he says.

He wants to be sure . . . Why does it matter to him? It's a rare man who thinks to ask what a woman wants. And even if they do wonder, she expects they'll say nothing. Maybe this one's a thoughtful lover, one who only wants a willing partner. Someone who doesn't play the ambiguities. He may have the face of a conquering Alexander but no wish to subjugate. And maybe he wants assurance that he is wanted. Maybe he is just as capable of becoming the wounded one.

"That other thing, it's over." She is amazed that she is talking about Theodorakis. After so many years, and so simply, he has drifted back to his place in the past.

So now there are only two of them in the room. And she realizes that with David, there must have always been three. Me and my two men. The husband and the man who would not leave his wife for her when she was single.

"I can't risk my sons," the Greek had said. She respected his not being able to bear separation from his children, although she never did really understand why he couldn't be a father and have her too. What she later suspected was that, in midlife, he could not risk a known life for the new.

But risk or not, she is ready to move ahead.

"Take off your shirt," she says, stunned by her pleasure in being so direct.

Her fingers chase his as they hurry to release the tiny buttons through the slits in the stiff fabric. Now, quickly, there is only skin. Stathis, his bronze chest glistening, puts his hand on her breast. It swells. She is surprised how out of control she is. No. She is in control. She is doing what she wants.

Silently, he slips the straps off her shoulders, touches the other breast. The tip stands up, burning a little. She is reminded how the unfinished limbs of Theodorakis's earth-mother sculptures expanded, magically, roundly, under his hand.

Now she is the dead clay coming to life.

She has forgotten what it was like . . . the sensations of her own body. Will her figure be sleek enough from its once-a-week jog? Stathis has that firm flesh that, at a certain age, comes with little effort. It was once like that for her. But it doesn't seem to matter to him as he nudges his way along the crease of the breasts where they fold over chest.

He is so young, and yet it is as if there is some ancient understanding between them. Their bodies fit so well together, like molded parts of the same figure. She can't draw away. She doesn't even want to. Her mind warns that acting impulsively can so easily end in disappointment, but she is biting the rim of his ear like it's an apricot, and . . .

"I want you," she says, feeling his penis bore into her, despite the fabric that separates their lower halves.

"Did you ever notice how everything in Greece moves more slowly than in the rest of the world?" he says. "It's how we eat, it's how we move, how we—"

He tosses her onto the white bed, anchors her firmly against the coverlet, and unspools her from the crumple of the linen dress. Her panties are gone fast, it's as if they were never there. His touch is so penetrating, so lingering—it's like he's writing on her skin with a pen.

He is searing her everywhere—licking her under the armpits

and behind the ears and between the deep valleys that link the toes. Even the tender skin that creases behind the bone of the knees has been found. Everywhere but that place men usually seek to go first, hardly taking the time to explore the other territories that might benefit from careful handling.

"Come inside me," she says, awed at her greed.

"There is time for everything."

The phrase "hurry up, it's time" pops into her head. Is that a line from a poem? But remembering the radio broadcaster's advice, she does not fill the silence. "There is time for everything," her new lover just said. So why not place some trust in him?

He pelts her with kisses and tiny bites, his headful of uncontrollable curls adding to the sensation with their tickle. Now it's the satin smoothness of his penis, dangling free, that writes on her. Her hand darts for it. He catches it. "Think only of yourself," he says.

And then, finally, he is between her legs. Hands or lips, after a while she doesn't know which, only that she is soaked as a squashed fruit whose skin the heat has caused to burst. The permission he has given her is freeing her to indulge in sensations in a way she has only been able to achieve alone, in her bed, with the help of an electrical appliance that she is suddenly not ashamed to admit using—not just in between the times when men wanted to have their way with her but on other occasions, when she wanted to have her own way with herself.

The double-gated lips of her lower mouth start to embrace him. And then his mouth is on her own, and she pleads, in muffled cries, that he come fully inside her. But the pulsing has already started, and she's seeing spots before her eyes, like after the camera flashes. Bright pink spots dangling in the particles of air—reflecting, she thinks, the hot spot igniting between her thighs.

Orange-red now, that round smudge of light she sometimes sees when she does this to herself, greedily orchestrating her sensations while lying on her back, her legs splayed in the position for giving birth, the light from the overhead bedroom fixture reflecting pinkish through her tightly clenched eyelids—the way the glare of the sun burns through the lids you've sealed for a bit of respite on a hot day.

And then it's the pink fire of the lower limbs she sees, fanned by that hard nub that causes her delicate membrane to pulse into a slow burning.

But there's no need for appliances now, and she thinks, how handy this man would be in a blackout. No socket, no plugs needed for this electricity.

And then she's reminded of David—how he could never do this for her. And she thinks how unfortunate it was there was only one man who could—until now.

And how, maybe, finally, she is allowing this for herself.

And then the focus of brain and body is again on the pink spot, which she sees as a projection of her own blood rushing through the purpled lips that guard the entrance to the womb, and which now, praise the lord, are screaming, for the man to enter.

And finally, he obeys.

"There's something I want to show you," Stathis tells her, after they have lain together for a long while. They pile on their clothes and enter the tight quarters of his white Volvo. For a quarter-hour they journey up along one of the steep hills edging the sea that define the island's landscape. Sometimes, while adjusting the clutch, his hand brushes her knee, causing her to feel a sting of intense pleasure. Since their route is crossed by high-pitched roads and trenched with valleys, he must make these adjustments often. She revels in such scrapes of his hand.

Another slide, this time into low land pinked with thyme and prickly with rosemary. They seesaw up again, on a path that seems somehow familiar, though many of the roads here look alike.

Terra-cotta stones keep the edges of the terraced farmlands

clinging to the hillsides from tumbling over. More tall cypresses, black-blue as raven feathers.

A sheer rise of red earth.

The path here, etched in dirt, is too narrow for a car to pass through. They go on foot, tackling a series of stone steps overgrown with island herbs.

"The front road's being worked on," he says, apologizing for the unruly landscape. "I live up this way."

"Just you, and your smile?"

He seems pleased that she cares to know. "Just me, and the constellations."

"I thought Greeks married young."

"After seeing my parents, I decided not to rush."

They trudge on. And then, suddenly, she sees it—the wide white archway of the house she once thought would be her home.

The breath freezes in her jaw. An instant chill, like when you're eating ice cream and your teeth sting because it's too much cold too fast.

The sharp slap of more than déjà vu, as more evidence that she has been here before reveals itself. The singular sapphire swirls of the pool where she once clocked laps. The chipless blue glaze of Mediterranean sprawled beneath the dry crust of cliff. The broad stretch of sky framed in the white archway of the villa's showcase room.

This room just as it was, with its high white ceilings, vaulted as in the island's whitewashed churches. But the furniture is different. He used it as a studio because it got the best light, but in this incarnation it's fashionably decorated, with a low banquette of indigo, green, and yellow pillow squares neatly laid out in a row like Chiclets and white leather chairs and sofas soft as sponges. The floor is now a sea of alternating swirls of mosaic blues and yellows.

A camera crew from *Architectural Digest* could come right in and start snapping—but it all has a friendly, lived-in air.

She supposes the house must have been sold after Theodorakis's death—the only thing that could have caused him to abandon the potential of its perfect light. And for an instant, the revelation wounds. After all, he did not find it *impossible* to shed her company. But she sees her host is watching her intently.

"I used to know the man who lived here," she explains.

"Did you?"

Only for a second, she sees one last flash of Theodorakis's bearish figure up on a hammock of white canvas that billows in the breeze like a sail. "He was a very talented artist. A sculptor."

"I know," says her lover. "I am his son."

I've always been fascinated by islands. There's nothing more seductive than a scratch of earth surrounded by sea, cut off from the mainstream, with its own distinctive personality. The right island can bring out aspects of ourselves of which we're not conscious, and, somehow, the intimacy and smallness of an island give perspective to the larger things of life.

LOVE IN THE WAX MUSEUM
❦❦❦❦❦❦

Nancy Holder

M ae West, Michael Jackson, and that new one, that country singer. Bonnie thought it very charming of her
nephew, Jay, to think of taking her and Clara to the wax
museum and to ask every twenty minutes or so if they were
tired. Of course they were—they were old ladies—but they
denied it in one voice, "No, no, not at all," on the off chance
that saying so might dull his pleasure. And they were born of a
generation when a man's pleasure should not, under any cir-
cumstance, be dulled.

Clara was hiding a yawn behind her fist; her gaze slid toward
Bonnie and she grinned an apology. But there was amusement
there too, in her eyes, so dark against her white, crepey skin. She
walked with a slight hunch these days, slowing down. It seemed
as if less than a year had passed since they'd first met instead of
decades.

Jay's wife, Alyssa, touched Bonnie's arm and pointed at a
mannequin dressed like Batman. That young man, that one with
the weak chin. Bonnie nodded appreciatively as Alyssa said, "I
almost got a part in the first one." Alyssa was an actress; she was
beautiful, luminescent like the statues around them. As firm.
Bonnie had never looked that way in her life.

When she was young, once she realized she was a lesbian,
she thought she would become exotic, a brittle New York art-
lesbian in a black turtleneck, chignon, and stiletto heels. Smok-

ing and painting, a highball in one hand while her lover, in a beret, played the bongos. Growing up on lesbian prison-warden movies, she knew she was not like *that*.

What she had failed to realize until later was that she was a small-town girl growing up in a small town, and she would grow into a small-town lesbian. She would hide herself amid church socials until she became the kind of woman who went to church socials, clucked her teeth at profanity, and bought pastel pantsuits and sensible and very ugly shoes to wear on her big trip to Los Angeles to visit her nephew.

Clara tapped her shoulder as Alyssa walked on. She whispered, "Do you think they'll be very hurt if we skip the Chamber of Horrors?"

"They've probably been here a million times. Taking all the out-of-towners." All at once she was depressed. She felt dowdy. Their neighbors back home had warned them about the superficiality of Los Angeles, but she liked it here. The sun was golden, the people clever, ambitious, and attractive. Their affectations made her envious. They opened up themselves, their lives; as they said, they "went for it." Exposing your dreams, wearing your heart on your sleeve. How could that be superficial?

Sometimes Bonnie used to imagine that she and Clara would move to the desert, two Georgia O'Keeffe's, and grow their hair long and gray and beautiful. In the twilight they would sit by the window because there would be no air conditioning, and Clara would brush her hair, and a bird would sing in the hushed, graceful silver-ending day.

In the wax museum, her group were beckoning her to move on. Clint Eastwood, Kevin Costner, that young, flat-chested actress—there were so many these days, so many, who were more boyish than any dyke of her day. Androgyny was stylish. Not so in her time. She lifted a brow at the munificent waxen breasts of Sophia Loren, Liz Taylor. They had looked great in black turtlenecks and stiletto heels.

Now the gift shop. Clara was looking for something to buy, not because she particularly wanted to. Bonnie watched as she picked up salt and pepper sets, spoon rests, scarves with the faces of movie stars printed on them. For the folks back home. To show Jay that she wanted to remember having come here. Clara was a bookkeeper and played bridge; Bonnie worked for the water district and had never gotten the hang of bidding and given up after a while because she made Clara lose. They knew people talked about them, although their public behavior never betrayed a thing.

Alyssa said brightly, "This is cute, Clara." She dangled a coffee cup from her thumb. Bonnie couldn't see it clearly from where she stood. Clara didn't like it, but she made nice noises and took it from the young woman's smooth hand. Alyssa smiled and turned away. Clara examined the cup and put it down rather absently. She looked tired.

"Are you getting hungry?" Jay asked, startling Bonnie.

"My, yes, I am." That was an answer that would bring him pleasure.

On the way home the kids—as Bonnie thought of them— couldn't bear the thought of missing one last sight for the day. They assured Bonnie and Clara that it was "on the way," but it seemed they drove and drove and drove. Bonnie had begun to doze; she jerked as Alyssa said, "Here we are!"

The Range Rover overlooked the city of Los Angeles, glassy structures like silvery mirages sparkling in the sunset. Incandescent, magical, brimming with possibility. Bonnie caught her breath and imagined herself describing this moment to the folks back home. She would not do it justice. She would use ordinary words, and they would see something ordinary. Her throat was tight with emotion. The city was so vast, filled to bursting with young dreamers.

Clara's hand brushed hers, just so; Jay had gay friends who probably held hands in public, perhaps even kissed. Wore those T-shirts with slogans and attended rallies. Still, she did not take Clara's hand, and she knew Clara did not expect her to.

Bonnie wondered if Clara felt the same regret, the same longing, for all the untapped . . . extremity they might have experienced. If she, too, felt as ridiculous as a character in an old Carol Burnett skit.

"The sun's this bright because of all the smog," Jay said. He put his hand on Bonnie's shoulder. "Kind of a downer, huh."

Bonnie smiled for him. The knowledge made no difference; it was still an exquisite sight.

"You must be worn out," Alyssa said.

"No, not really." Bonnie traded glances with Clara. They both smiled.

Dinner at Jay's pleasant stucco house was fish and new potatoes. And asparagus, always very pricey in the middle of Texas. Everything was wonderful and fresh. There was wine. When they sat down to the colorfully set table, Clara had murmured, "Oh, my," impressed in her subdued way. Bonnie was glad Alyssa wasn't some kind of health-food nut, had known when she met her that she wasn't. She was an utterly charming woman, and Jay clearly adored her. Jay worked at NBC as a cameraman. Not too glamorous, but a good union job. He was happy, and he owned his own home. He knew movie and TV stars, and tomorrow he was going to introduce her and Clara to some of them.

"Have some more wine, Aunt Bonnie." Jay filled her glass even though it was more than half full.

Clara said, "Me, too," holding hers up in a coquettish way. Women of their generation often flirted with men as a matter of course. It was a way of flattering them, smoothing their way. Their mothers taught them to do it, and how to do it; it was no trouble, and Bonnie didn't understand why the young women of today resented it. It was simply common courtesy, a social grace that cost one nothing.

Alyssa understood that; now she was bringing in a cheesecake she had bought at a bakery because it was Jay's favorite. His eyes were warm with gratitude and desire. Bonnie's gaze ticked toward Clara, whose head was bent. She had white hair now. It had been rich and brown when they had met. Bonnie felt a tinge of remorse, as if she herself should have prevented the change from happening.

Alyssa cut the cake, Jay poured Amaretto for everyone in cunning little liqueur glasses, and Bonnie realized that there was no reason for her to be unhappy, depressed, or sad, and that it was actually rather selfish of her to let herself go on like this when Jay and Alyssa were trying so hard to entertain her.

"Here's to my two aunts," Jay said warmly, raising his glass. "It's so great to have you here."

Bonnie got teary, murmured something about being so glad to be there, and meant it. She tossed off her Amaretto and poured herself another glass. Jay said, "All right, Aunt Bonnie!" and laughed. For a wild moment she thought about asking him if he had any marijuana, but it was beyond her even to joke about it.

"Oh, God, I forgot the chocolate sauce!" Alyssa said, jumping from her chair. "Jay loves chocolate sauce on his cheese-cake." She hurried toward the kitchen.

"It's in the bedroom," Jay called. Clara guffawed, caught herself, saw Bonnie, and chortled as she tipped back her glass. Jay said, "Sorry," but he didn't mean it. Everyone was giddy. Outside the crickets were scraping, the city lights were sparkling, and it was wonderful to be in the superficial city of Los Angeles.

Jay showed them bloopers of some of the shows on NBC. Bonnie didn't watch much television and didn't know the actors, but their awkwardness and fluffed lines were amusing. Clara was braying like a horse, pointing and laughing, holding out her glass for more Amaretto. She was having a wonderful time, and Bonnie thought she had never loved her more than in that moment.

Then it was bedtime, and there was no fuss or confusion: Alyssa showed them to a guest bedroom dominated by a huge king-sized bed. There was a black and gray quilt on it, very modern and elegant, and at least six pillows.

"You have your own bathroom," Alyssa pointed out. There

was a vase of fresh roses on the black lacquer bureau, a florist card that read "Welcome!" Tears sprang to her eyes at the thoughtfulness, the opulence. Alyssa kissed them each on the cheek and they were alone.

Clara flopped onto the bed and sighed. "I'm floating. Your nephew is wonderful. And his wife." She patted the bed and said slyly, "Turn on the radio, dear." It was their code. Even at home alone, they turned on the radio.

"I need a shower," Bonnie said.

"You don't." Clara half-turned her head and eyed her. "You smell good. Like wine."

Bonnie sat on the bed and began unbuckling her sandals. She saw the veins on the backs of her hands, her knuckles, gnarled from arthritis. She thought of Alyssa's hands, of the hands of the mannequins in the museum.

"Where are you?" Clara asked, and Bonnie jerked, realizing she had stopped taking off her sandals. She hurried with the left one and began on the right. Clara waited.

"Oh, I . . ." She shrugged. "Everyone here is so . . . nice, don't you think? Alyssa's very lovely. Pretty enough to be in that museum."

"Nice buns," Clara said, snickering at herself. They never talked like that about other women. She said, "Firm as wax."

"Yes." They should have come here, Bonnie thought fiercely. As soon as they had found each other, they should have flown here like witches on brooms, goddesses of the wind. She in her late thirties, Clara on the other side of forty—they would still have been young enough for Los Angeles. Maybe they would have become actresses or opened up an art gallery. Something fabulous would have happened to them.

Clara rolled up to a sitting position and turned the radio on. It was an easy-listening station; they were playing the theme song to a movie they had rented back home. Bonnie couldn't remember the name, but it had made them both cry romantic tears.

Then Clara reached for Bonnie and murmured, "Come

here, old thing," and laid her on the bed. Bonnie began to protest; she wasn't in the mood. She was tired and she wanted a shower. No, that wasn't it. She was old and she thought she might need a shower. She couldn't imagine Clara actually desiring her. All their years of lovemaking were distant from her now, as if she had only dreamed them; as if Clara were merely a friend who had had a little too much to drink.

Clara kissed her cheek, the hollow of her eye, her forehead. She clasped Bonnie's shoulder and cupped the side of her face. Her gentleness loosened Bonnie's muscles; she was so tense. Slacken and loosen as Clara helped her undress—dowdy jacket, blouse, slacks—until she lay in Clara's arms in her underthings.

"Oh, Bon." Clara kissed her mouth. Bonnie felt her lips part; she was becoming warm and languid and easy. Everything was sliding away, rolling away, like heated wax. It was all leaving her as Clara guided and manipulated her body. Her breasts, her stomach, the cleft between her legs that Clara kneaded, shaped, reshaped.

They used to wonder what they would do if either of them decided she needed a man. A penis, to be exact. Shyly, they'd purchased what was called in those days a marital aid. Now they called it a dildo, a very ugly word. Bonnie and Clara had never had any quarrel with men; they had simply preferred women.

Now Clara's fingers were a penis that slipped into Bonnie, and her vagina became molten. Liquid and malleable, golden and good, clear wax, pearlescent, excitingly unformed. Images flashed through her mind—what could have been, what they might have been.

New York and black turtlenecks.

French lesbians.

Movie lesbians with huge breasts.

She pulled herself against Clara, whispering, "Make me into what you want," with an urgency she had never heard in her own voice before. Saying her name, "Clara Clara Clara Clara," as if she had never spoken it before. Making it become the name of a famous woman, a brittle woman, the sexiest woman in the world, Clara Bardot Clara. Bonnie's hands ran over Clara's face, cupped her breasts as Clara undressed herself with one hand while she slipped her fingers into Bonnie's vagina and caressed her labia. "Clara Clara Clara Clara."

And Clara's answer, "Bonnie," was full of desire and love and need, but questions, too. Bonnie let herself forget that she had questions; she let herself forget that she was from a small town in Texas. All she remembered was that she was in Los Angeles with the woman she loved. She rose up and over Clara, parting her legs, and kissed her there because Clara loved it so. Her love, her dear love who smelled everywhere of wine and, yes, of wax; melting beneath Bonnie's burning adoration.

In delicious amnesia, they rode together along sensations that thickened and pulsed, pulled harder, harder; Clara climaxed and Bonnie held her buttocks to make her go further. As if in shame Clara pushed at Bonnie's shoulders; she always did. It was like a small battle that Bonnie forced her to win.

Then it was Bonnie's turn, and she shook her head and cradled herself against Clara instead, loving the urge in her body to finish it off, savoring the fact that she herself wasn't yet satisfied. Clara was panting, and that was so sexy and wonderful; and Bonnie wanted more than anything to be with her. Usually Bonnie drifted away into fantasy before she came, feeling distanced from the woman she loved. As if she were watching a movie, all alone. Preferable to coming now was staying in the moment with Clara, who didn't understand but did in bed whatever Bonnie wanted.

Bonnie's body quieted, although it did not rest. Her reality began to rush back in—her Texas dowdiness, the ordinariness of knitting and bridge and clerical tasks. The things they could have been, and had.

She lay so still that Clara whispered carefully, "Bon? You asleep?"

Tears spilled down Bonnie's cheeks; she didn't answer. Clara kissed the top of her head and settled into a more comfortable position. After a few minutes, Bonnie said, "I'm not asleep."

"Don't you want to come?"

Bonnie hesitated. "I . . . I want to do . . ." She took a breath, let it out. "I want to do something different tomorrow."

Clara cupped her breast. "Like what?"

"Not sexwise. I want . . ." She raised her eyes and Clara saw the tears. She was clearly surprised, concerned. She started to say something. Bonnie made a little moue of apology; if she didn't know better, she'd say it was her hormones. "I want . . ."

Clara regarded her. "What's wrong, Bon-bon?"

"I want to get a tattoo. Or something." Bonnie shrugged. That was all wrong. That wasn't what she wanted. Now Clara would say something like "land's sake!" and that would thoroughly depress her.

"Or something?" Clara kissed her breast. "What something?"

"I want . . ." Bonnie put her hand on Clara's neck. So many years of pillow talk. More tears spilled down her cheeks.

Clara got off the bed. "Come on." She grabbed Bonnie's hand and pulled her up. "Come on." To her feet.

Clara urged her to the door; she opened it and bounded into the hall. Looked in the direction of Jay and Alyssa's bedroom, gave Bonnie's hand a shake, and dashed toward the living room.

"Clara!" Bonnie whispered, shocked.

Clara giggled girlishly. Their feet made padding noises on the carpet as they went into the living room. Clara grabbed up the bottle of Amaretto and changed direction, toward the back yard.

She opened the screen door. They stood naked in the cooler air, both slightly out of breath, their hands clasped.

Below them, Los Angeles lights spread in all directions, a brilliant, vast wonderland. Cars crowded the freeway lanes, speeding; the moon was one more energetic current that glowed and charged and recharged the landscape with its potential.

Crickets chirped above the susurration of the traffic. An owl hooted.

In the moonlight, Clara was a glowing, pale figure, a perfect being of indescribable beauty. Her drooping tummy and breasts, her pudgy thighs, amazingly wonderful. She was the patron goddess of Los Angeles.

Clara took a swig of Amaretto and handed the bottle to Bonnie. She said, "We'll go in their Jacuzzi," and pointed to the wooden structure surrounding it, on a small slab of concrete to the left of the house beside a row of oleanders.

"Now?"

Clara let go of her hand and found the controls. Red lights glowed beneath the surface; soon the water bubbled and roiled. Clara climbed the two steps to the top of the structure and stepped in. She sat down and sighed delightedly. "Oh, you'll just melt," she said.

Bonnie followed. She put one foot in, the other. What would they do if Jay appeared?

Clara reached for her, rosy and wrinkled and from a small town in Texas. Bonnie went to her: two buck-naked old ladies—broads!—in the hot tub, sharing a bottle of booze.

"Is this something different?" Clara's hands were every-where, her mouth, everywhere; Bonnie got excited but found herself right beside Clara, with Clara, not leaving; the place beside Clara, in Clara were the most glamorous, dreamlike places, magical places Clara had never taken her before. Where old lovers know, and understand, and perhaps don't even realize they do, which makes it all the more fraught with chances for another visit, and another, and a lifetime of them: Potential. Extremity.

Seized opportunity.

If Jay showed up, they'd all just laugh.

"Yes," Bonnie whispered gratefully as her vagina gathered and pulsed and began to contract.

"I'm glad, hon. It was such a long day."

That wasn't it. Or maybe it was. Bonnie kissed Clara, their lips melting together as they swirled and flew among the lights and dreams of Los Angeles, their kisses like reflections in the hot, flowing pool of waxy, clear love, of Texas and bridge, of *them*.

To Dixie Barnum-Scrivener and Alan Scrivener, who took me to the wax museum. And to Claudia O'Keefe, who gave me the directions.

Being a native Californian, I'm one of those people who loves L.A. and all the strange and semireal dreams that are spun there. It is my own dream that my desire for sensual and erotic pleasures, like Bonnie and Clara's, will last my lifetime.

YARN

❦❦❦❦❦❦

Jenny Diski

For the purposes of the story, I never had a name. I was always just the daughter of a miller, and then later the Queen—meaning Mrs. King. But us millers' daughters have names, like everyone else, though the archetype makers would have you think different, even in a story such as this, where naming names is the name of the game.

Well, I bloodywell had a name and have one still—excuse the language, not suited to a Queen, I know, but, once a miller's daughter, always a fucking miller's daughter, I say. My name, I can reveal, was, and still is, Claraminda Griselda. The first confabulation of a name being an indication of the florid hopes my father had for his own flesh and blood to raise him up above his natural station in life (a hope rather surprisingly granted, now that he's been elevated, as the father of a Queen must be, to an earldom); the second name my father once heard in a tale told in the local inn by some accountant fellow called Chaser, or Chooser, or Chancer, or something, who fancied himself as more than just an ordinary customs and excise man. My father, the recently elevated earl, told me he had liked the sound of Griselda, and that the story the tax man told had held out great promise for the bearer of that name, who, though she had her troubles, came out well settled in the end.

However, not wishing to antagonize the rest of the village children (my father already having alienated us from our neighbors, on account of his comical fantasies and highfalutin ways), I called myself the rather simpler Clary, and even now, though the King has all the pretensions of a miller and insists on having my full name on documents of state, I think of myself as plain Queen Clary.

I spent my childhood in a miasma of flour dust; no matter how my mother wiped and washed while she lived, it was always possible to write my name with my finger in the film on every surface. Naturally or, rather, unnaturally, my father insisted I go to the village school to learn to read. So while most of my contemporaries were productive elements of their household—carrying water, carding wool, pumping bellows—I sat in school, alone except for the children of better families than ours, who would not talk to a mere miller's daughter, learning my letters, and what to do with them. I could not see what such an excess of learning achieved, apart from being able to write my name on stools and tables and windowsills.

Of course, the price of his flour reflected the extraordinary expense my father had in the raising of a mere daughter, so we weren't very popular on that account, either. There were plenty of people who passed through our village with tales of the price of a sack of flour just a few miles away. I say a few miles, but each one of them might have been a continent for most of the villagers, with their broken-down nags and rickety carts, and then only if fortune had smiled on them and the brigands kept away. It goes to show—me saying *a few* miles—the way you get used to a new station in life. What would a dozen miles be to me, with all the resources of the stables and a choice of exquisitely crafted carriages at my disposal? If I ever used them, that is. As for brigands: I should be so lucky.

So I grew up in a flour-pale house where even our eyelashes were dusted with pulverized wheat and rye, and learned, in readiness for the future in my pompous father's head, to read. Even now, in my mind's ear, I can hear his bellowing baritone carrying through the air from the mill next door to our cottage.

I care for nobody
No, not I
And nobody cares for me.

They were the truest words that ever came from a man's lips.

So we weren't a very popular little family, and I spent a good deal of time on my own. Often, I'd sit in a corner watching my father at work. Not from any admiration of him, but with fascination at the process he carried out. The two great granite grinding stones were turned by two pairs of donkeys at opposite sides of the stones, going 'round and 'round very slowly as if once they had tried to catch each other up but had finally tired out and, realizing they never would manage it, had slowed forever down to a dull and hopeless plod. Actually, there was a series of donkeys—they didn't last long, my father being mean with feed and generous with their work hours. I never cared for them much, they seemed so depressed. What interested me was the process they set and kept in action.

My father tipped grain into the hopper and it trickled down, like the sand in the hourglass in my husband, the King's, countinghouse, between the great stones that turned, thanks to the will-less motion of the donkeys, and crushed the grain into a gritty powder. I think it was the relentlessness of the process that fascinated me. 'Round and 'round, and on and on. Grain in at the top, flour out at the bottom. An endless process for the endless need of the village for bread. Those grinding stones were at the secret heart of all our lives. Whether they liked it or not, the villagers had need of my father and his mill. No one could manage without bread, and those who had fallen on bad times were obliged to go cap in hand to my father and ask for time to pay for the sacks of flour they could not do without.

He always obliged, but not very obligingly. There are two ways of having people in your debt. You can make it easy, taking the long view that everyone has periods of difficulty but also other times that are not so hard, and treat your creditors as if they were yourself at a different stage of fortune, so that people know when better times come they can take an extra chicken or whatever and the debtor will rejoice with them in their improved fortune. And there is the other way—my father's way. Everyone in the village owed him at one time or another, and he never let them forget it. He would mark the names of those who couldn't pay him on a slate with exaggerated care, listening with relish to the screech it made. Other people's hard luck made him feel richer, not just in what they owed him but in some more mysterious way, as if every degree by which someone else was down pushed him up in his own esteem. "They can't do without me," he would say, booming with self-satisfaction. Then he'd burst into the old chorus

> I care for nobody
> No, not I
> And nobody cares for me.

It was a song of triumph. And although the last line was as true as true could be, it didn't worry him. It made him feel bigger and more important in some twisted way to know that nobody, including his daughter, *did* care for him.

I never had much time for my father, and my mother for the handful of years I knew her was too preoccupied with drudgery and not getting on the wrong side of him to make much impact on me beyond pity for her lot. She died very quietly, apparently of nothing more than lack of will to live. She faded away, as if each day proved that there was little and increasingly less to live for.

So I was a solitary child. I watched the stones grinding and listened to the rhythm they made as the slight hollows and bumps in the granite altered the pitch. *Strraagga graast, scrummm, scrummm. Straagga grasst, scrummm scrummm.* It inhabited my dreams, that beat, becoming as much a part of me as my own heart's rhythm. And I was content in spite of my loveless surroundings. Somehow, the perpetual circling of the stones seemed to me very like the shape and movement of the world itself. The village, bread, work, children seemed to have a pattern I knew, for all the ups and downs of fortune, to be a good solid pattern. I felt a rightness about how things were, about all the circles that were drawn by each family and each village with the millstones grinding out the rhythm of being alive. And my father, for all his foolish pomposity and grandiose notions, could not help but provide the certainty as he ground the grain around which life made its circles.

Only once, while I was growing up, did the circle pattern fail. A blight on the crops, who knew why, one year, and for a while the grinding stones were silenced. There was no grain to mill, and it was as if my own heart had halted, the silence was so ominous. It was, that time, a localized problem, however, and soon enough grain was brought in from the outside world, and the stones began their *strraagga graast, scrummm scrummm* once again. It was a warning to me, though. That pattern, so close to life itself, was not immutable. The vital circles could be halted. It was a useful lesson to learn.

Of course, the King was nowhere to be seen during that time of hardship. It was not his way to go abroad among his people unless he was certain of their loyalty and affection. And no one in the village doubted that the King had enough grain stored away to get him through difficult times. However, once the millstones were doing their work, he passed through our village in a grand, triumphant ride, as if the return of the stuff of life was his doing. People lifted their heads as he passed, magnificent on his great white horse, weighted down with plumes and tapestries. They bobbed a curtsy or a brief bow, while he nodded graciously at them. No one took much notice. The King was not part of village life, except inasmuch as he taxed and tithed us. No one hated him, he was too remote, too irrelevant for that. They simply saw him as a fabulous creature passing through their byways.

Except my father, of course. He bowed and scraped so much that the King thought him his finest subject and actually dismounted and demanded to be taken on a tour of his miller's

mill. Oh, my father obliged, with such obsequiousness that I
thought I might vomit. I suppose the honor was too much for
his miserable mind. At any rate, that is some kind of explanation
for what happened next. My father entirely lost his head, faced
with the condescending attention of his liege lord. It was never
entirely true that he cared for *nobody*. For the rich and powerful
he cared, it seemed, beyond his own sanity and both our well-
being.

My father called me to him, hissing out of the corner of his
mouth while blathering to His Majesty, who was about to
remount and go on his way, back to the relative warmth and
comfort of his castle.

"Sire! Sire!," he said, bowing and scraping, while from the
other side of his smiling face he summoned me. "Where are
you, girl? Come here! Come *here!*"

"Sire, may I introduce you . . . she's just coming . . . here in
a moment . . . to, yes, here she is" ("Straighten your dress,
girl!") ". . . my daughter, Your Majesty. My daughter, Claraminda Griselda."

My father held me in front of him by my shoulders, his fingers digging into my flesh in his excitement. The King looked at
me and smiled a vague, royal smile. Frankly, I wasn't the pretti-
est girl a King had ever laid eyes on. Not *ugly*, you understand,
but nothing really special. He was again about to turn and go
when my agitated father, seeing no light in His Majesty's eyes,
let out a strangulated sound, a screech not unlike the sound of a
creditor's name being marked on the slate.

"Your *Majesty!*"

The King turned at the urgency of his cry. My father now
had to think up the rest of the sentence. But thinking isn't a
good description of what he did.

"Your Majesty, this is no ordinary girl. No mere miller's
daughter, Sire. No, she is a remarkable child. Not just dutiful
and clever, though she is that, of course, but something more,
much, much more."

We all waited to see how my father would complete his babblings. I supposed madness mixed with insatiable greed came to the rescue.

"This child, this young woman, Your Majesty . . . has an extraordinary gift . . . given to no one else. You see, Sire, she can . . . she has the ability . . . gained from God himself, it must have been . . . she can . . . spin . . . straw into gold."

There was an astonished silence while my father stared at the King, his eyes bugging almost out of his head as he himself heard the preposterous thing he had said. Everyone else looked at him; the King, myself, the whole retinue. I thought for a moment that the King was going to have my father arrested for ridiculousness, but when I dragged my eyes away from my demented creator and took in His Majesty, I saw his expression change from disbelief at what he was hearing to something very like my father's when someone came to him to put themselves deeply in his debt. I saw the King's eyes glaze over with lust at the idea of monstrous wealth and power.

"Your Majesty," I said, trying to think of something to excuse my father and prevent him from being thrown into the country's deepest, blackest dungeon for the rest of his life. I did not love my father, but still I felt that the blood between us was enough to want to try and salvage his life.

"Be quiet, girl!" my father shouted, though he needn't have bothered; I couldn't think of a thing to say that might mitigate the nonsense he had spoken.

His Majesty turned his head to me, and the former complete lack of interest in the plain miller's daughter was transformed, as if my fairy godmother had waved a wand and made me the most exquisite maiden in the land. I immediately understood my position, and a shiver of despair ran through me. I was locked between the gaze of two avaricious men, both of whom saw me as the means vastly to improve his own standing. What hope had I, imprisoned between the hungry stares of father and King? It was as if a sentence of death had already been pronounced on me, before His Majesty ever said a word.

"Is that so, Miller?" the King finally said, never taking his eyes off me for a second. "Straw into gold, you say?"

A look of fear crossed my father's face, as for the first time he realized what would happen to him (never mind me, of course) when his ludicrous boast was proved to be a lie.

"Your Maj—" he began, but what could he say to retrieve the situation? The words had flown from his mouth and nothing would make them unsaid.

Funnily enough, the King did not think to ask me about my unusual skill. Nobody thought to say anything to me at all. You could see the King wavering between his eagerness for such a thing to be true, because if so, he would be the beneficiary of a treasure beyond the dreams even of Kings, and the thought that he was being made a fool of. There was nothing he liked less than people trying to make a fool of him; just the idea put him into an executionary frame of mind. You could see him weighing up the benefits and the risks of believing my father. You might say that my father's story was so preposterous that no one could give a second's credence to what he said. But that would be to underestimate the power of greed. Our future, my father's and mine, hung in the balance, as the seconds passed. Our very lives depended on the King being as avid a greedy fool as my father. It was all we could hope for.

The King stared dangerously at my father when he spoke again.

"Well, let us see, Miller, what wonders this daughter of yours can perform. I will take her to my castle, and if she can indeed turn straw into gold, then I will marry her. If not, the pair of you will die so that the world can see I am not a monarch to be fooled with."

Now, it has probably crossed your mind that it's a damn strange thing for a girl to become a wife purely on the grounds of being able to spin straw into gold. She could become your bank, yes, but why a wife? Of course, it has to do with the needs of the structure within which we were all of us imprisoned—the story. That's how it goes in this corner of the narrative world; the prize for doing the impossible is to become the wife of a

King. Nothing to be done about that. Not even the fact that I cherished the idea of this particular King for my husband as much as I cherished the idea of my father being my father. But we have no choice, characters such as us. Nor could I, given my lack of regard for His Majesty, decide to sit in his palace and flatly refuse to change his straw into gold (if I could have done so, which obviously common sense would tell you I couldn't), preferring to die than live out a miserable life as Queen. Like the circular life of the village, I was caught up in a pattern, though this pattern was a great deal less to my liking than the everyday life of the world I inhabited.

My father threw a desperate look at me as I rode away, perched on the back of some flunky's horse, as if begging me not to let him down now that his life depended on me. Brilliant! All I had to do to keep us both alive was spin straw into gold. Why hadn't he made up something *really* difficult for me to accomplish? In fact, it seemed to me that straw into gold might be relatively easy; all I'd have to do was join the ranks of magicians and alchemists and tinker with potions of this and that, and perhaps, given a lifetime of esoteric study and all the luck in this world and the next, come up with the philosopher's stone to realize my father's boast and achieve the King's dreams. The real problem facing me, however, was a great deal more fundamental: I didn't know one end of a spinning wheel from another. I'd been far too busy being prepared at school for my social climbing to learn anything useful like how to spin. I was, quite frankly, absolutely useless with my hands.

I was installed in an out-of-the-way room in the castle. Up everlasting winding stairs, to a room at the top of a turret. Since it was circular, it had commanding views of the whole area. I suppose looking down on the world I had previously been a part of was what my father had intended for me, but, quite honestly, I had other things on my mind than the view.

Half the room, a semicircle as it were, was filled with a great mound of straw; the other half was empty except for a spinning wheel, and me standing staring at it. The deal was, I spin all the straw into gold by morning, or else. Some deal. Also, I knew my way around stories of this kind, being of them as well as in them. I knew as well as anyone about the rule of three. Once never does in this kind of tale, and I was certain that I'd have to perform my miracle times three. Frankly, it didn't matter this time, since I couldn't do what I had to do, anyway. But in general, it's a most dispiriting law. Knowing you have to do everything three times takes the sense of achievement away before you've even started. One might be thrilled to have done something brave or clever or impossible the first time, but knowing you have to do it twice more takes immediate gratification away. Even having three wishes loses its charm. You can be sure you'll get one of them wrong and lose the benefit of the other two.

However, that was all rather theoretical as I stood in the turret room, staring at the spinning wheel and not having the faintest idea how it worked. I grant you, it was an interesting piece of psychology, worrying about not knowing how the spinning wheel worked, as though if I'd known everything would be all right. But if you're going to die, you have to pinpoint a single, simple reason. The fact that I didn't know how to turn straw into gold seemed an absurd reason for dying, so I transferred it all on to the spinning wheel. It seemed more acceptable somehow to die because I didn't know how to do the simplest, rather than the most difficult, thing.

The question I held in my mind was: Did I really mind about dying and leaving a world where fathers and kings (and, it ought to be said, ineffectual mothers) caused one to be in such a predicament? Put that way, my fate seemed less unacceptable. Still, I was young, barely fourteen, and I had not used up all my optimism about what might lie ahead for me. So, quite honestly, I was not entirely reconciled to my forthcoming fate.

I perched on the wooden stool attached to the spinning wheel and identified a sticking-up thing in front of me as a spindle. That's education for you. What I was supposed to do with it, I had no idea, but I knew it by name. I pushed the wheel around listlessly, listening to its wobble and creak with growing interest. It had in some way a relationship to the pattern of sound made by my father's grinding stones. Not surprising, really, both being circular and designed to go 'round and 'round. The rhythm was a comfort to me. By morning, and the end of my life, I thought, I'd be quite consoled.

I can't say how long I'd been doing that when I heard a gratingly high-pitched voice coming from behind me.

"Quite a pickle you're in, isn't it?"

And there, of course, was a skinny little man with a most unpleasant leer on his wrinkled, disagreeable face. Well, I don't need to tell you that he said he could help me, but there would be a price. My ring, I said. All right, he said. And he set to work.

But knowledge is a terrible thing. How could I be delighted with my magical escape when I knew that tomorrow the same scenario would occur, and that the night after that I would have run out of ornaments to barter with? Yes, yes, I thought, so the room is filled with gold where there had been straw, but was I really any better off? At best I would become the Queen of this King, and what kind of compensation would that be for my suffering and anxiety? Riches, power, even, if I played my cards right. Nice frocks and servants to take care of them, but I had an intuition that all those things would pall before long, and when they did I would *still* be married to a pig of a man whom I disliked almost as much as my father.

On the third night, in the unwavering way these stories have, I'd promised the firstborn of my marriage. Things will sort themselves out, I thought, in the way things do. And I concluded it was, on balance, better to be alive than dead. More opportunity.

And then the marriage, the wedding, the raising of my father to his earldom, the wedding night. Each of those events, and in particular the latter, filled me with disgust. Best leave it at that. Suffice it to say that kings do not necessarily carry their royalty into the bedroom. Once the fur and finery were off I might as well have been at it with the local shepherd boy. As a matter of fact, having been at it with the local shepherd boy for several months before my new life began, I can tell you I missed him that night—and for a good few thereafter.

That shepherd boy was no slouch in the carnal knowledge and skills of love department, and he taught me a thing or two, but His Majesty had such a depressing effect on me I could not bring myself to practice any of the interesting tricks I had learned. Eventually, my Lord and Master tired of plowing into me while I lay there limp, with nothing more than my fists clenched, and went on to entertain himself with some of the likelier lasses from the village (all of whom, it must be said, had also learned everything they knew from that delightful young shepherd—how he had learned these things, I wouldn't like to say, but I wager the sheep could tell a tale or two if they had the power of speech).

Nine months later, as sure as fairy tales are fairy tales, I gave birth to a young son and heir to the throne. Huge celebrations, and the return of the wizened little man. Now, I wasn't all that attached to my offspring. Frankly, I would have given him away—I hardly ever saw him in any case, he was nannied and wet-nursed and kept in isolated splendor in the nursery wing of the castle. But I didn't fancy explaining to the King that I'd swapped his son for a load of old hay, even though he would have had only his own greed to blame for it.

"Very well, then," said the little old man, predictably. "I will give you a chance. If you can guess my name within three . . ."

"Oh, please," I interrupted. "Don't you get tired of this nonsense? Guess my name. Three days. And what would you want with a baby, anyway? Listen, I have an alternative suggestion."

He was not pleased to have been stopped in mid-cliché. He stood staring at me open-mouthed and was, I'm sure, about to ignore what I said altogether and simply carry on with his pre-programmed deal. I daresay he was unable to consider even the possibility of an alternative. I carried on before he could.

"I've got a better idea. More interesting for both of us. Why don't you give me three days to make *you* forget your name?"

He was flabbergasted, and screwed up his face in confusion, trying to think out this new angle on an old story.

"But . . ." he sputtered eventually. "That's not the way it's done. You have to discover my name. You've got to find it out. Names. It's about names."

"But actually it's not very interesting, is it? All that happens is that I send out my servants who creep about and listen in doorways, and eventually—though granted at the last minute—you can be sure one of them will come across you in a wood cackling your name to yourself in premature self-congratulation, and the game will be up. What's clever or amusing about that? A rich and powerful woman uses her servants to find something out. Big deal. Now, what I'm suggesting is another thing altogether. Think of how difficult it is to make a person forget his name. Especially someone with as rare and interesting a name as I'm sure yours must be."

Still bemused, he scratched his head.

"How would you do that?"

I smiled at him.

I'd better explain something about myself. Just as I wasn't your archetypal beauty of a miller's daughter, I also did not have the same hankerings after pretty golden princes as my peers were universally supposed to have. Don't ask me why. A matter of personal taste. The King, as handsome as a former fairy tale prince must be once he's stopped being a frog, left me cold. I had always been attracted to—how can I put it?—the unusual. The shepherd boy was no one's idea of an Adonis; he suffered badly from the aftereffects of chicken pox and had a body that at best could be called weedy. But once he did the things he did, I came to love each and every crater on his pallid cheeks and lay in my bed at night entertaining myself with visions of his skinny thighs and unmanly, thin, rounded shoulders. It's fascinating how human desire can find all manner of things exciting once it's been given a push in the right direction. Beauty, muscularity,

height, and thick manes of hair didn't do a thing for me. There
it was. Apart from the pockmarked shepherd, I had had another
regular liaison with the girl at the dairy—a blowsy, bulbous,
ruddy-cheeked creature, bovine like her charges but as lusty and
lewd as any you might hope to meet in a cowshed while collect-
ing the milk in the early dawn. I did not know what to call what
the two of us did in the hay together every morning, but I
enjoyed it no end, and our frolics added nicely to the detail I
was accumulating with my shepherd lad. My tastes were, there-
fore, catholic, and desire was to me to be found where it may. I
did not dismiss the possibility of lascivious, unlawfully wedded
bliss with someone simply because they did not conform to the
current form of beauty dictated by our fairy tale existence.

The little man, as stringy as a newborn foal and half my
height, with a face so wrinkled that his wrinkles had wrinkles,
intrigued me. All that nervous energy, hopping about from one
foot to another, his wide, thin lips all aquiver, and violent, corn-
flower-blue, stark-staring eyes. Everybody has something about
them that can be found attractive.

"Come here," I said. "I've got something to show you."

For the statutory three nights he came to my queenly bedroom,
and I did indeed show him such things as he'd never even
dreamed about. Each morning, at dawn, he'd stagger from my
royal room, moaning and murmuring things to himself as if he
were trying to lodge impossible truths in his brain. I used and
passed on everything I'd learned during my glorious times with
the shepherd and the dairymaid, and the scrawny, twisted little
man trembled and mewed, night after long, slow night, with the
results of my expertise. Each morning, as he limped, his muscles
wrenched and ragged, away from my bed, I stopped him and
asked him: "Little man, what is your name?"

On the first morning he stopped his muttering and turned
achingly toward me on the bed with a wild look in his eye. After
a moment of enormous effort, he managed to raise his voice
enough so that I could hear what he said.

"My name . . ." he croaked. "My name is . . . Rumpel-stilts—"

And then his eyes went vague as something disappeared into the mist that was his mind. I smiled and said how much I was looking forward to the coming night.

On the second morning, I asked him the same question as he was leaving. Again, he turned, but this time it took much longer to bring the words out into the world.

"My name . . . my name . . . is . . . my name is . . . Rum-ple—"

And he fell silent. I bid him a warm good-day.

On the third morning, he was barely able to reach the door, his thin little legs were shaking so much. Great sighs came from him as each foot touched the floor and sent a shuddering memory of bliss and agony shooting through him.

"Little man, what is your name?" I asked him gently.

A strange, almost strangulated sound came from his depths and stuck fast in his throat. His mouth worked and his eyes rolled while he quivered from head to foot, as if every ounce of himself were involved in the effort to think what I could possibly mean by my words. But nothing came.

"What is your name?" I said again.

But the little man had given up, and merely shook his head in wonder and confusion as he disappeared from my room, like a shadow slipping beneath a door.

And so my life is just as my father had dreamed. I am a rich and powerful woman. The Queen of all and everything. I am respected, even revered for my wisdom and carefully considered decisions. The King, these days, is too busy to attend to matters of state, so I make sure that everything runs well and for the benefit of all the people. My father, the *arriviste* Earl, assists the King in his neverending task, so he also doesn't have much time to visit his royal daughter or attend to the mill, and I have placed it in the safe and talented hands of the shepherd boy, who says it makes a nice change from tending sheep. In order to maintain this satisfactory state of affairs, I arrange for the turret room with the spinning wheel (I still have not learned how to use it—just as well, considering the risk and result of pricking one's finger on the spindle, in a world such as ours) to be filled every day with straw-spun gold.

So the King is in his countinghouse most of the time, these days, along with my father, counting out his money. There's so much to count, I'm afraid they will never get to the end of it. And while they are thus engaged, I run the country, dispensing just law and keeping the millstones grinding and all the necessary circles turning. And for entertainment? For entertainment, I have my milk delivered fresh to the castle every morning, and at night I summon my little man from his day's spinning, and, over and over again, make him forget his name.

This is a story about circles and cycles, with a raging perversity at the center.

A DISH FOR THE GODS

Kay Kemp

My mother went to graduate school in English and became a feminist at an awkward time for me. I was sixteen and falling in love regularly. She went to seminars, fell in thrall to the feminist critics, and came home boiling with rage: "Look at the way all the poets made women into comestibles! Who needs this 'dish for the gods'? There's no end to it: Her *milk-white* skin, her *cherry* lips, her *tender* flesh. We're positively masticated by these guys—look at this one, 'Spearmint Girl with the Wrigley Eyes.' Huh! Eat or be eaten, I say."

She cooked well but it was never easy. Her lips did not drop as honeycomb, nor was her mouth as smooth as oil as she stood over the stove counting the seconds to stir the chocolate sauce. She cursed the pastry when it stuck to the rolling pin. Nothing came naturally: She measured everything, she never guessed, she never tasted, she never experimented. And always she fulminated over her labors, savagely gnawing on her lower lip, her eyes dark with resentment.

Her bravura collapsed, however, when she served my father. The roast beef may have been the same tawny red, like a pair of penny loafers, but sometimes he waved it away.

"How many times have I told you, a flat platter, please! I can't carve on a platter that's concave!!"

We didn't eat potatoes because my father thought they were pig food, but there were always three vegetables—broccoli, car-

rots or cauliflower, and a salad composed of a few leaves of lettuce, transparent slices of radish, and two strips of purple cab-
bage, maybe, in fluted wooden bowls bought on a trip to
Hawaii. Dessert was heated chocolate sauce over ice cream or
nonexistent.

If my mother pulled this off without spilling on a burner or
smoking up the oven or scorching one of her stainless steel pans,
she was relieved. They both hated cooking smells. She sat down
to eat, but her face stayed in knots of tension as she chewed.

I had probably just come in from necking to the breaking
point in the front seat of the car, pants down, bra unhooked, my
boyfriend poised over me, his cock buried in my belly, him dripping, me dripping, gasping, "We can't, we can't!" No doubt I'd
ridden home in the car with my face in his lap. I'd watch my
mother and father eating and try to imagine them making love.

How trying it must have been for them both! I couldn't see
my mother enjoying all that finger dipping and licking, the
yeasty smells, the smoke, the heat. And you never knew how it
was going to turn out! As for my father, if it wasn't served up
flat he'd get mad. It must have been no fun, no fun at all.

As it happened I married a nudist. Not a card-carrying member,
just a man who likes to walk around the house with his clothes
off. He's been known to go out and fetch the paper off the
front porch that way, which was a problem when we lived in the
city. Now we have no near neighbors: We moved up to our cottage, where I grow strawberries.

The strawberries are finished; it's August now. My husband
drives up from the city Friday night. He likes to shop at the
market first thing that morning. In his business suit he runs
from farmer's stand to farmer's stand, hearing them boast,
watching them fondle their produce. Then he puts all the food
he buys in bags in his car and goes to work for half a day (he's in
hospitality). At three, he jumps in the car full of warm eggplant,
softening Brie, baguettes, and new potatoes.

When I meet him at the marina the food is at the critical

stage. We drive the boat full throttle to the cottage and rush up the dock with the lettuce, the green, red, and yellow peppers, the croissants in their buttered bag, whiskered corn on the cob, first apples so hard they explode at your bite, the trembling beige eggs. We stash it all in the cooler, the fridge, and the baskets that we hang on pulleys from the ceiling so the mice won't get them.

Then we pour ourselves drinks and sit in the declining sun on the screened-in porch. Last night I made guacamole with an avocado that had survived the week. We sipped and we dipped our tortilla chips in the soft green mash. I never eat like this when he's not here. Food tastes better when I look at this man. My husband is big and there's nothing faint about his intake.

We ran our fingers around the rim of the bowl and sucked them. He pretended innocence as I took him by the hand and led him into the little bedroom we have up here, which is only large enough for the bed and a few hooks for clothes on the walls. We have to fall over forward to get onto the bed. There was a wind blowing and the faded chintz curtains flew over us like a shower of petals.

We started kissing hungrily, as we always do. It's a long week when he's gone. His mouth is wide and he sucks as if he could take me all in. Then I get on top of him and gather his lips in mine. I love the way they crush up against his teeth, the wet of his mouth that seems to run from them. He bought those concord grapes today, the ones that are meant for making wine. His concord lips are velvety, crushable, slightly sour, and stain purple the harder you press.

While we're kissing we're wriggling to get as close as we can on that large, soft old bed, and out of the angle of that last searching beam of the sun, which pierces the western window. He hitches me up against him, and I run my hands over his back, his neck, his head, down the back of his thighs. I get my hands on his belt as soon as I can without seeming greedy. I just love to undo it and get my hand inside his pants.

By this time—and it has taken some time—we've rolled

around enough so that he's erect, all tangled in there in the opening of his shorts, and my hand goes in and there is this great, warm, bristling, satiny root vegetable that pulsates in my palm. Perhaps it is a yam, one of those long ones with hair and eyes, a vegetable so rich I want to taste it, so febrile I want to cool it. I have a whole lot of places where I want to take it in, but that's for later.

I run my hand down its length to feel, at the place it springs from, the hard, sour plums in their furry sac. I hardly touch them at all—when they're cool like this it's best not to. Later they'll be hot and soft.

I actually enjoy the awkward business of pulling our wrappers off. Now we can see what we've bought, taking away the sticky plastic, the manmade markings, and finally bringing it into the light of our own home, getting our hands on it. Sometimes we don't quite remove the last tie but are so tempted we begin before we're bare.

Shirts we push up. Pants we untangle from ankles. I can separate my legs now and I'm kneeling over him while I undo my bra and let my apples spill over his face. They're Empress, the best for eating raw, rose on the outside, very white flesh. He goes for them, takes in as much as he can in his mouth. His lips go as black as eggplant meanwhile, his neck flushes, and his hands become white and his cock goes purple with blood. Under his skin, you can see all the juices begin to run.

He can take nearly a whole apple in his mouth, and does, and pretends to bite, but doesn't, then lets the full part slip out and nibbles daintily on the nipple. He bobs for a while, catching one and letting it go. We play that game. I'm the water, too, moving up and down, teasing his teeth. He's trying to sink his teeth in, get a purchase on me. Meanwhile I can feel that root vegetable test and try my thighs and my belly.

When I can't stop myself any longer I roll off him, turn, and take the yam between my two hands, rolling it slowly and bringing the tip up to my lips. He is over me now, and he has his hands on my pelvis bones. My belly goes concave as he presses those two horns, handles, really, and lifts my hips like a two-handed cup from which he can drink the sweet, warm, white milk of my pelvis.

But he doesn't drink, not yet. His lips graze the inside of my thighs, those straight white stalks, he takes a nip here and here and here, moving up, yes, it is like eating a cob of corn. So hungry now I can't stop, I take him between my lips and make circles with my tongue. I dip him in and out gently until he responds and moves a little more, and I know he's too distracted for more corn.

My thirst is overwhelming, and now I'm drinking his wine, and finally he too finds the narrow mouth of the cup buried in the folds of linen. All the fine food in the world is lost without wine.

We're calmer when we turn again to face each other, and we take a little time to look at the feast we have. The sun is sinking fast beyond the window, and before it goes it gives a boost of pink to our cheeks, our bruised lips.

The finest meal is nothing without music. Now I am wearing him across my front, like a cello between my legs, off at an angle over my shoulder. But this cello is reversed, its strings are toward me, they run through me, from crease to clavicle. I have my arms around the neck of the instrument, I let my hands play over the white swell of his hips. He moves up and down, sideways. The sounds that begin to flow are not mine or his but both of ours.

I lie here on my back and hold the white back of this man and follow with my body the undulations he makes. I find the crease between his white loaves of bread, I even find those plums I saved before, which are different now, they're soft, they slide inside their sac and they are warm as life. I run my hands from the back of his neck—his face is buried somewhere over there in the pillow—along his spine, and down his legs. I feel the pressing within and my mouth yearns for one more thing to take in. I fasten on his shoulder, mouth the flesh there, feel the muscles working under the skin.

You are my nourishment, my food, I tell him.

And then it's over. The stained remnants of our feast are cast with abandon across the bed. The silence of fulfillment is soft as twilight.

Already I'm thinking about what we'll have for dinner. Before long he'll get up naked and light the gas barbecue, standing on the front porch where the whole bay could see, if it had eyes. It will be dark by the time we dine on his market offerings. The end of the meal will be my strawberries, so small and ripe and sweet they run without sugar.

––––––––––

Of the two lusts, desire is more elusive than hunger. Too frequently these days we hear about those arid phases of our lives when we are dead to sexual desire, when we must seek out the bizarre and the dangerous in order to reawaken a longing, which, in truth, has always been there. I wanted to write about the sort of desire that is kindled as easily and as naturally as the passion for delicious food. "Mouth-watering" is the word that comes to mind, the one I wish to attach to this story.

LAST TANGO IN GENEVA

❦❦❦❦❦❦❦

Jacqueline Ariail

It was 1973. Geneva. Our honeymoon—though neither of us was so sentimental as to call it that. A working honeymoon, at least for Barry. He had a conference in Naples; in Geneva, there was an Institute to visit. Capelle, it was called. A few cities we threw in for pleasure: Florence before Geneva; Paris, after. But it's Geneva I remember best.

We stayed in a guest house in the Commune de Carouge, a suburb on a hill outside the city. We had a private bedroom; we shared a kitchen and bath with another guest. The ferocious Madame Vicquerat was our *propriétaire*: a petite woman, with perfectly coiffed black hair. She wore old-lady flowered dresses and a demure half-apron, though she was not old. She was brusque in her dealings with us, nearly inhospitable, and Barry and I wondered aloud together why she bothered to take in boarders, except, of course, for the money.

She kept the place immaculate, and at every turn there were signs, penned by Madame. In the kitchen, above the counter, hung two hooks, and above each hook hung a small hand-lettered sign: *essuie-mains,* hand towel; *torchon,* dish towel. In the bathroom, over the john: *Prière de tirer la chasse d'eau,* please flush. Above the light switch in our room: *Prière d'éteindre les lumières,* please put out the lights. And in every room, including the large upstairs hall, onto which the guest rooms opened, *Défense de fumer.*

Our room was at the back of the house; it had a French door onto a tiny balcony that overlooked the garden. Our fellow boarder—a red-haired man, an American—had the room across the hall from ours. I watched him on the afternoon we arrived from behind the lace that covered the French door. I was putting our things away—Barry had gone out for a few groceries—when I heard some commotion outside. Opening the door a little, I saw the boarder emerge from the woods and enter the gate of Madame Vicquerat's garden. He had a red beard as well, a close-trimmed one. It was Madame who was shouting, as he walked toward the house, and it took me a minute to understand what she was saying as she came into view, waving her arms at him. "*Et le jardin—interdit—aux pensionnaires.*" The garden—forbidden—to guests. He stopped and stared at her. He was tall and thin. He pulled his glasses off and rubbed his eyes wearily—he looked bemused, then he said something quietly in French. Madame Vicquerat was not satisfied; she gestured at the gate behind him and pointed along the edge of her garden to a path outside the fence. He turned and went out the gate, and I watched him walk along the path with a wry smile on his lips. He went to the front of the house. The door closed behind him, and I heard his footfall on the steps.

I stuck my head out of our door as he got to the landing. "*Liberté, égalité, et le jardin,*" I said.

"*Mais oui,*" he told me, as he went into his room.

The Europeans, it seemed, had a penchant for single beds, even in rooms meant for coupling. Often these rested a foot apart; sometimes they were pushed together; always there was a gap where the frames met but the mattresses didn't. Our beds in Madame Vicquerat's room were no exception. They stood with a corridor between them. So Barry would visit me, but without the sexual charge you'd expect a single, narrow bed to elicit. Our lovemaking that summer was no different from what it had been in my dormitory room or in Barry's apartment: It was too quick, too hard, too quick. Before I knew it, he was gone, back to his own narrow bed, asleep. I didn't have the words to protest. I didn't know how to ask for more. I was young then, and he was so much older.

Silently, I resented his not lying in bed with me all night, not coming to lie with me in the morning. He was up early. I'd wake to the sounds of him making coffee for the two of us in the kitchen below. Our fellow boarder—the intruder in the garden—seemed always to sleep late. We never met him in the kitchen. Hearing Barry's morning noises, I'd get up and dress and go down like a dutiful wife to share coffee and bread in Madame Vicquerat's spotless kitchen. When he left for the day, I'd wave from the door, then go back upstairs to read Henry Miller. I carried *The Tropic of Cancer* with me that summer. *The Tropic of Cancer* and George Eliot's *Daniel Deronda*—unlikely bedfellows. I was supposed to be making notes for my dissertation, which I actually did some mornings, after my rendezvous with Miller. I sat at a small writing table across from the separate beds. On the wall behind the table, from the ceiling down to the floor—where, if I stretched my legs out, I could touch it with my feet—hung an enormous snakeskin. I suppose it was a boa constrictor's. At its widest, which was about at eye level, it was a good eight inches. Sitting at that table, trying to take notes but catching myself staring at that dry, speckled skin, drove me out every morning into the quiet streets of Carouge. We were on the edge of a forest. Madame's fenced garden backed up against a thick copse of trees. Nearly every other house on the street had a front fence of some kind—a high stone wall, or wire strung between heavy round posts, curling over forbiddingly. Dogs barked as you passed. Mourning doves cooed. They reminded me of home.

I walked a lot that summer. In every city we visited, I walked, and walked again, stopping in shops, stopping in museums. Sometimes I'd lunch in a small café. I told myself that it was an adventure, but, in truth, I was lonely and bored. I wanted company; I wanted affection. I bought pastry or fruit at the end of the morning and, following an afternoon stint of notetaking before the snakeskin, made myself coffee and had my treat, with my back to the beds and the table, and the lace-covered door onto the balcony flung open to the garden and the woods.

On one such desultory day I wandered out of the Promenade des Bastions with its grim statues of the Protestant reformers and over to the Rue de la Cité. There were people, lots of people. Up ahead I saw a marquee and on it *Le Dernier Tango à Paris*. I went in to the cool dark of the theater and watched Brando fuck Maria Schneider. Watched Schneider unzip her jeans and reach her hand in to make herself come, rolling giddily onto the bare wood floor. And suddenly it struck me: If Barry couldn't please me, if I couldn't tell him how to please me, I could please myself.

I went out of the darkness into the harsh afternoon light, thinking, how could she shoot him? thinking, I'd take the streetcar back to Carouge. I wasn't meeting Barry until seven, at a restaurant near the Capelle. The afternoon stretched invitingly ahead. I stopped at a little market before I caught the streetcar and bought some luscious red strawberries. They smelled so good. In Madame Vicquerat's kitchen, I washed them, leaving the stems on, putting them in a shallow white porcelain bowl. I took them upstairs and set them on the writing table. I opened the French door onto the balcony. The afternoon was hot; there was hardly a breeze. The whole room smelled of strawberries. They made the room come to life; they made the snakeskin less sinister. They were lovely.

Then I went to the bed, propped the pillows against the headboard, and lay back on them, pulling my shirt out from my jeans, reaching a hand under and up to my breasts, rubbing them gently. It was the newness of it that excited me—this possibility of pleasing myself. I unzipped my jeans and reached inside. They were still too tight and I wriggled my hips out, aching for my own touch. It was lovely, this gentle probing with my fingers between my swollen lips. I took my hand away. It was too good not to prolong. I pulled my shirt off, reached around and unfastened my bra and let it slide from my shoulders. I wet my fingers with my own saliva and circled my nipples, first one and then the other, while the ache grew. I rolled onto my stomach, up on my knees, pulling the pillow down, brushing just the tips of my nipples on the cool cotton, and with my fingers once again—not needing any saliva now—rubbing my spot, gently at first, then harder and harder, and my hips moving, as they were never inclined to move with Barry, in slow waves, back and forth, with my ass in the air, my breasts against the pillow, until with each twitch of pleasure, each rocking motion, my legs widened and spread, my ass touched the sheet, and I came, moaning, sinking, spreading myself wide onto the bed.

I teased Barry over dinner that night about working too hard. He was in no mood to be teased.

"All day," he said, "I've been trying to understand the makeup of this virus. And nothing." He threw up his hands. "Nothing."

I murmured sympathetically.

"It's not the same for you," he told me. "You can spend the day reading and writing and actually get somewhere."

"Yes," I said, "I suppose I can."

We walked back from the restaurant in silence and were growled at by several dogs along the way. A German shepherd barked and ran at us and leapt against the crisscrossed wire of its owner's fence.

"I bought strawberries," I told Barry as we let ourselves in. "I saved them for you. They're in the fridge. You won't believe how beautiful they are, how good they smell."

"No, thanks. I'm bushed. I'm going to bed. You have some, though."

"I already have."

The *minutier* went out just as we reached the landing, and I noticed a narrow slit of light beneath the door of the red-haired boarder. After our door closed, his opened; and I heard his footsteps on the stairs. I sat on my bed, fidgeting for no good reason while Barry took off his clothes. He was handsome and hairy. I loved to run my hand over the thick curly dark hair that covered his back and his chest. When he got into bed, I leaned across the space that separated us and kissed his forehead. "I'm going downstairs," I said.

When I got to the kitchen, I found the red-haired boarder standing at the open refrigerator, admiring my strawberries.

"Go ahead," I said. "Have some."

He turned, startled, but then he smiled. "They're gorgeous."

"What's your name?" I asked him.

"Alan. What's yours?"

"Laura. Too bad we don't have any cream."

"Ah, but we do." He reached into the fridge and produced a small carton, then took the bowl of strawberries and set it on the table between us. He poured the cream on. I got spoons from the drawer.

"I don't think we need those," he said. He held a strawberry, glistening with cream, to my lips. We sat at the table and fed each other strawberries as if we were old lovers. And when we'd finished them off, he got up and set the white bowl with all our discarded stems in the sink. "Let's leave that for Madame, shall we?"

"I saw your encounter with her from my window. The garden is forbidden," I said, laughing. I felt giddy. "You were very gracious," I told him.

He leaned against the sink. "And you have good taste," he said.

I went to the sink to wash my hands as he crossed to the door. Our arms brushed. It was like a charge of static on a crisp winter's day—only nicer. It made my stomach dip.

He was in the doorway, leaning against the jamb. "Night, night," he said. And if I hadn't been a newly married woman, I would have followed him to his room.

When I came down the next morning to the aroma of Barry's coffee, he told me that he was going overnight to a lab in

Lucerne, where someone else had a lead on his virus. He looked sheepish. "I forgot to tell you last night. Jurg is taking me. He said it'd be better if we stayed overnight. Do you want to come? There's a wonderful bridge in Lucerne. A covered bridge with paintings inside."

"No. You go. I've gotten into a rhythm here. Walking, working. It's fine."

"I'll be back in the afternoon. We could go to a movie."

After Barry left, I didn't know what I wanted to do: read, walk, get into bed. I opted for my usual routine minus Henry Miller, whom I thought I might save for the afternoon. Walking into the city, I decided I'd buy myself a dress. There was a shop I'd noticed a few days ago, with vivid, bright things in the window—in particular, a maroon dress with a wonderful batik pattern. I walked in, asked to try it on, and liked it immediately. It had slender straps and a low, scooped neckline that showed my shoulders. There were buttons all the way down the front, from the fitted bodice and waist to the full, long skirt.

"I'll take it," I told the smiling clerk. "May I wear it?"

"*Oh, oui.*" She cut the tags off for me, put my shirt and jeans in a bag.

I walked out feeling good and went back to the same open market I'd visited the day before. There were raspberries today, big ones, and small oval purple plums. I bought some of each.

From the bottom of the street, I saw a small knot of people outside Madame Vicquerat's house, heard shouting voices, a dog barking. A car with a flashing light was parked at the curb. They were all at the formal front entrance, standing under the eaves on the wide stone steps. Alan was there, his red hair bright in the afternoon sun. He did not look happy. He bent down just as I drew closer, putting his hand to the bare calf of his leg. Madame Vicquerat's voice rose above all the others. There were two policemen and a man with a German shepherd, straining at its leash.

When I came up, the policemen were laughing and Madame Vicquerat was arguing, in furious French, with the man with the dog.

"What happened?" I asked Alan.

"I was bitten."

"Let me see it."

He was holding a crumpled, bloody handkerchief to the bite. He took his hand away, and I winced at the wound. It was deep. It had to be painful.

"What are they arguing about?"

"Whether the dog should be impounded. The police think I'm an idiot for having her call them."

"Let them argue," I said. "Let me take care of that."

I led him inside and up the stairs and into my room, closing the door behind us. Barry's socks, which I'd washed the day before, hung over the radiator near the French door. I made him sit on my bed.

"I don't know why I'm shaking," Alan said.

"I do. I would be, if I'd just been bitten by that dog."

"I really didn't see him coming. That sounds silly, I know. But I heard him barking and thought he was inside the fence. Do you know the one I mean—the wire one?"

I nodded. "Hold your leg out."

He had on khaki shorts that came to just above his knees. "You wouldn't have been much better off in pants," I said.

"I know."

"Here's a clean handkerchief. Keep holding it there. I'll get some soap and water." I propped the pillows from Barry's bed and mine behind him.

He eased himself back and stretched his leg on the bed. "I'll bloody her damn duvet," he said.

"So you will."

When I came back with a small bowl of water, soap, and a clean towel, he was smiling.

"You're taking awfully good care of me."

I smiled back. "I'm happy to. This isn't going to be fun," I said.

It was still bleeding. I tossed the handkerchief aside, dipped the towel in the warm water and wrung it out, then pressed it against the bite. I held it there for a long time and ran my other hand up and down the front of his leg to distract him. His skin was smooth, and the hair on his legs was fine, a light blondish-red.

"That feels nice."

"It's to make up for what's next, which probably won't feel nice. I think it's time I cleaned it."

He nodded. "Go ahead."

I rubbed some soap on the towel and swabbed the wound as gently as I could.

His muscles tensed.

"This may need stitches."

"Oh no," he said. "No doctor's office. No hospital. I've had enough of Swiss authority. We'll use adhesive tape if we have to."

"I'm nearly done."

I had my free hand on the back of his leg just below his knee as I dabbed at the wound with the soapy towel. "Do you run?" I asked him.

"Yes. Why? Do you?"

"One at a time, please. I'm concentrating here. Because you have wonderfully strong calf muscles. And yes, I do."

"Have you run here in Geneva?"

"No. There're too many dogs."

We both laughed.

"I've got good old American Bactine in my toiletry bag, but I don't have the kind of bandage this needs. Let's see what Madame has."

"Find out, if you can, what's happening to the dog."

He was lying with his legs slightly apart, one arm across his chest and his eyes closed behind his glasses, when I came back with the bandage. His hair was mussed; he looked very attractive.

"This is going to sting," I said quietly, and he sat up and opened his eyes. He turned his leg toward me and I looked at the smooth white inside of his thigh. I squirted the Bactine on.

"That hurts."

It seeped into the wound and went running in little rivulets down to his ankle. I dried his skin with the towel and put the bandage on.

When I finished, my hands were trembling.

He saw that they were and took both of them in his. When he looked at me, I saw his eyes register the snakeskin behind me on the wall.

"What the hell is that?"

"You mean you don't have one? I figured it was Madame Vicquerat's reminder to her boarders that this *is* a Protestant city. Knox, Calvin, original sin. Actually, I hate it."

"Let's take it down," he said. "Stuff it in the closet."

"There is no closet."

"In the wardrobe, then."

"I don't know why I never thought of that."

"Because you're too gracious a guest," he said. He started to get up.

"Don't," I told him. "I'll do it." I climbed from the chair onto the table and took the snakeskin off its hook. Holding it in my hands, touching it, made it less menacing. I rolled it loosely and set it in the wardrobe atop Barry's suitcase.

"Better?" he asked.

"Much." I sat at the foot of the bed. "Oh—the dog *will* be impounded. That's why the owner was so incensed. Madame Vicquerat says the police want to speak to you again, but I told her not tonight. I said you didn't want to see anyone tonight."

"Thank you."

"You're welcome." I looked at him for a moment, then bent my head to his leg and kissed him gently just above the newly dressed wound. When I raised my head to look at him again, he took his glasses off with a quick, impatient tug that made me want him. Then he reached for me and pulled me toward him on the bed, up between his spread legs.

He kissed my hands first, both of them. "How can I thank you?" he asked.

"You have," I told him, "you are."

He touched my hair and my face, tracing the line of my cheekbone, and I put my hand on the back of his neck, at his hairline. His hair was thick and a little wiry. I could push my fingers into it.

Then we kissed—a long, slow, exploratory kiss that relaxed us both.

"Where's your husband?" he asked.

"In Lucerne for the night."

"Good," he said and kissed me again.

Then he drew back and looked at me. "This is what you want?" he asked.

"Yes."

"Tell me," he said, "tell me what you'd like."

"I'd like you to unbutton me." I scooted up on my knees, pulling my dress out from under me. He sat up, against the headboard. First he kissed my face, then my neck, and just above my breasts where the dress began.

"It's a pretty dress," he said, as he started to unbutton it, kissing me as each button came undone.

How delicious it was to feel the dress come open, to feel myself open, slowly, to him. I had no bra on. When he'd opened the buttons down to my waist and my breasts just showed, he reached in with his tongue and licked them.

"Keep going," I said.

He unbuttoned every button with the same measured calm, licking his way down. And I unbuttoned his shirt as well, pushing it off his shoulders and down over his arms. When my dress was completely open, he slipped it off and smiled at me, and I felt as I had never in my life felt before, desirous and desired.

I lay on my back and he ran his hands over me, down my arms, over my breasts, across my stomach, as he pulled at my underpants. I wiggled out of them.

"How did you get skin so soft?" he asked.

"It's a gift from the gods," I told him. "Like you are."

I unzipped his shorts then, and we took care to pull them gently over the leg with the bite.

Beneath *his* underwear, he was hard and ready. I touched him, cupping my hand to his crotch, feeling his hard penis, his soft balls. Then I reached inside, holding him, stroking him, as he pulled his briefs off, and we were naked on the narrow bed together.

"This is what I want," I said.

It was twilight. The last light of the day filtered through the lace on the door. We pushed the bunched-up duvet out from under us. It fell off the bed.

He kneeled over me, caressing my breasts with his hands, kissing them again. And with his fingers, he touched me where I was so wet and ready.

I reached for his penis, but he took my hand away. "Not yet," he said. "It's your turn first."

He ran his tongue across my belly, then spread my legs wide and put his mouth to my hot, wet, full lips and licked me there, flicking his tongue back and forth till I couldn't stand it.

"Stop. Please stop. And come inside. That's what I'd like. It's what I want. For you to come inside me."

I pulled him up. He stretched out over me, and now it was my turn to run my hands over his chest as he leaned on his elbows. To reach around and feel his taut ass, to put my hands in the deep hollows just inside his hip bones. I guided his penis to me, and the sensation of him pushing in and moving—not deeply, not yet—inside me was the most exquisite thing I've ever known.

"Now," I said, "come in now." And he did, all the way, and we moved together, slowly, and then faster and faster in quick inevitable waves of hot, lovely motion until we both were open and spent and done.

"Don't move," I said. "Stay where you are." I took my hands from his back and felt the sheet on either side of us. We were perfectly centered in Madame Vicquerat's narrow bed. I smiled.

"Now you can move," I said. And he slid down beside me, tucking his arm beneath my head, gathering me to him.

"I want to sleep like this," I said.

"So do I."

With his free hand, he fished on the floor for the duvet and pulled it over us.

"I don't want to think about tomorrow."

"Don't," he said, "just sleep."

And I did. And I remember that in the morning, in the first light, we lay together quietly on that narrow bed and listened to the mourning doves coo in the forbidden garden.

I started to write this story without giving the man and woman in it names, calling them simply "he" and "she." Then I realized that they had actually been with me a long time; in fact, they are the main characters in the novel I'm currently working on. Only Alan, the man bitten by the dog, is new—as new as the heroine's sexual awakening.

POLISHING MY SKIN

❦❦❦❦❦❦

Nazneen Sheikh

They have come for me. Two women carrying wicker baskets covered with cloth and a small charcoal brazier. My mother and sisters have left. All my mother whispered into my ear was "let them prepare you." This time it is a gentle entreaty quite unlike her usual stern maternal injunctions. This time her gaze softens as she strokes back the strands of hair sculpted across my forehead. I am startled because in the shining depths of her brown eyes I see the iris ringing out as though it is trying to contain something that smolders . . . unfurls inside. I have never seen this expression in my mother's eyes before, and I move closer to her, but she has turned away and moves beyond the door. I am left with the two women who have already shut the door to the bathhouse in my grandmother's ancestral home.

The wedding is five hours away and the city of Lahore scorches under a July sun. Not here, though, in this plaster and tile room equipped with water faucets mounted above a tiled bathing trough. I have heard about this bathhouse since I was a child. All the women of the family have come here before their weddings to be "prepared." When they are viewed many hours later as brides, each one shimmers with an uncanny luminosity that we all know is nothing to do with cosmetics. No one shares the secret and nothing is ever discussed. Now it is my turn, and I can hardly wait. I am not like the other women. I am my mother's wayward daughter who has lived in the West and is not a virgin. The man I have chosen to marry is much older than me and a Hispanic American. I have brought him to my father's home so we can have a traditional wedding. This is the land of soft women with hard yet resilient minds. So I am here not to indulge my mother but to satisfy my curiosity. My favorite aunt has guessed it, though; she looked at me with a diamond winking in her pierced nostril and said, "The West cannot teach you the mysteries of the East." Her comment is clichéd and outmoded, yet I am ensnared. I grew up surrounded by these women who had husbands chosen for them. Educated women, who managed to escape abroad for prized vacations with their husbands so that they could get their hair permed in Paris and pick up shoes in Rome. Their conversations were dotted with anecdotes of their husbands, children, tailors, and maid servants. Some of them held political debates and exercised intellectual freedom in unique ways, but they never spoke about sex or desire, let alone their orgasms, and their fantasies. It was their lot, I had decided, and nothing whatsoever to do with me. I had my hair cut at Vidal Sassoon and poured myself into denim and offered my body to men I desired. My only innate female vanity is to envelop myself in rose-scented fragrances.

The two women are busy removing objects from the baskets. The older one moves slowly, giving instructions to the younger one, who is plump and given to giggling. They are professionals in the rituals of their trade, which has been passed along from mother to daughter. The items they use are indigenous, organically grown, dried, and then pounded in primitive mortar and pestle and finally stored in delicate earthenware vessels. I am told to remove my clothes. The older woman makes this request as casual as asking for the time. The younger one pulls down a *charpai* that is leaning against one wall. It is the traditional hemp woven bed bolstered by four wooden legs. The legs are ornately carved and painted in lurid colors. As I step out of my clothes, the younger woman covers the bed with a white cotton sheet. I am naked in front of two other women who are fully clothed. The older woman looks at my body, and a smile plays across her lips. I am convinced she is taking some sort of inventory. Then she puts a hand on my shoulder and pivots me around. I almost stumble, but she holds my waist to steady me. The palms of her hand are soft, and I feel as though a silken sash is holding me in place. She is behind me now and I know that some sort of examination of my back is being conducted without my being touched. She steps out from behind me and leads me to the bed. In that minute and a half I am made aware that some transformation of my body is imminent, and I instinctively trust my benefactress.

Silk, she says, looming over me, as I lie on the bed knotted with anticipatory tension, is always packed in tobacco leaves. But when we take it out, it is silk. I can make you into a river of silk and he will never want to cross to the other side. I will turn you into the milky flesh of the green almond, which he will hold in his mouth without ever swallowing. I can do without machines what they can never do in America. Amused, I gaze up at her face and nod. Then she deftly adds: It may hurt a little. Plump and giggling Safia hands her strips of muslin coated with heated brown sugar and lemon juice. It starts from my ankles, the primitive depilatory process. The sticky heated embrace of the cloth, the quick caramelizing on the skin, and the sharp yank. A three-tiered process in which I go through a contracting, relaxing dance of my own. The discomfort is minimal. Silk and pearls, croons the woman, moving upward to my knees, deforesting my skin, making me truly naked. Defoliating, deforesting . . . denuding. Like some lyrical poetess, she hums with similes and metaphors. Then she takes my hand and trails the fingertips across one of my thighs. This is his hand, she whispers, these are his fingers. All you will have to do is look into his eyes and you will feel your own skin. I am instantly catapulted into the heavy-lidded gazes of Eastern men gazing from old portraits. Were all those smoldering orbs reflecting the opalescent skins of their hairless women? Was this the reason perhaps that women were hidden, veiled, and closeted from the eyes of men? How quickly would the warring instincts of their men be derailed by images of desire. All those pear-shaped Mughal women with complexions the color of yellowing clotted cream had kept this secret buried. But I return again to this century and this room, where I sense that, although something else is about to begin, I am not certain if my hazel-eyed lover with his sensuous smile will attain the mystery of the East in his arms tonight.

Now this, she says, tapping my pubic mound, is like a ball of wool. What will he say when he gets here? There isn't any way to tell her how my soon-to-be-husband separates with almost surgical delicacy all the strands of the ball of wool. How the anticipation of the moment as he deliberately prolongs finding my clitoral bud is also one of the more enthralling aspects of our lovemaking. You pant, he always chuckles, like a little animal. I say, record them, I want to hear these pants of mine. These half-breaths drawn out from my primeval self where I am neither human nor animal yet miraculously sensate. But a strip of muslin is already settling into place, and the following yank ricochets with a stinging pain that shocks me into silence. It is repeated three more times, and when it is over I discover a new sensorial receptor in my body. Now, says the woman, helping me up to a sitting position, we will polish your skin. I glance down between my legs, seeing a continuous line of skin and the pale flesh rise of my pelvic mound a freshly revealed contour. I know I suddenly want a full-length mirror in order to pose for a moment like the heavy-hipped women of Botticelli and Titian.

Plump Safia's giggles hiccup softly in the room, and the gleam of approval mirrored in the older woman's eyes makes me rise slowly. I walk like a piece of statuary toward the bathing area. I walk like Cleopatra, Nefertiti, but most of all I walk like the Mughal Empress Nur Jehan, who hunted tigers and created Attar of Rose. I sit on the wooden stool placed in the sunken area near the taps, and as I reach toward a faucet, a hand encircles my wrist. It is the older woman, holding a clay jar in the crook of one arm. I am told to extend my arms and be still. There is more to come. The pale yellow paste is rubbed into my entire body and massaged vigorously. The base is turmeric, I am told. The other ingredients have names I cannot even pronounce. The movements of their supple fingers are circular. Both women work on my body as if they are polishing a metal object. I know for the first time how the skin folds over my elbow and how it dissappears into a dimple behind my knee. How the spill of my stomach is guarded on either side by the angular thrust of my pelvic bones. Where the weight of my breasts create a niche in my midriff and how far my navel is embedded in my stomach. Every protrusion, each folded crevice is sought out and attended to.

Safia now turns on the water and collects it in a bucket, which she pours over my body. The older woman removes the paste with a coarse loofah. Each section of my cleaned body draws a satisfied murmur from the older woman, and I, who have suddenly been gifted with this polished and tingling skin, am overwhelmed by the desire to rub myself like a cat against the fold of a curtain, the leg of a chair, and most of all the softly crisping hair on my lover's chest. My breasts begin to stiffen, and I cannot be certain if the liquid between my legs is water or my own sex juices. A heaviness, almost a languor, roots me to the wooden stool. When my feet are lifted one at a time and scrubbed with another paste, this one abrasive, I know that I will insist his tongue pay homage to every inch of this glistening nudity I call my body. When I am finished I feel ready to jump into a car and reach the hotel room, where he lies, waiting for his foreign wedding to begin. I don't want to cover myself with the stiff gold tissue outfit that has been stitched for me. I don't want the heavy, encrusted gold jewelry to pinch my throat and earlobes. I just want my nipples sucked into hard pellets and his sweet hard cock riding high inside. I want the women now to disappear.

The older woman is rubbing my American shampoo into my wet hair. She sniffs at the mouth of the bottle once in curiosity and then the second time in obvious disdain. Yet she sees the warning in my eyes, so she works a lather in my hair. After Safia has poured the cool well water through it eight or nine times, I become aware of a hissing sound and a fragrance rising around us. It is coming from the small iron brazier that is lying close to one end of the bed. I inhale deeply, just the way you do with marijuana. It is sandalwood, pure with its almost sickly sweet draw, coiling through the bathhouse. I am motioned toward the bed and told to lie down. Now, says the older woman, I will rub oil into your body; you will carry its fragrance through the first night into the second. I am eased up toward the edge of the bed so my hair hangs over the edge. Safia, positioned behind me on the floor, uses a fan to push the heated, fragrant smoke through my shoulder-length hair. Her fingers are parting my hair, coiling strands around and around. My head feels warm and cool simultaneously. I long to smell it, inhale the sandalwood, but I can't as yet; the older woman is massaging my feet with slippery hands. Jasmine oil, she says to me. It is the lightest and the most delicate of all flowers. It is better in the heat, she adds. When you perspire, even your sweat will be scented.

Where is my lover, says my perfumed skin, I want him to ride me like a centaur in the heat of Lahore, pounding his haunches into mine, making me slippery with scented sweat. You will put it between your legs, yourself, she requests politely, this high priestess of flesh . . . this polisher of skin. Into my cupped palm she pours some oil, light as water, and I am dabbing between my legs around the lips, cautiously, toward the bud and then around the soft sides. I cannot go further because there is music pounding in my skull entirely made up of a palpitating state of desire. I want to escape this room and end this drawn-out erotic exercise where I have felt the power of my femininity only filtered through the ritual of this most exquisite of toilettes. This preparation which my mother had slipped into the chaos of my East/West marriage had been done only to remind me of the reverence paid to the act of love. Now the legions of Eastern women, shrouded by their stultifying conventions, assume a new aura for me. Their silence is understandable. They have memorized the ultimate sex manual, not with the aid of text or illustration but rather through the most conscious examination of their own bodies.

You, says the older woman, massaging my earlobes with jasmine oil, may wish to have something to drink. We give it to the younger brides. She had guessed, this polisher of skin, this titillator of nerve endings, that I had come back from the land of free and easy women. I am interested; I normally see things to the end. I sit up on the bed like a column of incense. Hair of sandalwood and body of jasmine, ready to swallow the libation of the moment. It is offered by giggling Safia in a metal glass. I am drinking milk with ground almonds, laced with powdered cardamom. It is cool, with a bit of an aftertaste. Nothing comes to mind. The older woman watches me intently. I drain the glass and wonder how much time has passed. Will anyone remember to collect me from this place? Safia brings the pile of fresh clothes for me to wear home. I am stepping into them slowly when I realize that my body has lost some contact with the outer edge of reality. I am floating in etherized form. There is no substance to my limbs as a series of minute explosions press out the unconscious tension that has always pulsed inside.

You are not even waiting now, whispers the older woman, as she leads me toward the door. You are in the moment, and what you have drunk heightens it so that it does not end even when you have taken him.

Much later, when a monsoon-like torrent cools the night and we lie in the flower-strewn debris of this great white bed and I am covered by the blanket of his limbs and he whispers, You are in my nostrils, in my hair . . . aah, the feel of you . . . I can hear the older woman wearing the face of Ikbal recite:

It must be known, this world of scent and sheen,
They must be plucked, the roses in the dene;
Yet do not close thine eyes upon the Self,
Within thy soul a thing is to be seen.

I wrote this story because I wished to put women from the East and the West into the great white bed together. When the face of a Moroccan or Bengali woman peers out from a shrouded form, her sisters in Boston or Toronto conjure up images of deprivation and oppression. But the kaleidoscope needs to be tilted so that the celebration of erotic power is not stifled by geography. In the culture in which I was raised, the physical act of love becomes a form of worship, and at this altar the most glittering and precious offerings are our bodies.

VALENTINE'S DAY IN JAIL
❦❦❦❦❦❦❦

Susan Musgrave

Western wind when will thou blow?
The small rain down can rain.
Christ that my love were in my arms
And I in my bed again.

ANON.

T he bus dropped me in the heart of town, across from the
funeral parlor, where a sign in the window read, "Closed for
the Season."

"No one dies much this time of year?" I asked, making small
talk with the taxi driver taking me the rest of the way to the
prison. "Not if they do it around here," he replied, and then
asked me if I minded if he smoked.

Before I could answer, he lit one and blew the smoke out his
window. I sat in the back watching rain streak the windshield as
he talked about the justice system and how "sickos like drug
dealers" should be shot to save taxpayers' money. He must have
thought I worked at the prison because he kept glancing in the
rearview mirror, waiting for me to agree. I explained I was visiting a convicted marijuana smuggler, a Colombian, doing life,
that it might even be love. He apologized, saying he should

have kept his trap shut. He said there must be one heck of a lucky guy waiting for me inside, that all he'd ever wanted was a soft girl in his bed every night, and all he'd ever been was disappointed.

I looked away into the mountains above the distant town of Hope, the snowy ridges few had ever set foot on, and tried to picture what Angel, the lucky man, might be doing at this moment. I imagined him lying on his bunk, staring up at the dull green institutional gloss on his ceiling, with not even a crack or a ridge he could use as landmarks.

"So when's the honeymoon?" the driver pressed. The window had steamed up, and he wiped a little space with his hand. "You going to escape? Go someplace tropical? Swimming pool, palm trees, hula-hula. You wish, huh?"

We rounded a bend at the northern end of the valley, and Toombs Penitentiary came into view. All that separated it from its sister prison, Toombs Penitentiary for Women, was the Corrections Mountain View Cemetery. Both prisons were cut off from the world by mountains so high their western flanks were always in shadow.

I'd met Angel when I visited both prisons, and the adjoining cemetery, a year ago. I had just begun free-lancing and hoped to cover the story behind the high rate of inmate suicides over Christmas. "No one but the law ever wanted them when they were alive, and now *no one* wants them," an official told me, indicating the forlorn tract of land, overgrown with scagweed, where the unclaimed bodies of lifers were laid to rest. Escape risks, he told her, were even buried in leg irons.

My driver let me off in the parking lot, a hundred yards from the front gate, and wished me luck. "You know, you make me jealous," he said. "You get to go in there and be all lovey-dovey while I go back to work." I paid him and stood for a moment watching him drive away, then turned to face the prison.

The heavy gold watch on my wrist told me it was 12:45, and I had to stand outside in the rain, waiting, until the big hand on the clock inside gave its single digit salute to the sky. Then the guard buzzed me in. I waited some more as he went through my handbag, taking apart my fountain pen and getting ink all over his hands. I was allowed to take in with me a tube of mascara and lipstick, but not the lozenges that Xaviera Hollander, the *Penthouse* columnist, had recommended as a prelude to oral sex.

"Leave these in there," he said, pointing me toward a metal locker. "And this, too." He held up the loose tampon he'd found at the bottom of my bag. "Security measure," he said. "An inmate could suicide himself by choking on one."

He repacked my handbag, saying they would supply me with a substitute if I needed it. "The matron will see you next," he said, pointing to a door marked NO EXIT. On the other side of the door I could hear a woman protesting.

I sat on a hard chair and waited. Angel's sister emerged, with the red-faced matron, Miss Horis, behind her. Consuelo, which was her current alias, had told me to trust her—she could hide *anything*. Why wouldn't I trust a woman who had smuggled herself and three kilos of cocaine into the country so she could pay her brother's legal fees, and be near him? Angel told me, too, she had once smuggled a grenade in her vagina into Bella Vista prison in Colombia. The condom she'd offered to carry for me today seemed like small beer in comparison.

"Miserable enough out there for you?" Miss Horis asked, sighing as she ushered me into the NO EXIT room, then telling me to remove my coat, suit, blouse, underthings, and "all other personal items." Naked, I placed both feet firmly in the middle of the mirror.

"Straddle the mirror, please, one foot on either side. That's it. Now relax, and cough twice."

I coughed, and Miss Horis peered in the mirror, then asked me to lift my breasts one at a time, before opening my mouth where she checked under my tongue. "Enjoy Valentine's Day," she said, as she left me to get dressed again.

She hadn't mentioned the watch—obviously meant for a

man's wrist. I got dressed again and she popped her head in the door a moment later, offering me a sanitary napkin to replace the seized tampon. I shook my head no. No inmate, evidently, had yet thought of trying to suffocate himself with a Kotex.

Once inside the Visiting Room I headed for the washroom, where I found Consuelo fighting with her hair. A sign informing visitors that there was No Necking, Petting, Fondling, Embracing, Tickling, Slapping, Pinching, or Biting Permitted During Visits was posted above the condom machine (foreplay might be prohibited, the machine's presence seemed to suggest, but fucking was not). Today the machine bore another warning: "Sorry. Out of Order." The word "Sorry" had been crossed out.

I turned to Consuelo for the condom she was supposed to smuggle in for me, but she held out her empty hands. "I had to swallow it," she said. "That woman she wanted to look me in the mouth." She said Angel and I should get married so we would be approved for private visits. But Angel and I weren't waiting for approval. Today our names were at the top of a clandestine list for a different kind of private visit—the unsanctioned kind. I borrowed Consuelo's comb and dragged it through my own damp tangles.

At half-past one, Mr. Saygrover, the Visitors and Communications officer, led us into a hallway painted the same avocado green as the outside of the prison. He nodded to the young guard in control of the first of the iron-barred gates blocking our passageway, and the heavy steel doors parted on their runners. We crossed five more identical barriers before reaching the gymnasium.

I could see the men pressed up against the last gate, awaiting their visitors. All were dressed in green shirts and pressed trousers the same shade as the prison walls. The ritual had been the same ever since I first started visiting Angel—the men standing behind the barrier waiting and waving, and the women approaching, awkwardly, looking at one another for reassurance, like girls at a junior high "turnabout" sockhop. The closer we got, the longer it seemed to take the guards to open the barriers. A female guard with sweat stains in the armpits of her uniform opened the last gate. Janis Joplin's voice came rasping out of two coffin-sized speakers strapped high on the gymnasium wall. She didn't need to tell anyone here how freedom was only another word for nothing left to lose.

The gym was decorated with red balloons and white streamers. The streamers had been affixed from corner to corner the night before and had lost their elasticity. A prison sculptor's *papier-mâché* heart, trapped in barbed wire, lay on display next to the Coke machine, which was also "Out of Order."

Visitors found seats around the long banquet tables, each one laden with the institution's version of hors d'oeuvres: mini-sizzlers on toothpicks, rolled cold cuts, radishes that had been sculpted to look like roses too terrified to open, a pyramid of mystery-meat sandwiches and plates of heart-shaped cookies baked by prisoners in the kitchen. My eyes moved from table to table, searching. Angel sat upright on a metal chair, arms folded across his chest. Our eyes locked. He stood up.

Nothing had changed. He didn't speak. I couldn't. He had a smile bittersweet as a pill for the sick at heart, a pair of lips you wanted to lick under a mustache that would keep you from getting close enough, and sad night eyes. His hair was straight and black and today he wore it tied back in a ponytail. In my last letter I'd written, "Tie your hair back so it won't get in the way. I want to see my juice all over your face."

Angel pulled two chairs together so we could sit facing one another, and he leaned forward and put both his arms around my neck. "I'm always afraid I'll never see you again, that you won't come back," he said, breaking the silence. "I'm afraid you might find me—too available."

I laughed as I cupped his dark face in my hands. "I wouldn't call any man doing life behind bars *too available*." His moustache, smelling of the red-hot cinnamon hearts he sucked every time I visited to hide the smell of the dark tobacco on his breath, scoured my upper lip. More than his smile or his eyes, I think it was his smell that attracted me most the first time we met, like the air before a storm, long before there is any visible sign of it.

"You look thin," I said, sitting back in my chair. "Are you getting everything you need?" Angel sat back, too, straightening the sheet that served as a tablecloth. He picked up an orange and poked his finger into its navel.

"I'm getting your letters every day. And you're here. What more do I need?" He kissed me, but I pulled away. "And you?" he asked.

I needed privacy. I wanted to be with Angel, alone. We'd had one chance, at the Christmas social, to spend five minutes in the toilet stall of the men's lavatory, but I needed more time than that to fondle him, embrace, tickle, neck, pet, slap, pinch, and bite—it was all I had thought about since we'd met. I pictured him alone every night in his cell, penis erect and shining, sad as tinsel at an unattended party. When we were together I was aware of how close he stayed beside me and how every time we brushed against one another I felt a shiver of something long lost stirring inside me, the same longing I'd felt for a brown-eyed boy in the fifth grade, my last painful crush before the crash of puberty.

I'd been afraid, too, I told Angel, afraid I had "gone too far." In my last letter I'd quoted Kurt Vonnegut, who said the only task remaining for a writer in the twentieth century was to describe a blow-job artistically. I told Angel I'd rather *show* him a blow-job than write about it, then went on to discuss the calorie count in a mouthful of sperm (one swallow contained thirty-two different chemicals, including vitamin C, vitamin B12, fructose, sulphur, zinc, copper, potassium, calcium, and other healthy things). I said I had a One-a-Day Multiple Vitamin habit but figured I could give these up if he were willing to have oral sex once a day.

Angel told me "far" was the only place worth going, and he kissed me again. This time I didn't stop him. He shifted on the hard chair, adjusting the bulge that strained to break out of his trousers. I squirmed on the warm metal, forcing my knees together, my sex swollen, struggling to escape. I caught two guards staring at us; I nudged Angel and we pushed back from one another. Angel held my hand underneath the table, stroking it with his thumb. "I haven't been in the yard yet today," he said, after a silence. We'd been having the same thought. Out there we might be alone. "How is it, outside? The weather?"

"Wet," I said, taking a heart-shaped cookie and breaking it in half. Angel took the other half from my hands, and I watched it shrink under his mustache. "Raining."

"Good," he said. "Let's walk."

We had the yard to ourselves, almost. Two guards in a patrol vehicle slowed to look us over as we stopped to watch a pregnant doe browsing on the thick grasses outside the perimeter fence. It was the same spot, Angel said, where a half-blind bear had been shot in the autumn. Angel said the guards had fired warning shots at her, but she kept coming back. A handful of yellow-and-purple cartridge shells lay in the wet grass.

"She couldn't see well enough to get away while she had a chance?" I asked.

"Few see that well," said Angel, and when he looked at me this time I saw, in the gleam of his shadowy eyes, a depth of wanting that promised heaven.

We kept to a well-worn trail Angel called the warning track. Walking, we lifted our faces to scale the double high-wire fences but stayed well inside the dead line, the line beyond which any prisoner would be shot. Angel pointed to where a man had been picked off by the tower guard "before his hands were even bloodied by the razor wire."

I squinted up through the rain, beyond the gun towers, to the sky. Angel slid his hand in under my thin coat, cupping my breasts, milking my nipples between his thumb and forefinger, and I felt the wet silk of my panties sticking to me where I was open, and a thin seam of silk rubbing back and forth across my clitoris with every step. But Angel, his faraway eyes on the towers, seemed to have scaled the high-wire fences and left me behind. Then, as we rounded a bend in the warning track, he said someday he would take me so high, so far up in the Andes, nobody, not even God, could stare down at us.

"You're dreaming." I screwed up my face at him. I didn't need to say it out loud: "You're stuck in here doing life." Angel knew my thinking.

"Life can be shorter than you expect," he said. Then he looked at me and laughed, in a way.

I laughed, too, but pulled him closer. For now this was good enough.

When the call came over the loudspeaker to clear the yard we went back inside, elbowing our way through a cluster of guards who'd been checking us out from the door. We sat in our wet clothes holding each other and waiting as more guards pinned two sheets together to make a screen on the gymnasium wall. The Inmate Committee had planned to show *Carmen* before the food was served. Angel whispered what he wanted me to do when the lights dimmed, but now, without the condom for protection, and surveillance from every corner of the room, my heart started looking for an emergency exit. I told Angel we had too much to lose, including our visits. But then the lights went down, he lifted the hem of the tablecloth with his foot, and pushed me under.

Beneath the table, in a private world, I sat hugging my knees, feeling lost and uncomfortable. The Inmate Committee, in charge of all forms of entertainment, had transformed the space under the table into a low-ceilinged motel room. We had a foam mattress, two arsenic-green blankets, and a pillow, upon which someone had placed a long-stemmed rose. My mouth felt dry. How was I going to give Angel that blow-job? I longed for those lozenges and thought about the editor from *Elle* who'd phoned a few months ago asking for reminiscences of "my most embarrassing sexual encounter" for their Valentine's Day issue. I'd been unable to come up with anything, but now, as I sat composing the story in my head, I concluded a guard must have seen me and apprehended Angel. I would be forced to wait it out under the table until such time as they chose to humiliate me publicly; precisely the ending I needed for my date from hell for *Elle*.

I felt a hand go over my eyes, then (the smell of him!) Angel began kissing me all over my face and head, sniffing my hair along the part line. When he took his hands away from my eyes I saw he was wearing dry clothes.

"I went back to my house to change," he said, laughing, taking off his jacket and draping it over my shoulders. "Your dress is soaked," he said. "Wear this, too." He began to unbutton his shirt.

He peeled back the blanket, gave me his dry shirt, and made me get under the covers. I told him he was the first man I'd been to bed with who tried to make me put more clothes *on*, and he told me I was the first woman who could make him hard and make him laugh at the same time. He wanted to know if all Canadian women could do that, and I said as far as I knew there'd never been a poll.

We kept our voices low. The room, too, grew quiet, as the credits began to roll. "Are you sure this is safe?" I whispered. "What if a guard saw us?"

"No one saw us," he said, as he pulled off his undershirt. For the first time I saw the hollow place in his chest. It looked as if his heart had been excavated, like the ruin I once visited in the remote Yucatán. Everything of value had been dug out and taken away. Only a pit remained, which, over the years, had been reclaimed by the jungle.

"I was born with this . . ." He took my hand, curled it into a fist, and placed it in the little hollow. "My mother used to say by the time I died it would have filled up with the tears she would shed for me during her lifetime."

I laid my head on the pillow, waiting for the table to be pulled out from over us. It took an effort of love to get in the mood, staring up at the words PROPERTY OF CORRECTIONS CANADA MORGUE stamped on the underside of the table. I shut my eyes tight as Angel picked apart the rose, then laid the cool crimson petals on my eyelids.

"You're not like any woman I've ever known," he said, pressing his nose in my armpit and edging one finger under the elastic of my bra.

"What's that like?" I shook the petals away.

"Uuuummmmmmmmm," was all he said. I wanted to undo his zipper and take his cock in my mouth, but something made me hold back, an old memory, perhaps, of my first "most embarrassing date" in the old boathouse smelling of high tide, fish, and water rats. I was twelve and Dick Wolfe (not his real name, but close) showed me how to light a banana slug on fire, how it would melt into a pool of sticky stuff if you had the right touch. Then he undid his pants, and I remember it looked so eager, so trusting, as he said "put your mouth on it," and when he came I thought I'd cut him with my tooth, the crooked one my parents could never afford to have fixed. I believed I had a mouthful of his blood but did the polite thing, I thought, and swallowed it. "I've cut you," I said, thinking we'd have to go to the hospital and how was I going to explain cutting a boy "down there"? Then he said, his brown eyes more open to me than ever, "That wasn't blood, sweetheart."

"It's been a long time," Angel said, as I lay still, dreaming, half-listening to someone at our table tuning a guitar. My arm was going to sleep, and I shifted position. The movie had begun, and the man who'd been tuning his guitar began strumming on it so passionately that Angel and I could no longer talk. Then the projector shut down and the lights went back on. The voices up above us grew louder, as if an argument were taking place.

"Something's up," said Angel. "It sounds like there's a problem with the projector."

"The lights have come on," I said. "How are we going to get out of here without someone seeing us? What sort of person will they think I am?"

"No one is going to blame you," Angel said. "The guards will just think I corrupted you. They think all inmates are criminals."

He put his arms around me as if to reassure me. Then he saw the watch I was wearing and asked if it was a gift. He didn't say "from another man," but I could hear it in his question. I unstrapped it from my wrist and said yes, a gift for him. It was guaranteed to be shockproof and never to lose time.

"I've never owned a watch that didn't break down," he said. "I think watches get nervous being on my wrist."

I pushed him back so I could move my pillow away from the end of the table, where a pair of knees was invading our love nest.

"This one comes with a lifetime warranty," I said.

Angel settled his body back alongside mine and blew a strand of hair out of my face. He shifted again so his chin rested on my shoulderblade. The person with the intruding knees began tapping his feet and calling for more music.

It was growing stuffier under the table, and neither of us had enough legroom. But I'd waited long enough: I slipped my arms out of my dress, pulled him close to me, and kissed him, for a long time. It didn't matter that up above us there was a world of men and women arguing and laughing. (The film, I learned, leaving the social, had turned out to be *Carne,* sado-masochistic pornography, not *Carmen* the opera, and the guards axed the show.) We were alone in the new world of our flesh, and the occasional appearance of the toe of a running shoe under the hem of the tablecloth, or a hand slapping the table-top, no longer felt like an intrusion.

"But will you still respect me after this?" I smiled.

He took my hand and guided it to his cock. "My respect for you knows no limits."

I unzipped his trousers. Erotic texts from ancient India claim there is a definite relationship between the size of an erect penis and the destiny of its owner. The possessors of thin penises would be very lucky, those with long ones were fated to be poor, those with short ones could become rulers of the land, and males with thick penises were doomed always to be unhappy.

For now, I was destined to make Angel happy. I began licking the end of his cock, which was already swollen. I thought it was going to burst as my tongue busied itself.

"I'm going to die," he said. When I looked up at his face, across the nut-brown expanse of his body, he smiled back, that slow smile, and I took his cock in both my hands. I could barely get my fingers around it. Its head had a ruddy glow and was grinning. It glistened. I kissed it. Sniffed it. Sucked it hard, taking as much of it into my mouth as I could, then licking it again, making a lot of noise while I sucked and licked.

"I'll come if you keep doing that," he said.

Then he pulled me up so I lay next to him and reached inside my panties. He said my cunt nuzzled up to his hand like a horse's soft mouth when you feed it sugar. He moved down between my legs, pulling my panties aside, sliding one finger inside me, sliding it out, sliding two fingers in, then sliding them out, then sliding three fingers in. I arched my back, spreading my legs wider to give him better access, and he tugged gently upward on my pubic hair, baring my clitoris. Then he began licking me, slowly, teasingly, moving in small circles with his lips and tongue, his kisses falling on me, gentle as the scent of rain in a lemon grove. My body strained against his face, and when he looked up at me, his skin was alive with my juices.

I sat up and pulled him down on top of me.

"I don't have any protection," he said.

There are some exquisite moments from which we are not meant to be protected. I slid him inside me, achingly. I had never had anything so hard inside me. I held my breath as he kept coming into me, we were breathing and then not breathing in unison, and I brought his hand up to my mouth to cover it, suppress any sound, and then I began sucking his fingers, one at a time, then two at a time, then three. His fingers tasted of salt, of my own sweat and juices. "Suck," he said, and pushed into me, harder still, as if by trying he could disappear up inside me and escape forever into the rich orchid darkness of my womb.

When he came his face became contorted as if it hurt him to come so hard, then we lay quietly for a while, and then he began licking me again, making me come with his own come, with his tongue, his lips, and his fingertips. I cried when I came, and doubled up, curling into myself. He began kissing me, from my toes up along my legs and the insides of my thighs, over my belly and breasts, up my neck and onto my face and in my hair. He said this was his way of kissing me hello and goodbye at the same time.

Afterward as I lay on a bed of bruised rose petals, licking the drops of sweat that had rolled down his chest and collected in the hollow above his heart, Angel said coming inside me was like coming on velvet rails. And later when we'd crawled out from under the table and were standing alone once more in the slanting rain, we kissed again. We kissed as if to seal our fate, to finish a life together we hadn't even begun.

Years ago, on an island in the tropics, I had been lured from my bed in the night by the air pregnant with the scent of vanilla. I found giant cauldronlike cactus flowers opening in the moonlight and thousands of tiny sphinx moths fluttering from one pod to another. In the morning, when I came to show them to a friend, the flowers had disappeared.

I missed the next visit because I had a deadline to meet (a piece about these cactus flowers that bloom one night a year, conduct their whole sex lives, and vanish by dawn) and the one after that because the prison was locked down. There'd been a stabbing, and a hostage-taking, and rumblings of a hunger strike. I wrote to Angel, concerned about his health. He wrote back, worried about mine. He hoped I wasn't pregnant, for though he liked the idea—that way part of him had already escaped for good—he didn't want to leave me with a burden.

Angel must have sensed it: Visits weren't the only thing I'd missed that month. I made a doctor's appointment. In the evening I tried to phone Angel, but good news was not enough of a reason to bring an inmate to the phone. I asked to book a

Special Visit to see him the next day. An officer informed me that Special Visits were granted for death or bereavement only. So I had to save my news until I could sit across from Angel in the Visiting Room and touch his face, let him take my hand under the table and stroke it with his thumb.

But the next time I saw Angel, he was in the news. "Two men are dead after today's daring escape attempt from Toombs Penitentiary" was all I heard; my heart began to pound to the staccato beat of a police helicopter, a throaty thwap thwap thwapping. I moved closer to the screen and turned up the sound. "Earlier this afternoon two Colombian nationals tried to climb aboard a waiting helicopter that had landed in the prison yard . . ." There was a shot of the dead line where Angel and I had walked, then a file-photo closeup of his face.

"*Life can be shorter than you expect.*" Consuelo and I rode the bus to the prison in the rain. She said Angel hadn't confided in me, hadn't been able to tell me about his escape plan, out of respect . . . *my respect for you knows no limits* . . . but that he'd been insistent: He would send for me when it was safe. My good news—that I wasn't pregnant—seemed like sad news now. All of him had escaped for good.

Mr. Saygrover asked Consuelo to sign for Angel's property, which fit in a gray plastic suitcase. Consuelo looked inside, then handed it to me. Angel, she said, would have wanted me to have everything. He had left his battered *Pocket Oxford,* a key chain with no keys, a toothbrush, an unopened bag of Cheetos, and $2.37 in change. And, he had left me. So much for respect!

A service took place in the prison chapel. A handful of fellow inmates gathered to pay their last respects, the chaplain mumbled a few words and asked us to pray. Consuelo said Angel wouldn't have wanted hymns, so she sang a song from their childhood, "*Si me han de matar, que me matan de una vez*": "If they're going to kill me tomorrow, they might as well kill me right now."

I wanted, for a moment, to kill him, myself, all over again, until I saw him lying that still in his gray Styrofoam coffin. I tried to hold one of his hands—awkward because of the hand-cuffs—then stroked one of his thumbs instead. He wore the watch. I could hear it ticking.

I moved my hands down over his body, saying hello to Angel, saying goodbye. And when I felt the leg irons at his ankles, I wanted to rip open his shirt and let my tears collect in the hollow place in his chest.

But I didn't weep. Through the bars of the chapel window I watched the slow rain falling on the fake-fur trim of the guards' brown jackets, and thought how lonely it would be, how cold and cramped the earth Angel was going into. In this world, I knew, there was an unending supply of sorrow, and the heart could always make room for more.

Romantic love flourishes when there is intense passion along with a monumental impediment to its fulfillment. Erotic love, even more so. This story is drawn in part from my relation-ship with Stephen, my life partner, whom I met in 1984. He was then serving a twenty-one-year sentence for gold robbery, and in prison he'd begun a novel, which I was asked to read. I began to edit it and fell in love with his main character, then with Stephen himself.

ABOUT THE AUTHORS

Some of these names are real, some invented.

Jacqueline Ariail lives with her two sons, Isaac and Jacob, and
her daughter, Hannah, in Durham, North Carolina, and
teaches expository writing at North Carolina State University. She has published a number of short stories and is
working on a novel about Barry and Laura.

I. Buiguise is an anthropologist living in London. This is her
second piece of fiction.

Marion Callen lives in Peterborough, England, where she is an
area organizer for the Cambridgeshire literacy and numeracy
program. She has contributed for five years to the Peterborough Writers' group and has recently become a member of
Cambridge Women Writers.

Elizabeth Clarke is a professional erotician who writes, dances,
models, and performs for men and women. She does safe

sex education for lesbian and bisexual women as part of the Peer Safer Sex Slut Team. "Queer" is the first chapter of a novel in progress. Most recently, she has been living in San Francisco.

Jenny Diski, who lives and works in north London, has published six novels. The most recent, *Monkey's Uncle,* appeared in England early in 1994.

Susan Dooley is a writer living in a small New England village.

Francine Falk is an actress, poet, and short story writer born in Washington state and long a resident of Pennsylvania. She is the mother of a twenty-one-year-old son.

Phaedra Greenwood is a writer and photographer living in New Mexico. In 1988 she was a finalist for the Katherine Anne Porter Award.

Laurel Gross lives in New York City. She has been an entertainment and television editor and critic for the *New York Post* and an editor at *Variety.*

Nancy Holder dropped out of high school to become a ballerina. She has published eighteen novels and numerous short stories. Two of her erotic horror novels, *Making Love* and *Witch-Light,* were written in collaboration with Melanie Tem. She lives in San Diego with her husband and three dogs.

Kay Kemp is the alter ego of a Canadian novelist and short story writer. She was born in Edmonton, Alberta, and has lived in Washington, D.C., and London. She now lives in Toronto with her husband and two children.

L. M. Lippman is a writer and journalist living in Baltimore.

Susan Musgrave, a native Californian, lives on Vancouver Island. Her eleventh book of poetry, *Forcing the Narcissus,* was published in Canada in the spring of 1994, along with her second collection of personal essays, *Musgrave Landing*.

Lawanda Powell lives in Washington, D.C. The mother of two grown daughters, she has been a social worker and an administrator.

Francesca Ross is a midwestern writer of Regency romances. She also teaches literature and composition at a state university.

Susan St. Aubin lives and writes in a turn-of-the-century cottage in northern California. Among the places her short fiction has appeared are the three *Herotica* collections and both the magazine and the anthology *Yellow Silk*.

Nazneen Sheikh was born in Srinagar, India, and was educated in Pakistan and Texas. She lives in Toronto with her husband, Gustavo, and is the mother of two daughters. Her second novel, *Chopin People,* was published in Canada in the spring of 1994.

Toby Vallance was born in London and educated in Cambridge and London. She is working on a collection of short stories and a novel.

ABOUT THE EDITOR

Michele Slung's works include *The Absent-Minded Professor's Memory Book; The Only Child Book;* and the best-selling *Momilies®* books, *Momilies: As My Mother Used to Say®* and *More Momilies.* Among her successful anthologies are *Crime on Her Mind: Fifteen Stories of Female Sleuths from the Victorian Era to the '40s; I Shudder at Your Touch: Tales of Sex and Horror* and its sequel, *Shudder Again;* and *Slow Hand: Women Writing Erotica* (HarperCollins). Most recently, she has published *Hear! Here! Sounds Around the World* and coedited the collection *Murder for Halloween.*

ACKNOWLEDGMENTS
❦❦❦❦❦❦